BROKEN WOLF HEART

MAFIA PACK #3

HEATHER HILDENBRAND

Broken Wolf Heart

Mafia Pack Series Book 3

By Heather Hildenbrand

For more information, contact the publisher at 4300 Portsmouth Blvd. Unit 9152 Chesapeake, VA 23321.

E-book & Paperback Cover Design by Blackbird Covers

Hardcover Design by Malice & Mayhem

Proofread by Dawn Y

www.heatherhildenbrand.com

1

LEXI

Today is supposed to be a beginning. The moment the nightmares of my past give way to something real. A future. A husband. A life I choose for myself. Instead, it's an ending—for the last living family member I had and undoubtedly for me too.

"He's dead."

Santiago's words hang in the air like a poison cloud. The suit-clad male with a paunchy gut stands halfway up the aisle of the crowded church, which is as far as he got after returning from my upstairs dressing room. As one of Franco's mafia generals, he hadn't been willing to accept Dutch's claims about his high alpha's sudden demise. Not without seeing for himself.

Now, he looks stunned.

At his pronouncement, the wedding guests—*my* wedding, which might as well be a wake now—look at me with shock and awe. And more than a little skepticism. I can't blame them for the latter. Mostly because Dutch just claimed *I* killed the mafia pack's high alpha… which is a total lie.

The question is: Why?

One look at my fiancé—husband? Did we make it that far?—and my stomach sours.

"What are you doing?" I whisper.

"Trust me," he whispers back.

Something flashes in his eye. Desperation. And something darker.

I blink and pull back as the realization washes over me. Grey killed him, but he's giving me the credit.

I don't know how he did it. Franco was supposed to be the most powerful wolf in this city. But somehow, my grandfather, Franco Giovanni—the man who ruled Indigo Hills with an iron fist, the man who had no qualms about being my enemy, yet failed to denounce me as his heir, is dead.

I also don't know why Grey isn't just declaring himself the new alpha. But I won't betray him. So, I keep my mouth shut and do my best to make my expression devoid of the truth. It's not hard, considering all my other half-panicked thoughts vying for attention.

Santiago looks from me to his brother, Conrad, who sits in the second row. They're both generals in Franco's pack hierarchy, which probably makes them in charge now that the old man is gone. Then, they both look at Toros, the third general. The worst of them, from what I've heard. His scars stretch across his face, pulled taut with the tension of the moment. After a shared look, they all nod like they've just made some unspoken agreement.

Fear squeezes my chest at that nod. Is it a "yes" to killing me? To shifting into their wolf forms and decimating this entire church full of people? A yes to retribution for what Grey took from them? For what they think I've done?

I can't breathe around my racing thoughts as I try to decipher my next move. Or how I'll possibly survive the next few moments with murderous wolf shifters hovering over me and my own inner wolf intent on clawing her way out to join them.

The serum Vincenzo gave me to access my wolf has finally started to kick in. I don't know what's considered normal for a new wolf, but I've never felt quite this unhinged before.

The guests become restless.

Murmurs echo off the walls. They start low but get louder fast. Shoes scrape against the floor as people shove to their feet. Threats and curses are tossed my way, the most vicious of them from Franco's lieutenants sitting in the second row. The loudest voice, though, belongs to Vincenzo Diavolo. Grey's father. If there were an award for Most Likely to Kill Me Where I Stand, it would go to this man, no contest.

While Santiago, Toros, and Conrad seem to debate who gets to murder me, Vincenzo shoves to his feet, yelling, "What the fuck have you done?"

But he's not looking at me.

He's shooting venomous glares at his son. Like he knows the truth. Or has at least guessed it.

"Lexi," Grey warns, pulling me back just as a couple of Franco's pack members surge toward the dais. Toward me.

I tense, bracing myself for their vengeance. Before they can reach me, a couple of bodies slide in front of me and Grey. Razor and Dutch. They shove the two men back and face the crowd with their arms crossed—a veritable wall between us and them. It won't last long, though. Not with the looks Franco's generals are giving me.

Inside, my stomach rolls with nausea. Anxiety slams through me. The need to run wars with the urge to fight. I shove both of them away and try to breathe.

"Hey," Grey says, but I can't look at him. I can't do anything except suck in oxygen and try not to lose my shit.

My next inhale is an assault on my senses. Suddenly, I can smell every single person in this room. None of them smells like friends, not to *her*.

"Whatever happens next, know that I love you."

Grey's words break through my inner battle.

I blink, finally forcing myself to look at him, to focus on the intensity in his dark grey eyes. The way they are fastened so completely on me. As if this room isn't full of people who want to kill us both.

Whatever he sees in my expression startles him.

"Is it your wolf?" he whispers.

"Yes," I manage, gritting my teeth against the pain of what feels like my insides being ripped apart.

I watch as his expression goes from resolute to worried and back again.

He reaches down and runs his thumb over the twist-tie wrapped around my finger. I look down at it, my heart squeezing.

"Focus on this," he says.

I nod, doing my best.

But when I look up at him again, I can feel the pain winning. My focus slips. My breaths become ragged.

"Shit," Grey mutters, and I know he can see how close I am to losing it.

He grabs my elbow, pulling me close. His mouth crashes down on mine, fierce and possessive.

And despite my wolf howling to get out, I relax.

Somehow, I know everything he's doing now is to save me, even if it gets him killed in the process. The idea of losing him sends me panicking again, and I try to pull away. But he only kisses me harder, his lips bruising against mine. His thumb rubbing that damned twist-tie like it's a wishing stone. A promise, flimsy and fragile—and somehow stronger than anything holding either one of us together right now.

I kiss him like he's my last grip on sanity before I lose myself forever. Before I lose him forever.

Vaguely, I hear Razor threatening someone to step back or he'll remove their legs from their body.

My hip is bumped, and I'm jostled.

Grey's grip tightens around my waist. Despite the chaos, he kisses me with singular focus, as if pressing his mouth to mine will somehow stop everything that's coming.

But it won't.

Because before his lips even leave mine, hands are already snatching me away. Razor curses viciously. Someone grunts. Rough fingers clamp down on my arms, wrenching me backward.

Grey is ripped away from me.

Strong hands keep me upright while binding my arms helplessly behind me. I struggle like a wild animal, panic blotting out all reason. My nails rake across flesh, and blood pools where I've scratched my captor's skin.

The sight of the blood and the coppery scent of it leaves a thirst in my throat. My wolf wants more of it. She wants to drink it while standing over their dead body. To bathe in it underneath the light of a full moon and—

Ugh.

I shake my head to clear it.

My wolf is clearly a psycho.

Her murderous daydream is like a bucket of cold water to my senses. I stop struggling long enough to identify my assailant.

Santiago.

Beside him, Toros looms in front of Razor, whose skin has already sprouted fur in a partial shift. Razor's eyes are wild and unfocused, but it's Dutch holding him back, talking him down with quiet words. On the other side of the dais, Conrad holds Grey in place by his arms, though barely.

A snarl erupts from Grey's chest, savage and raw as he glares across the space at Santiago. "Take your fucking hands off my wife."

The remaining guests go still at the steel in his voice.

But Santiago doesn't listen.

With a malicious grin, he hauls me off my feet and begins carrying me away, his grip unyielding. My wolf strains inside me, desperate to free herself. To fight them. To kill.

"Where the fuck do you think you're going?" Dutch demands, the words laced with a growl. He and Razor surge toward the steps—toward me.

My panic escalates at the inevitable brawl coming. I make a sound that's more animal than human, and it's enough to make Santiago stop in his tracks.

Dutch eyes me with suspicion, but it's Grey who speaks.

"Put her down, or I swear I will kill you and everyone you've ever loved," Grey snarls.

"This is Giovanni pack business," Toros tells him. "You have no authority here."

Grey stops struggling then. He blinks as if letting those words really sink in. "You're taking her to Franco's." It's more of a question than a statement.

"We're taking her home," Toros snarls. "Where she belongs."

Grey looks at Dutch and Razor and gives a swift nod. They back off.

My stomach twists as I realize they're going to stand down.

Santiago carries me down the steps.

The crowd, mostly Franco's people on this side, parts for us.

"Wait." Grey surges forward. He yanks out of Conrad's grip hard enough to send the man staggering. "I'm coming with you."

"That's not your call to make," Toros shoots back.

Grey's eyes narrow. "I'm her fucking husband."

The air between them thickens, the tension slicing through the ruined sanctity of the church like a blade.

"Husband or not, you know the price," Toros tells him. "Denounce your father. Publicly. Swear allegiance to us."

"Like hell," Vincenzo snarls. He's watching this unfold like he can't decide if it's a good thing or a nightmare. But at the mention of Grey defecting, he looks like he's settled on the latter.

Grey's breathing is ragged, his hands curling into fists at his sides. He wants to do as they demand. I can see it in the way his entire body strains toward me. In the way his chest rises and falls like he's seconds from shifting and ripping them all apart.

Mia appears at Grey's side. She gives him a look that conveys something I don't understand. Grey's eyes flick to mine, stormy with anguish, apology, fury. His jaw clenches. The growl that rips from him is pure rage, his wolf so close to the surface that his pupils blacken, his body trembling with the force of his instincts.

And then—he goes still.

Toros watches him, waiting.

Grey doesn't speak.

He doesn't have to.

The decision is made.

Toros nods. "Didn't think so."

Then they carry me out.

And Grey lets them.

2

GREY

Watching Santiago carry my bride away like she's nothing more than the spoils of war is a bittersweet sort of agony that leaves me both relieved and strangely lost. I'd known it was a gamble, convincing them to let me come with her. I hadn't counted on such a public ultimatum, though, and not being able to choose Lexi in that moment gutted me.

If it had been only my own fate hanging in the balance, I'd have let them see the truth in a heartbeat. My wolf, more powerful than ever, would have torn through anyone who challenged me, anyway. But admitting my new status as alpha would have exposed Dutch, Razor, Crow, and Mia. I couldn't live with myself if something happened to my pack.

Lexi will understand.

That's what I tell myself as I watch her disappear through the church doors, clutched in the hands of my enemies. Even if my wolf howls inside me, furious I didn't choose her. But I did. I just chose all of them too.

The moment she's gone, my father is in my face.

"What the fuck just happened?" he demands.

"Lexi just became the high alpha of Indigo Hills," I tell him calmly, despite my heart hammering my rib cage. I want so badly to rip out his throat and be fucking done with him. But this church is still full of his pack. And I don't have nearly the numbers yet to fight them all.

Soon enough, I promise myself, *I will*.

"She couldn't possibly have killed that bastard," my father says.

His face is flushed with rage, but beneath that anger, I see it. The kernel of doubt. He thinks maybe, just maybe, she could have. He also suspects I know more than I'm sharing.

"Couldn't she?" I ask and allow myself to slip into character. A confused, erratic mate. A groom without a bride. The son he lives to torture by taking away the things I love most. "Her eyes were different. But they… The way she looked at me—" I stop and look at him dead in his face. "She felt like a wolf."

My father blinks with zero surprise at my words. And I almost forget every logical reason not to kill him.

I knew it the moment I'd seen that animalistic flash in her eyes during our vows. Then again, the way she'd kissed me—with a hunger only a predator possesses. Not to mention the feverish temperature of her body as it had pressed against mine, like her skin was on fire from the inside out. But seeing him confirm it now… it's almost too much.

He triggered her wolf. And he doesn't look the least bit sorry—or worried—about what will happen to her next.

"What the fuck did you do to Lexi?" I demand, dropping the weak, scared act as I crowd into his face.

"Watch your fucking tone," he warns.

Mia, Razor, and Dutch press in behind me. They want answers too. But my father clearly doesn't give a shit what we want. He turns to my mother. "Serena, I need to deal with this."

"Of course," she says, glancing at me.

I recognize the look she wears. It's a warning, a plea to let it go, to stop stirring his temper. I look away from her and back to the asshole who I've hated for so long that I can't remember any other way.

He doesn't offer anything else before turning and striding up the aisle.

I start to follow him, but Dutch grabs me, holding me back. "Let him go," my best friend says quietly.

"He did something to Lexi's wolf," I snarl.

"And you're an alpha with Franco's power in your veins," he reminds me in a low voice.

"Excuse me?" Mia hisses, eyes wide as she looks back and forth between us. "Did you just say—?"

"Yes," Dutch cuts her off.

"When the fuck were you going to tell me?" Mia demands.

"In about five more minutes when we're in the damned car," Dutch tells her. She huffs at that, but he ignores it and levels a pointed stare at me. "Unless you're ready to play your hand, we should go."

Fuck.

He's not wrong.

Using the hex blade to secure our pack's bond was bad enough. Killing Franco and taking his alpha power is like having a blinking neon sign over my head. With Lexi standing next to me, it was easy enough for folks to assume that power was hers, but now that she's gone, anyone who looks too closely will see the truth.

I'm an alpha now.

A powerful one.

"Get the car," I mutter.

"Crow's waiting with it out back," Razor says.

My pack wastes no time ushering me out the back door and into the car waiting in the alley. It's not one of the SUVs from my father's fleet. This is Crow's personal vehicle. For some reason, the sight of it makes me remember the way he drove it as a getaway car the day we rescued Lexi from Altobello's when Franco tried to toss her into a cage. Dutch drove Lexi and me while Crow and Razor drove separately to take the heat off.

I shake off the memory of that day—when I'd almost killed Dominic Albero to get her back even though I barely knew her yet—and refocus on today.

My wedding.

Fuck, I'm married to that girl now.

Life is so fucking wild.

And I did end up killing Dominic Albero in the end. For her. I'd do anything for Lexi Giovanni. Even start a war, which I may have just done by killing Franco and naming her as his murderer.

Crow drives, and I sit shotgun. The others pile into the backseat, and Crow chirps tires as he drives away.

"What the actual fuck," Mia says as soon as we're moving.

"Mia, calm down," Dutch warns.

She ignores him, and I can practically feel her eyes

drilling holes in the back of my head as she accuses, "You killed Franco."

"Wait, what?" Crow says, eyes wide as he gives me a double-take.

I blow out a breath and lean my head back against the seat, letting my eyes close for a long moment.

"When? How? Why?" Razor asks.

"Last night," Dutch says.

"You didn't call us." Mia sounds pissed, but I recognize the hurt underneath it.

"There was no time," Dutch says.

"But there was time to call *you*," she snaps.

"Can we talk about this when we're out of the car?" I ask, pinching the bridge of my nose to ward off a headache starting to form.

"Uh, speaking of which," Crow says, coming to a stop before pulling out of the alley onto the main road. "Where are we going?"

"My house," Mia says darkly before anyone else can answer.

Crow looks at me questioningly, and I nod. Mia's apartment is the most secure place for us to talk. Mostly because it's one of the few places I know isn't wired with surveillance. The only spot more private would have been the warehouse, but since there's a good chance we're being followed by my father's people, I opt for a place they'll expect us to regroup.

Crow punches the gas, and we speed through the streets, the tension in the car thick enough to choke on.

The moment we pull into Mia's parking garage, she's out of the car, slamming the door in Dutch's face and striding for the elevator like she's gearing up for a fight. The rest of us pile out, and we ride up to her high-rise apartment in silence. I can feel Razor shooting me daggers with his pointed stare, but I ignore him. My thoughts are on Lexi —where is she now? What have they decided to do with her?

We barely make it out of the elevator and into Mia's colorful living room before she rounds on me.

"You killed Franco fucking Giovanni, and you let Lexi take the fall for it."

I don't flinch. I don't break eye contact. Because she's not wrong, even if she's glaring at me like I've committed a cardinal sin. "Yes," I tell her evenly as the others fan out around us.

Dutch and Razor remain close, more than willing to participate head-to-head. Crow hangs back by the windows that look out onto the rooftop patio, just watching.

"Why the hell would you do that?" Mia demands.

"Why do you think?" I ask her. "To save her."

"Is that what you call it?" Mia shoots back.

"That's what it is."

When I don't give her more than that, she opens her mouth, clearly ready to blast me again.

Dutch interrupts before she can. "She's alive because of it, Mia."

"She's *gone* because of it," she counters, arms crossed, fire in her eyes to match the fiery red of her hair.

Mia's always been the mom of the group and sometimes even the boss, especially when we're all being dickheads about something. But she's not the alpha. And my wolf won't let her act like she is. Not after what we did last night, binding ourselves together with that hex blade. Making me our alpha—officially.

I can feel it in my beast and in my very blood. Our pack dynamic is changing. Mia's no longer going to be able to pull rank. Not unless I give her that rank as my second.

Shit.

I have to choose a second.

The thought hits me just as Dutch steps between us. "We don't have time for this. We need a plan."

"I have a plan." I rake a hand through my hair, willing the headache away. "We let this play out."

Razor barks out a laugh, but there's no humor in it. "Let this play out? Are you out of your fucking mind?"

"She's in their hands, Grey," Mia says, her voice softer but no less furious. "A girl whose wolf is inaccessible. Whose namesake wouldn't even recognize her as his heir. Whose veins supposedly run with the power of their high alpha. You think they're just gonna keep her alive out of the goodness of their hearts?"

"No," I admit. "But they need her. She's their high alpha now, even if they don't want to admit it."

"And if they decide *not* to recognize her as the alpha?" Mia asks.

"They won't kill her—not yet," Dutch adds grimly. "Not until some kind of hierarchy can be established for who gets to do it and take Franco's alpha power along with hers."

Mia gawks at him then at me. "*That's* your plan? Hope they don't kill her *yet* for a power she doesn't even possess?" She shakes her head, muttering to herself that we're all idiots.

"Would you rather I let my father have her?" I snap.

"Your father—" she starts, but I don't let her finish.

"—was going to kill her," I roar.

She falls silent for a long moment, glaring at me as my words echo around the room. The power in my voice is unmistakable: alpha power. They all blink at me as if seeing me for the first time, and I know they've begun to realize what I have; our hierarchy has changed. And we have to change along with it.

If I'd been arguing with anyone else, I doubt they would have kept pushing after such a display. But Mia isn't just anyone, so I'm not completely surprised when she says, albeit a little less forcefully, "We can protect her, but only if we get her back."

"She can protect herself," says a voice I'm not expecting.

We all turn to look at Crow.

He's always so quiet, especially in arguments. The fact that he's speaking up now is more proof of our dynamic shifting.

"She smelled like a wolf," he says to me. It's a question and a statement.

The others turn to look at me again, questions brimming in their expressions.

"I think my father gave her something to trigger her wolf," I say.

"Wait. She's going to shift?" Dutch asks. "When?"

"Probably today," Crow says quietly. "If her scent was any indication."

I nod, hating that Lexi's going through her first shift alone. "If not today, then soon."

"And you let them take her," Mia says, eyes wide as she looks angry all over again.

"Mia," I warn.

She shakes her head, muttering things to herself.

"She shouldn't be alone for it," Razor says. There's no accusation in his voice. Not for me anyway. "Your dad's a bastard for doing it this way."

"He's a bastard for a lot of things," I say wearily.

"But they'll sense her wolf on her," Dutch adds. He looks at me. "When they gather to decide, they'll know she's a wolf. That's something at least. Besides, she's safer as a leader of her own pack than she is as one of us."

"Dutch is right," Crow says, and then to me, "You know your old man's going to come for us when they realize you're an alpha now."

"Not just yours," Dutch mutters.

"Shit," Razor says. "I didn't even think of that." He exchanges a worried look with his half-brother. "Maybe we should have waited."

Crow looks away guiltily, and that's the thing that has my worry spiking.

"Waited for what?" Mia demands, clearly reading the same look I did.

"What did you do?" Dutch asks.

"We, uh, might have done something stupid last night too," Razor admits.

"The list of possibilities is endless. Can you be more specific?" Mia prompts.

Razor straightens like he's bracing for her wrath, but it's me he looks at as he says, "We freed Ramsey last night."

There's a full beat of silence while we all absorb those words.

Mia breaks it by screeching, "You what?"

Dutch snorts at that.

Razor's jaw tightens.

Crow is categorically silent.

Razor says, "Ramsey knew things, things about Lexi and her involvement with Franco. Her deal to spy for him." He glances at me stoically. "I didn't think you'd want that kind of information being shared with your old man."

I sigh. He's not wrong. And even though I want to bust his balls for doing it on his own rather than asking us to back him up, I can't say shit. I did the same thing.

Then again, our first night as a pack doesn't exactly scream "unity."

"Where did you take him?" Mia asks, her voice low and contained—like she hasn't yet decided how pissed to be over this.

"We didn't take him anywhere," Razor says, his forehead crinkling. "We just unlocked the door to the cell where Vincenzo was keeping him and distracted the guards."

Mia stares at him wide-eyed. "How the hell did you make it on and off Vincenzo's estate grounds undetected?" she asks, but that's not the question I want answered right now.

"Did you speak to him?" I cut in, "Let him know you were the ones who helped him escape?"

"No." Razor shrugs. "We weren't trying to bring him home or anything. Just keep him away from Vincenzo."

"So, he doesn't think he's coming back to us?" Dutch presses.

"Of course not," Razor says. He looks at me. "We'd never offer that without full agreement from everyone."

But part of him wants to.

Something inside me twinges. Ramsey pledged his loyalty to me. For better or worse, that makes him pack.

"Can you feel him?" Dutch asks me. "Through the pack bond? Because I can't."

I shake my head, frowning. "No. But he didn't do the blood ritual, so it might be a weaker connection."

"I don't believe this," Mia mutters. "Everyone was out doing gangster shit last night but me."

"It's not a bad thing to get a good night's sleep in this town," Dutch tells her.

"Who said I was sleeping?" Mia counters. "I was booking a honeymoon for you," she says, jabbing a finger at me. "One that has gone to complete waste."

"I'm sorry," I tell her.

"You owe me," she fires back.

"Add it to my tab."

She rolls her eyes but remains silent.

"It's fine," I tell Razor, who simply grunts.

I look at Crow. "Do you think Ramsey told them anything about Lexi's betrayal before you released him?" I ask.

"No," he tells me in an eerily calm voice, given everything we're discussing.

"How do you know?" I ask.

He shrugs. "If he had, your old man would have brought it up today and tried using it against you. Or her."

"He's right, man," Dutch says.

I don't say anything. My dad is straightforward in his hatred and manipulation, so they're probably not wrong, but I refuse to let my guard down without being sure. And even then…

I can't rest until Lexi's truly safe.

"But either way, now that you have Franco's alpha power, now that we're a pack not to be fucked with, we have a bigger target on us than Lexi has being in her own pack," Dutch says, nodding grimly.

"Do we have a plan for what we're doing about that target?" Mia asks.

"First, we make sure Lexi is accepted as alpha," I say.

"How long do you think it'll take them to decide?" Mia asks.

My phone dings before I can answer. I pull it out, tension radiating through me as I read the text.

"It's time," I say, heading for the elevator.

"Where?" Razor asks, already following.

All of them are. It reminds me that the kind of pack I've made here with them is so different from the one my father has. Even when they're pissed or confused, they have my back without question or hesitation.

"The generals have called a vote on recognizing Lexi as the new high alpha of Indigo Hills," I say.

"How do you know?" Mia asks. "Lexi didn't exactly take her phone with her."

The elevator dings, and the doors open. We all climb back inside. "I have a source," I tell them.

"Who?" Razor asks.

"You'll see."

I only hold back so they don't give it away when they do, in fact, see who I've managed to bring over to our side. The last thing I want to do is expose someone willing to risk their own neck to help us.

"Are they going to let us into this meeting?" Mia asks, frowning as we ride the elevator back to the garage.

"Since the outcome affects all of us, the meeting is open to all pack members."

"All?" Razor echoes. "Even your dad?"

"Who do you think called the meeting?" I tell him.

"Whoa." Razor grabs my arm before I can step off the elevator into the parking garage. "You can't go in there."

"What are you talking about?"

"If Lexi's threatened—"

"Shit, your wolf will rip throats," Dutch says.

They all pull up short.

"I can control my wolf," I tell them.

"Maybe. But what if someone tries to hurt one of us?" Mia demands. I scowl, but she answers for me. "Your control won't mean shit if one of your pack is threatened."

Dutch sighs and shakes his head. "Fuck."

I don't argue, but only because there's no time for it. The meeting will start without us if we don't hurry up. "Fine. New plan," I say, filling them in as we go.

3

LEXI

I don't remember getting into the car. I don't remember the drive. All I know is, one second, I'm standing in a church with my marriage vows still warm on my lips, and the next, I'm being dragged up the marble steps of a house that isn't mine.

No, not a house. A mansion. A goddamn empire.

The Giovanni estate is everything I imagined it would be—cold, grand, and suffocating. And that's just my impression from the outside with its white concrete walls, imposing arches, and multiple stories offering balcony overlooks with iron railings. Not to mention the grounds that seem to sprawl as far as I can see in either direction.

None of the windows have bars on them like Vincenzo's house did, but there's something intimidating all the same. A sense that, once you go in, you don't come out unless the person in charge of this place allows it.

Inside, gilded sconces line the endless white walls, casting eerie, golden light onto high, vaulted ceilings. The floors beneath my feet are pristine marble, polished so smooth I can see my reflection staring back at me.

Massive portraits of men I don't know, men who ruled this mafia pack empire long before I ever existed, glare down from their brushed bronzed frames, their eyes full of the same judgment I've been drowning in since the moment I arrived in this city. My father's name isn't among them, but then, he didn't live long enough to become an alpha.

The house is opulent. Immaculate. A museum for a legacy built on blood and control. And even though Franco lived here, even though my father would have grown up here, it feels nothing like a home.

It feels like a tomb.

My stomach churns as Toros leads the way up a grand, winding staircase. At the second-floor landing, we turn left, and I follow him down an endless hallway to a large ornate door at the very end. He pushes it open then steps back, ushering me inside with a scowl.

The animal inside me cringes at showing this man our back. But I do it, too afraid of what he'll do if I don't play along. Rather than leave me alone, he steps in behind me, and my heart squeezes with fear as I turn to face him.

This is it.

This is where I die.

On an expensive rug where generations of Giovanni blood has probably already been spilled before me. Where more will undoubtedly be spilled again.

The bedroom is cavernous, the furniture dark and heavy. A four-poster bed looms in the center, too big, too gaudy. There are no personal touches, no warmth, just expensive things meant to impress. The air is too cold. The scent of polished wood and leather mixes with something fainter—something rotten.

Franco lived here.

And now he's dead.

A fact that should bring me some kind of relief, but instead, all I feel is the sick, pulsing weight of my future pressing down on my shoulders. I'm hyper-aware of the fact that my future might only last me the next ten seconds.

Toros takes a menacing step toward me. There's no trace of welcome or civility. Only calculated ice.

"What are you doing?" I blurt, hating that I take a step back. But it's either that or let him invade my space, and I refuse to allow that kind of violation.

He ignores my words—and me—and brushes past me to fling open another door behind me. Through the opening, I glimpse a walk-in closet full of suits. I inhale the scent of Franco. He's everywhere in here. Reminding me I'm the intruder.

"Closet's here, bathroom's through there," Toros says flatly. He sweeps a pointed gaze down the length of my wedding dress. "Get changed, and meet me downstairs."

"Where am I supposed to get changed?" I ask.

He looks at me like I'm a complete moron then flings his arm out to gesture to the space. "Here."

"Here?" I echo.

"This is your room now."

My room.

Right.

Toros turns for the door. "You have ten minutes."

The way he says it sends a cold shiver down my spine.

Ten minutes for what? To live? To explain how I killed a man I didn't actually kill? I don't ask, don't let myself react, but even as he shuts the door behind him, my body betrays me.

Suddenly, every nerve is on fire, every hair on my arms and neck standing on end. My senses come rushing in with a roar in my ears. From up here, I can sense six others inside the house. More than that, I can smell their breath, hear the way their heartbeats thud slow and steady in their chests. The lace fabric of my dress scratches at my skin like needles. My mouth is dry. My lungs feel too tight.

Panic claws at my insides, a sharp and sudden fear that I'm about to come undone right here, right now. My wolf is close to the surface. I can feel her teeth in my skin, the low, rumbling growl curling inside my ribs, demanding release.

With a strangled snarl, I tear at my dress. The buttons and snaps are impossible to reach, which only makes me more desperate to be free of the stifling layers against my skin. My nails lengthen into claws, and I tear through the lace and tulle, shredding it until I stand in only my bra and panties with a pile of luxury fabric at my feet.

My chest heaves with breath after breath as my blood swims hot inside me.

I've traded the dress for my wolf. A husband for a pack. Happiness for duty. Somehow, I always knew this was how it would go. Even before Ramsey forced me to spy on Grey, I understood nothing would ever be so easy as remaining in Jericho Grey Diavolo's arms.

Ramsey.

Who is probably selling me out at this very moment to Vincenzo and his generals, detailing every covert thing I did to betray them. Once that truth is out there, I'm as good as dead anyway.

I only hope I can find a way to warn Grey it's coming.

Maybe then he can be ready to face his father rather than get caught up in the crossfire. The last thing I want is for him to get hurt because of me.

The beast inside me stirs as if even the thought of Grey being threatened is enough to unleash her.

Downstairs, someone curses, and my sensitive ears pick it up easily.

I jolt back to the task at hand.

Four minutes left.

I step out of my shoes and pad into the closet. My stomach sinks as I take in Franco's clothes. Starched white shirts. Expensive silk ties. The scent of his cologne clings to the fabric, sharp and acrid. There's nothing here for me.

I can't breathe.

At the back of the closet, I clutch the edge of the armoire, fighting the pressure in my chest, the rising heat under my skin. My fingers dig into the wood, and for a second, I swear I feel my nails sharpen, my bones shift.

No. Not yet.

A knock at the bedroom door startles me, and I poke my head out of the closet just as it opens.

Andy.

Toros' wife. I met her only once, briefly, at a funeral. Closer to my age than she is her husband's, she struck me then as far too young and sweet to be a willing love match for the monster she's married to. But I was very wrong once already, and I'm not willing to let my guard down so easily again.

I cross my arms over my chest, still hovering half-inside the closet. "What do you want?"

She steps inside, a bag slung over her arm, her brown eyes wary but not unfriendly as she sweeps the bedroom.

"They left you with Franco's clothes?" she asks, her voice laced with something close to disgust.

I swallow hard, nodding.

She sighs and holds up the garment bag. "Good thing I figured they'd be assholes about it."

She walks over, placing the bag on the bed. When she turns back, her gaze lingers on my face, my still-shaking hands, and her expression softens.

"You don't have to be scared," she says, but there's no mockery in her tone. Just quiet reassurance.

I force out a breath. "Are they planning to talk or to kill me?"

Andy studies me for a long second before shaking her head. "They're not going to kill you."

I want to believe her, but I know better.

"They're loyal to Franco," I say.

Andy's lips press into a thin line, but she doesn't argue. Instead, she nods toward the bag. "Come on. Get dressed."

With resigned steps, I walk over and pull out the outfit she brought—a simple dress, black and sleeveless, with a skirt that ruffles out loosely. Expensive fabric, elegant but plain. Easy to move in.

"We're close enough to the same size. And it beats wearing one of your grandfather's suits."

I don't argue as I yank the dress over my head. It fits well enough, hugging my frame without suffocating me. Most importantly, the fabric is smooth and soft and doesn't make me want to claw it off my body or peel my skin off with it.

When I'm done, I shove my feet back into my shoes and stand before the mirror, studying my reflection. My gaze is hollow, but my face is flushed, and my chest rises and falls with heavy breaths. Heat still sings through my veins even if I'm managing to mostly ignore it.

Through the reflection, Andy watches me, arms crossed. "I know pants would be more practical, but I think projecting your feminine power is smart."

"You don't have to do this," I say when I finally meet her gaze.

"Do what?"

"Help me."

Something flickers across her face, too quick for me to name. "You're not my enemy, Lexi."

I let out a humorless laugh. "I don't think your husband would agree."

She tilts her head, studying me. "He will. Eventually."

I don't know what to say to that.

For the first time since walking into this house, my chest loosens, just slightly. Not because I feel safe but because—for now, at least—I'm not alone.

And that has to be enough.

Toros is waiting at the bottom of the stairs. Andy slips around me to tap his arm. I can only stare at where she willingly touches him.

"What do you think?" she asks him, gesturing to me.

Toros' phone dings. He glances at it then at me, and merely says, "We need to go."

"Go where?" I ask, my heart thudding as reality presses in again.

"Pack meeting," he says as he starts for the door with Andy still at his side.

I stare after them, my thoughts racing. A pack meeting right now can only be about one thing: me. About whether to kill me or let me be their alpha. I can't tell which side Toros is on, but it won't matter. Majority will rule, and by the end of the day, I'll know my fate.

I swallow hard and force myself to follow them. Refusing will only prolong the inevitable. And I need to get this over with before my wolf takes me over completely. I'm not entirely sure what that will be like, but I know I don't want to do it in front of these people.

Already, I can feel the heat from earlier returning. It's like a pressure building and building until I finally combust. All I can do is hold it off as long as possible—and hope I live through the experience.

We take the SUV again.

Andy rides in the back with me while Toros sits up front with the driver, who wears a black security uniform. No one speaks, and I concentrate on keeping my shit together. When we slide to a stop, I recognize the luxury high-rise office immediately. It's the same one where the last pack meeting was held. When Franco put a bullet in Anthony Greco in front of a full auditorium like it was nothing. But it's not the sight of the building I've had nightmares about that gets me. It's the crowd that pulls my attention and renders me immobile in my seat.

People are lining the sidewalk on both sides of the street. Men in black shirts and suits—some I recognize from Vincenzo's pack—are acting as a barricade, pushing people back. Police cars have pulled sideways with their lights flashing, using their cruisers to barricade the street ahead of us as they direct traffic, one car at a time, through the narrow opening between pedestrians.

I've never seen this many people gathered in one place. There are easily five times as many people here as there were last time during the protests.

It's insane.

They're all yelling, but I can't make any of it out.

Toros gets out and opens my door, but still, I don't move. What if they're all here to witness my execution?

"It's okay, Lexi," Andy says from beside me.

I don't believe her. But what choice do I have?

Sliding out of the backseat, I force my knees not to buckle as I step from the car. Andy slides out behind me, her presence behind me urging me to move farther onto the sidewalk.

The crowd glimpses me and goes wild. People scream my name. They point their phones at me, snapping pictures or even filming me just standing here. Some wave homemade signs in the air, but I don't read them. I'm too afraid they'll be calling for my death in print, and there's no way my control can handle that. Instead, I scan the faces for anyone familiar.

I tell myself I'd take Mia, Dutch, Razor—even Crow right now. But it's Grey I'm really looking for.

I don't find any of them among the people treating me like I'm some kind of A-list celebrity.

My heart sinks, and the wild animal inside me thrashes harder in its disappointment.

I've never felt more alone.

"Guess the word is out," Toros says with a menacing frown.

Andy appears at my elbow. "Just breathe," she says so only I can hear.

Toros takes the lead, and Andy nudges me to follow.

We climb the steps to the high-rise office building. Someone opens the door for us, and I hurry through behind Toros, exhaling as the volume of the crowd lessens through the glass.

GV Industries is exactly as I remember. The same pristine marble floors, the same cool sterility with all its white, shiny surfaces. And the same auditorium with its stadium seating and sunken center stage. The last time I was here, I witnessed my first execution. Now, I'm the one in the crosshairs.

As if to prove what I'm up against, the first face I see inside the crowded auditorium is Vincenzo Diavolo. Grey's father and Alpha of the Diavolo pack. Right now, he's the most powerful man in the room. And the way he watches me reminds me I'm only alive as long as he finds me useful.

Still, there's not so much murder in his eyes that I worry about Ramsey's confession just yet. Instead, I think of the deal I made with him in exchange for my wolf. So much has happened since then, but the way he looks at me says he hasn't forgotten what I promised him.

He gave me back my beast, and for that, I swore to give him the entire kingdom. It was a title I never thought I'd own, much less be able to pass it to him. But now, it may very well have just fallen into my lap. And the gleam in his eye makes it clear he expects me to toss it right into his.

"Hello, Lexi," he says, managing to make the simple greeting sound like a death threat.

He sits in the front row with his generals beside him. Alvaro—Razor and Crow's father—glares at me. Rocco, Dutch's dad, simply lifts a brow as if he's measured me and found me lacking. Charlie, Mia's dad, won't meet my eyes.

I'm not sure what that means. While Vincenzo held me

hostage at his house, Charlie warned me that I should find another way that didn't involve trusting Grey's father with my fate. It had been a little too late for that, but I haven't forgotten that he tried to help me in his own way.

I don't look at him either as I pass by them all without a word. My gaze sweeps upward into the stadium seats, and I suck in a breath when I see a head of flowing red hair halfway up.

Mia winks at me.

Beside her, Dutch and Razor lean over the seat in front of them, their attention focused intently on me. The sight of them bolsters my courage, and I think for just a second that maybe I'll make it out of this room alive after all. But then my chest squeezes as I realize Grey is missing. Why isn't he here? Especially when everyone else clearly is. Even Serena, his mother, is seated a couple of rows behind Vincenzo, next to Sonesta, Rocco's wife. She offers me a kind but fleeting smile before I turn away from her.

"Everyone, listen up," Santiago calls from the center of the sunken stage. The murmurs in the room ignore him, so he tries again. "Sit the fuck down and shut your mouths. We're going to begin the vote."

Andy motions for me to sit beside her on the far end of the front row. Before I can sink into my chair, Conrad steps forward, blocking my path and forcing me to face him.

"Here's how this is going to work," Santiago says from the podium behind me. But Conrad ignores him.

His sneer is a sharp blade meant to cut, and his voice carries the venom of a man who thinks he should be king. "You don't deserve a fucking vote, much less an alpha title," he says, his voice ringing loud enough to silence the low murmur of the assembled packs. "Can you even shift?" He snorts. "Of course not." He leans in, close enough to me that I can scent his stale breath. "You're just some orphaned street rat who got lucky."

Lucky. Right. Because getting kidnapped just screams good fortune.

I force myself to stand tall, ignoring the way my muscles coil like I've been backed into a corner. Or the way the beast inside me wants to come out of that corner, claws swinging.

"That's funny," I say, my voice calm even as my pulse hammers. "Coming from Franco's fourth in line…out of four."

Conrad's expression flashes with rage. "What the fuck did you just say to me, bitch?"

"Oh. Did I misunderstand the hierarchy?" I ask, watching a vein bulge in his neck at my taunting.

"You don't know shit," he spits out.

"I know Dom was first in line," I say, vaguely aware of the crowd now hanging on our exchange. "And then Toros, Santiago, and then you. Oh wait. Dom's dead, so I guess that makes you third."

Conrad's gaze flicks over my shoulder to where I know Toros stands watching, but the elder general remains silent.

"What the fuck do you mean Dom's dead?" Conrad asks in a voice laced with deadly calm.

Right. No one knows this yet.

Some vaguely sane part of me tries to nudge me to shut up. But we're so far past that now. Besides, walking back a statement like that will only be seen as weakness.

"Would you like me to spell it out for you?" I snarl, anger swirling through my veins as I remember that night.

The way Dom tried to attack the moment he saw me alone and vulnerable.

I refuse to ever be seen like that again.

"Dom's throat is no longer attached to his body. He's dead. Gone. But at least that's a promotion for you, right?"

A ripple of agreement spreads through the room.

I hold my ground, but the beast inside me is rising again. Just like at Franco's, I can feel her scratching at my insides, trying to claw her way free. Sweat coats my face and neck as I struggle to hold her off. To focus on how to respond to this room full of powerful predators who are one majority vote away from ending me where I stand.

"You need to back off," I manage, my hands fisting at my sides.

Conrad studies me. Through hazy vision, I see him frown. "What's the matter with you, anyway? You smell like a damned rabid she-wolf."

Someone touches my elbow. I yank away from the unexpected contact, backing toward the center of the floor in order to gain some space. Everyone is suddenly too close. Too loud. Their scents overwhelming.

I can't breathe.

"She definitely smells like a wolf now," someone else comments.

Santiago maybe.

I can barely make out the voice through the roar in my own ears.

"She *is* a wolf, and she's the rightful heir," says a female voice full of authority.

Mia.

I squint up at her, but she's not in her seat.

She's standing in the aisle less than ten feet away. Dutch

and Razor are behind her, looking like they hope this ends in a pummeling.

"She looks like shit," Conrad says. He sounds smug.

"Hurry up and vote," someone else calls. "Get her the fuck out of here. She looks ready to hurl."

"All who recognize Lexi Giovanni as the high alpha of the Mafia Pack," Santiago begins, and very few hands begin to rise.

My heart pounds.

Conrad grins. "Time's up, you stupid, entitled bitch."

At the sight of that smile, a voice inside me whispers, *We will bathe in his blood.*

And I suddenly know I'm going to lose myself to my wolf. And I can do it here—in front of this asshole. Or I can run and hide first to make sure I don't hurt anyone else.

But I'm done running. And hiding.

"You want the title, Conrad? Then take it." I step forward, the challenge thick in my voice even though I know I'm a trembling mess. Seconds, I have only seconds before I'm not human anymore. "Right here. Right now," I add in nothing more than a whisper.

A wicked grin spreads across his face. "With pleasure."

He lunges.

I expect my instincts to take over, to let me dodge, to find an opening. But what happens next is not instinct.

It's something else entirely.

Heat erupts beneath my skin, like molten fire pouring through my veins. My breath stutters. The room sways. And then—pain. Blinding, unbearable pain. It shatters through my bones, stretching, snapping, twisting me apart from the inside out.

I scream, dropping to my knees. My nails gouge the carpet as my spine bows.

"Don't fight it, Lexi," I hear Mia say. She doesn't have to worry. I couldn't if I wanted to.

Something inside me tears loose.

My wolf.

My fucking wolf.

For the first time in my life, I feel my wolf rising to the surface of my skin—and she's out for blood.

A furious snarl rips from my throat, but it's not my human voice anymore. It's a raw, guttural thing. A predator's growl.

Power and strength flood my muscles, my cells.

Conrad stops mid-lunge, his face paling as his eyes go wide.

Too late.

I don't hesitate.

I launch.

The shift is seamless, muscle and bone reshaping as I slam into him. His body crashes against the wall, his bones snapping with a deafening crack, my claws slicing through his chest. He screams as he slides to the floor, but the sound barely registers beneath the pounding of my heartbeat, the rush of blood in my ears.

His hands shift—his own wolf trying to emerge—but he's too slow. Too weak. The beast inside me revels in knowing that. My fangs find his throat, and I tear through flesh, through sinew, through everything.

Santiago comes for me next. He half-shifts before he reaches me, his rage and grief contorting his expression. But he doesn't even fully change before my claws are raking down his flesh and his torn body is lying at my feet.

Power runs hot in my veins. The kills make me stronger. Deadlier. Hungrier.

Not me.

Her.

I can't even find me anymore.

If I could, maybe I'd hear Mia screaming for me. Or Razor and Dutch trying to get to me in the panic of the crowd pushing at them as they try to flee.

But all I see is Toros coming for me at last. I want to tell him he shouldn't, but I don't have a voice, nor do I have any sway with the wolf whose body I now inhabit.

Franco's scariest, most deadly general of them all shifts into an enormous wolf right before me. He leaps, claws and canines out. This fight isn't as easy as the others. His claws snap too close to my throat. It both terrifies me and enrages my wolf. She fights harder, and he does too. But in the end, my wolf cuts him to ribbons.

He falls at my feet just like the others did.

I can hear the moment his heart stops. The stillness where his breath has left his body.

My wolf tips her head back and howls, the sound echoing off the auditorium walls.

When I'm done, the panic subsides, and everyone in the auditorium is suddenly still. They watch me with wary eyes, as if trying to guess who I'll target next.

My wolf basks in their fear as she scans the room, daring anyone else to challenge us.

No one does.

Instead, they bow.

A glimpse of red hair draws my eye. I watch as Mia kneels first, but then, one by one, every member of the Giovanni pack drops to one knee. Even the Diavolo crowd, including Rocco, Alvaro, and Charlie. Then Vincenzo himself, though his reluctance is clear.

When he refuses to lower his eyes from mine, my wolf nearly goes for his throat. I don't know how I manage to hold her back. Maybe it's the silence or the sort of violent reverence of it all. A quiet room decorated with the blood of my enemies.

It's disgusting.

But my wolf seems placated by it.

Slowly, Vincenzo rises again and steps forward, his expression unreadable as he surveys my wolf—his new alpha. I growl just so he knows who the fuck he's dealing with. Just in case Franco's dead generals aren't enough indication.

He doesn't challenge me, but I can see him warring with the desire to try. When he speaks, his voice rings through the auditorium like a death knell. "Lexi Giovanni is the new high alpha of the Mafia Pack."

And just like that, I am no longer a girl caught between two warring families.

I am the alpha wolf at the head of them all.

4

GREY

Waiting alone for Lexi's alpha vote results is a more excruciating experience than the war I fought with the Black Moon Pack. Worse than being beaten by my father. Worse than that moment when I watched Lexi disappear through the church doors, clutched in Santiago's grip. At least, then I believed I'd done the right thing to secure her future. In the quiet of this room with only my doubts to fill the silence, I have no idea if my crazy-ass plan worked—or if I've only hastened the inevitable for us both.

And if I'm wrong, it's too late. Because she's already inside the auditorium, surrounded by wolves who will either offer her salvation… or demand her execution. And I can't do a goddamn thing to help her.

Not without exposing everything.

I pace the length of the small office tucked off the main lobby. Dust clings to the edge of the desk shoved into the corner, and the only light comes from the hazy dusk bleeding through the blinds. Even with my wolf hearing, I can only hear murmurs—low voices rising from the hall where they're holding the vote.

If I step one foot into that room, they'll know.

Know what I've become.

Know the power that pulses just beneath my skin like a second heartbeat.

Franco's power.

And a Diavolo with Franco's strength in his veins?

That'll get me and my pack killed before I can even explain that I don't want Franco's title for myself.

My phone buzzes. Unknown number.

I answer, expecting maybe Dutch or Razor checking in.

Instead: "Miss me?"

Ramsey.

His voice drips with that same confident drawl I remember from childhood. But there's something colder now. Detached. Like the last shred of familiarity between us has been scrubbed clean.

"Where are you?" I ask.

"What? You can't sense me, alpha?" His voice twists with cruel humor.

"No," I admit.

"That's because I'm free," he says simply. "In more ways than one."

"You left the pack."

No wonder I can't sense him.

"I left your stupid imitation of a pack," he corrects. "Which you should be thanking me for. If I hadn't, Rocco would have sensed it on me the moment that fucker got the drop on me. And then your old man would already know you've defected."

"You went back to my father?"

Even after everything Ramsey's done to me, I can't quite believe he'd run back to his previous alpha either.

"Of course not. Vincenzo can go fuck himself." His words fill with venom before lightening again as he says, "And I'm not calling to say thanks for unlocking my cage if that's what you're fishing for. We both know you did it for your own interests."

So, he knows we freed him. Thinks I gave the order.

I clench my jaw, not bothering to correct him. His lack of gratitude irritates me, and I can't keep that from my voice as I say, "You didn't tell my father about Lexi. Why?"

"Because, despite what you think of me, I'm not a snitch. Yet."

"Agree to disagree," I snarl.

"Be that as it may, I can change my mind at any time and spill what I know."

"That supposed to scare me?"

"No, Grey. It's supposed to warn you. I didn't say anything this time. But don't think I won't if it gives me an edge."

"An edge for what? What exactly do you want, Ramsey?"

"From you? Nothing."

A pang of regret hits me in the chest then. Ramsey and I grew up as brothers. His betrayal is a loss I'll feel for the rest of my life.

"How could you do this, Ram? You know Razor and Crow—"

"What? Thought, by unlocking that door, I'd come running back to you?" He scoffs. "Sorry to disappoint, Grey, but your little wannabe pack officially has one less lapdog."

"Good to know that's what you think of them," I say, the quiet in my voice rippling with fury on their behalf.

"It's what we are," he spits. "What I was."

"Is that why you betrayed us? You got tired of feeling like you weren't the center of attention?"

"I refuse to keep following a guy who can't claim what's his. I waited, Grey. I waited for you to be who you were always meant to be. Even after you left, I held out hope for years that you would come back and lead us to independence. But you never did. Even when you found Lexi, you never saw the big picture. Never took what you were owed."

"That's bullshit. You don't get to rewrite history just because you're bitter."

"I'm so far past fucking bitter," Ramsey says, voice sharp. "My dad followed yours and got killed for it. I'm done following—you or anyone else."

I remember the moment his dad got shot. Something changed in Ramsey that day. I didn't realize then how bad it was. Maybe if I had, I could have prevented this irreparable break between us. Then again, he'd already been informing against us by then, so maybe the damage had already been done.

The silence stretches between us.

I don't fill it.

Then he adds, almost as an afterthought, "Besides, sounds like your mate's got her own mess going on. That wolf of hers? Can't say I didn't see that coming."

My pulse spikes. "If you touch her—"

"Relax. I didn't have to. Looks like your father beat me to it as usual. But you might be less concerned about me and more concerned about whether your pretty alpha wife can keep from snapping someone's neck mid-negotiation. Just a thought."

"What are you—"

"See you around, brother."

He hangs up.

And I stand there, staring at the phone in my hand, trying not to punch a hole through the wall.

He's here. At the meeting. And I'm not.

I clench my fists and lean over the desk I'm sitting at, pressing my forehead against the cool wood. My skin itches, my wolf prowling beneath the surface like he wants out, like he knows something's wrong and is ready to rip the fucking walls down to get to her.

"Keep it together," I whisper, even though I'm not sure if I'm talking to myself or to the beast inside me.

I send a text to Dutch, asking how it's going. Silence follows.

And then—

Shouts.

A crash.

From the direction of the auditorium, something heavy hits the floor.

I freeze, spinning toward the door. For a second, everything goes still. No voices. No movement. Just the deafening roar of blood in my ears.

Then—chaos.

Screams echo from the hallway. Footsteps thunder down the corridor outside the office. The metallic sting of blood floods the air, even through the closed door.

My heart stops.

Lexi.

I shove the door open so hard it slams against the wall.

Pack members—Giovanni and Diavolo alike—are rushing past me, eyes wide, expressions twisted.

"What the hell—?"

A female voice gasps, "She's crazy—she would have taken us all out—"

My blood turns to ice.

I tear down the hallway, my boots pounding the tile until I hit the open double doors leading to the meeting room. The scent hits me hard enough to stop me in my tracks. And then I see it.

Blood.

Everywhere.

The metallic scent clogs my nose, fills my lungs. My wolf rears up, snarling, wanting out, needing to protect—

Lexi.

She's not here. A quick scan of the room proves that.

But three dead bodies are.

It takes me a moment to identify them around the blood and exposed tissue, but then I see enough of their facial features to recognize them.

Toros. Santiago. Conrad.

Franco's generals.

All of them lie in crumpled heaps on the floor, blood pooling beneath them, staining the ornate carpet that runs the length of the room.

Their throats are shredded. Deep gouges rake across their chests and throats like they were torn apart by something wild.

By *someone* wild.

Dutch stands at the edge of the carnage, eyes sharp, body rigid like he's waiting for another attack. Blood streaks his shirt, but it's not his. Not from the scent of it.

Mia and Razor are near the back, helping people up who were either hiding behind the seats or tossed back there. Some have cuts and bruises.

"Lexi?" I rasp, scanning the space, searching for more bodies, more danger, *her.*

"Back door," Dutch says quickly, jerking his chin toward the rear of the room.

My legs move on instinct, but I pause just long enough to grab his arm. "What happened?"

"She shifted," he says grimly. "They threatened to vote her out. Conrad got in her face. Called her a fake alpha. Said she'd never rule." His jaw tightens. "She shifted and went straight for Conrad. Ripped his throat out before anyone saw it coming."

I swallow hard, chest burning.

"Toros and Santiago tried to stop her," he continues, quieter now. "They barely got a growl off before she eviscerated them."

"Fuck," I breathe.

"After that, it was like she lost it. Started going for anyone in her path. She got a lucky shot on Razor. Slashed his arm pretty good."

I glance up and see where Razor's arm is wrapped in his shirt, blood soaking through, while he continues to help others get out. Some of them look worse than he does.

"She probably felt trapped. Threatened by all these people," I murmur.

"I don't think she has anything to worry about there," Dutch says quietly. "They fucking bowed to her the moment they saw what she did to Franco's guys." He grabs my shoulder as if to make sure I hear him before adding, "They voted her in. She's High Alpha now."

"Good," I say, relief mingling with my worry. "How'd she get out?"

"Busted through the back door." He points at where the door at the end of the aisle is dented and hanging crookedly open.

"Alone?" I ask, the word like an accusation.

"No one was going to fuck with her," Dutch says. "Not like that."

Mia joins us, her eyes wide and worried. "I've never seen a wolf act like that, even in a closed space. She was... feral."

"I have to find her. You two track down my father and see what he's doing about Lexi suddenly being his boss. And see if you can find Ramsey."

"Ramsey?" Dutch echoes. "Why?"

"He was here. Watching. And he left the pack. I don't trust him not to hurt Lexi."

"Okay, we'll see if we can find him," Dutch assures me.

"We'll talk later." I start walking.

"Grey," Mia says gently. "Be careful. She wasn't *herself.*"

"She's still mine."

I push past them both and run up the aisle, two steps at a time. I hit the exit doors, race down the stairs behind the meeting chamber, and shove through the back exit.

All I can think about is how Ramsey was here. And now he's not. And neither is Lexi. If he tries to hurt her, fuck our history together. I'll kill him.

Outside, the alley is steeped in early twilight. Trash bins line the brick walls. The sky overhead is smeared with purple and gold, the edges of night creeping in.

Her scent hits me like a punch.

Bright. Wild. Tangled with panic.

Lexi.

I rip at my clothes as I move, yanking off my jacket, shoving my pants down as I stumble into the shadowed alley. The moment I'm clear of sightlines, I drop to my knees, calling on the beast inside me.

The shift tears through me like fire and ice, my bones snapping and stretching, my skin splitting open to let my true nature emerge. My wolf erupts, thick grey fur spreading across powerful limbs, paws hitting the ground hard. My nose lifts, catching the trail Lexi left behind like a flaming torch against the darkness.

She ran northeast. Toward the industrial district. Toward the river.

I leap forward, claws scraping concrete, muscles burning as I sprint after her. I don't know how far she's gone. I don't know what state she's in.

I only know I need to find her before someone else does.

I will not lose her.

Not now.

Not ever.

I push harder, my paws blurring beneath me. My heartbeat is a war drum in my chest.

I'm coming for you, Lexi. Just hold on.

THE CITY FADES BEHIND ME, swallowed by asphalt and distance. The air shifts as I hit the tree line on the southwestern border—cooler, sharper, rich with the scent of pine and moss. The last of the sun slants through the thick canopy overhead, dappling golden light across the forest floor. Birds scatter as I charge past, the world blurring into a mess of trees and shadows and the ever-stronger pull of *her*.

I know these woods like the back of my hand. From here, it's a straight shot northwest to the lake house my family owns. I've done countless pack runs between here and there. Some with Dutch and the others. Some with my mother. Good memories still linger among these trees. But I don't think about any of that now.

I think only of her.

Lexi's scent is thick now. Blood, sweat, fear. But underneath it all is *her*. Wild. Raw. Unmistakably mine.

She ran here to hide. To breathe. To fall apart where no one could see.

But I see her. I *feel* her.

And I'm not leaving until I bring her home.

My paws hit damp leaves and roots, kicking up the earthy perfume of loam and fallen pine needles. This place has always felt peaceful—there's a clearing to the right that opens onto a soft patch of moss, and the quiet there feels ancient, sacred.

Indigo Hills was created with the magic of a hexerei witch coven. That fact is never more obvious than inside the western part of the forest. Like the city has managed to wash it away with its own veneer but nature remains coated in that ancient alchemy. The trees rise overhead like cathedral walls, tall and patient, whispering stories only wolves can hear.

But tonight, even this beautiful place isn't enough to calm my mate.

I see a flash of white fur ahead.

She's fast—fuck, she's fast—but not faster than me.

Lexi glances over her shoulder, large green eyes glinting

in the dark. Her fur is streaked in blood, dried and dark across her chest and front legs. But even so, her wolf is stunning—long-limbed and built for speed, her white-blonde coat glowing in the moonlight, despite the carnage that's matted her fur. She's like something out of a dream. A dangerous, broken, beautiful dream.

Our eyes lock, and my wolf recognizes Lexi instantly for what she is to us: mate. If I'd ever doubted it, I don't anymore. For a second, I think maybe the sight of my wolf will be enough to settle her—but then she bolts.

I surge after her, my heart slamming into my ribs. The predator in me growls in pleasure. Despite the blood coating her fur and the reasons that drove us out here, my wolf howls with lust and need and raw instinct.

Chase her. Catch her. Bite her. Make her yours.

My alpha instincts ride the edge of control, pushing me faster, harder. The mate-bond is a wildfire in my veins, and everything inside me is screaming for me to chase her down and claim her with my bite.

But I can't forget the look in her eyes. The fear. The pain.

She's not running from me.

She's running from herself.

Still, I chase. I *have* to.

I keep her in my sights as we wind through the trees, leap fallen logs, splash through a shallow ravine. She's not heading anywhere. She's just trying to escape the weight of what she did.

I would do anything to carry it for her.

Hell, that's exactly what I'm trying to do by giving her the credit for Franco's kill.

Finally, she stumbles into a small clearing at the edge of

a narrow stream. The water is dark in the fading light, flowing over smooth stones and between banks covered in moss.

Lexi skids to a stop at the water's edge, sides heaving, blood still streaked across her fur. Her ears flick back, and she turns as I slowly approach, her paws sinking into the soft moss.

She's watching me.

Waiting.

Mate.

The word clangs through me, making it hard to take this slow. When I get close, her hackles rise, and her wolf bares its teeth, so I do the least threatening thing I can think of.

I shift, the change rippling through me with heat and fire and a burst of pain. Bones snap, flesh warps, and then I'm standing upright again, naked and breathless, chest rising with exertion.

"Lexi," I say softly.

She growls low.

"It's me," I continue, cautious, calm, crouching slightly to make myself smaller, less threatening. "It's okay. You're safe."

She takes a step back, her back paw dipping into the stream. A soft whine escapes her throat. I hold my breath, hoping like hell she doesn't run again but ready to chase if she does.

"I know you're scared. But you don't have to be." I take a slow step forward. "You didn't do anything wrong. They forced your hand. You defended yourself."

She growls low in her throat, a sound more broken than angry.

"Lexi… I need to talk to you." I let my own desperation creep into my voice. "I need to *touch* you. But I can't do that while you're like this."

She lowers her head, ears pinned back. Her breath rasps in and out in short, panicked bursts.

"Can you shift back?" I ask gently.

She whines again. Tosses her head side to side.

"Hey," I say, voice low and steady. "Just listen to me. That's all you have to do." I press a hand to my chest, right over my heart. "Listen to the sound of my voice. The beat of my heart. Really listen. It's all for you, Lexi. *I exist for you.* And my wolf…" My throat tightens. "My wolf belongs to yours. Always. Feel the truth of that inside your wolf. She already knows I'm your mate."

Her breath hitches.

"Find our connection. Let it ground you. Let it bring you back to me."

The recognition that she's my mate is nothing more than a vague, tenuous connection between us. But I wait, hoping it's enough.

She trembles. Her paws shift on the grass, claws digging in. She lets out a strangled whimper, eyes flashing as her body begins to twist, bones cracking, fur rippling.

Her shift takes longer than mine. It's rougher, like she's fighting it—or doesn't know how to surrender to it. And it's clear how much pain she's in.

But she does it.

By the time her knees hit the ground and her human form settles into place, I'm already moving. I cross the clearing in three strides and lift her up, wrapping my arms around her before she collapses. She's trembling violently, slick with sweat and blood and river water.

"Grey," she gasps, her voice raw and broken. She clutches at me, her fingers digging into my shoulders, her body shaking like she'll shatter if I let go.

"I'm here," I whisper fiercely, one hand cupping the back of her head, the other anchoring her to my chest. "I've got you."

She sobs against my neck, her body bare and battered and so goddamn precious I could fall apart just from holding her.

"I didn't mean to," she chokes out. "I didn't know— My wolf—"

"Shh," I breathe into her hair. "You did what you had to do. They would've killed you."

"But I-I *wanted* to kill them. I didn't even think. I just let her—" Her breath hitches again. "I'm a monster."

I pull back just enough to cup her face, forcing her to look at me. Her green eyes are wide and tear-filled, glassy with guilt.

"No," I say, voice rough with emotion. "You're not a monster. You're a wolf. A leader. An alpha. You did what they pushed you to do. What your wolf was made to do. You survived. You let her protect you. And I love every part of you, including the one that fought for yourself today. Including the one that killed today."

She shakes her head, tears slipping free. "They were going to vote against me."

"I know."

"They would have killed me."

I hold her tighter, wishing I could change that moment for her. But so damn proud of her for letting her wolf out. "You are not alone in this, Lexi. You never will be again."

And with that, I pull her back to me and wrap her in

my arms. She presses her face into my chest and lets the tears fall, and I hold her tighter, whispering words I don't even realize I'm saying, stroking her hair.

I don't care that we're sitting naked in the woods. Or that someone might find us here. All I care about is the girl in my arms.

My mate.

My alpha.

And I will burn this whole fucking city to the ground before I let anyone take her from me again.

5

LEXI

I'm trembling in Grey's arms, curled against his bare chest like his body is a lifeline to my sanity, but the chaos inside me is finally starting to still. The rhythm of his heart against my ear is the only thing keeping me from unraveling.

He hasn't let go of me once.

Almost as if he's the one who needs this moment instead of me. Realizing I'm not the only one who fell apart today is weirdly comforting. His heartbeat is a steady rhythm against my skin. I focus on that. On the way his presence seems to pulse all the way through me.

When my heart rate finally calms, I let myself notice my surroundings for the first time. And I'm struck by the otherworldly feeling of this place.

It's as if the forest breathes around us.

Not in the obvious way, with wind and leaves and branches swaying overhead, but something deeper. Older. Like the trees themselves remember what came before us—and maybe what's still to come. I never spent much time in nature before coming to Indigo Hills. And even once I arrived, my days here have been spent mostly inside high rises, mansions, and pool houses. But this place makes me want to claim a spot and never leave it… it's captivating and the perfect distraction to bring me back to myself.

"Talk to me," Grey finally says. "Tell me what else I can do."

The pleading in his voice alerts me that, despite his calm and steady heartbeat, he's still freaking out.

"I'm okay," I whisper, my voice rough and barely believable, even to me.

"You sure?" His voice rumbles through his chest, low and protective.

"No," I admit, because he deserves honesty. "But I will be."

He doesn't answer right away. Just holds me a little tighter. Lets me feel the truth in his silence: that I don't have to be okay right now. Not as long as he's here to carry the weight for both of us.

Eventually, my skin starts to itch. I rake my nails over what I realize with disgust is dried blood coating my face and throat. Grey watches my reaction with darkening eyes.

"Come on," he says gently.

Before I can ask what he means to do, he moves, lifting me effortlessly, like I'm light as air. I wrap my arms around his neck, holding on in a way that, if I let go, my wolf might take me over again, and I'll lose myself forever.

He wades into the stream with me still cradled to his chest. The water is deeper than it looks, and I gasp as it hits my legs, the cool temperature jolting to my senses. But Grey doesn't stop, and I press myself against his warmth as the water laps against our hips, the current rushing gently around us. I expected to be chilled, but after a moment, my body adjusts, and it feels warm. Comforting. Like the earth itself is trying to soothe us.

Or maybe my flushed skin is still overheated from my run. Then again, maybe wolves just run hotter than humans. I can still feel her inside me like a foreign presence beneath my skin. She's not nearly as controlling as before, but I am hyper-aware that she could take me over again in a second if she wanted to.

She seems happy enough now that Grey is touching me, though.

She likes him.

In fact, her emotions concerning him are clearer the longer I tune into her.

Mate.

The word jolts me back to reality. To standing in the stream naked with the man I just married.

"Let's get you cleaned up," Grey says, yanking my focus back to the way he's sinking a little and submerging my body.

"What?" I look down at myself—at the dried blood streaking my chest and arms—and flinch. I don't know whose it is, but I can still feel the way my claws sank into their flesh. The way my wolf reveled in the taste of violence. A predator. Never prey.

My stomach clenches, and I nearly pull away, but his hands tighten around me underwater.

"Let me," he murmurs.

He brings my hand to his lips and kisses my knuckles before dipping it beneath the surface. Then, with slow reverence, he begins to wash the blood away with his calloused hands.

I watch him in silence, my throat tight.

The way he touches me—careful, patient, thorough—undoes me more than any words of reassurance ever could. He's not afraid of what I did. He's not disgusted. He's still here, treating me like I'm some fragile goddess to be worshipped.

He rubs his hands over my arms, trailing his fingers over my skin as he brushes away all the imperfections. When he reaches my chest, he pauses, his hands hovering mid-air.

"Is this okay?" he asks, eyes locking on mine.

I nod.

His hand slides over the swell of my breasts. Down my sternum. Across my abdomen. The way he looks at my body is almost reverent, like he's not cleaning blood off me as much as honoring something holy. Something broken but beautiful.

"You don't have to do this," I whisper, suddenly embarrassed.

His eyes snap to mine. Fire burns in his dark gaze. "Yes, I do. This is what it's like to be touched by someone who *sees* you, Lexi."

At his words, I get a lump in my throat, and it takes everything in me not to shed another tear. Not trusting my voice, I nod and lower my eyes.

When the last of the blood is gone, he shifts his grip and walks us out of the stream. I'm not cold, but I shiver anyway. Naked and raw in every way a person can be.

He carries me to a mossy patch on the bank and sits down with me in his lap, tucking me into his chest like he's afraid I'll vanish if he lets go.

I sit with my arms around his neck, breathing him in.

The night air is laced with pine and moss and moonlight. His skin is warm against mine, his hands splayed over my hips, grounding me. It's not sexual, but somehow, that makes it even more meaningful. I've never been held like this in my life. My heart shudders and then clicks into place with the full and complete knowledge that no one else ever will. It's only Grey.

And now, I'm finally a wolf like him.

"I didn't know," I murmur.

"Didn't know what?"

"What it would feel like. To shift."

He waits, giving me space.

"I was scared," I admit. "But when it happened, it was… like waking up. Like I'd been half-asleep my whole life and didn't realize it until I opened my eyes as her." I pull back just enough to meet his gaze. "I felt powerful. Not just strong—*free.* Like nothing and no one could ever touch me again."

A slow smile spreads across his face. "That's what it's supposed to feel like."

"And the rest of it, the attack…"

He tenses slightly but doesn't look away.

"It wasn't like defending myself as a human," I say. "It was some kind of animal instinct. My wolf—she's… brutal. And I had no control. That scares me."

"You protected yourself," he says firmly. "And you didn't just survive—you claimed your place as alpha. Dutch says they all bowed to you at the end."

"At which point, I continued to take chunks of flesh out of them as I fought my way out." I cringe at the memory of all that blood. Not to mention what I'm pretty sure is tissue and maybe even organs. Gross. I had someone's skin in my mouth. "I don't know if they'll still see me as alpha after that."

"They will. Or else."

I arch a brow. "Or else what?"

He shrugs. "Or I'll make them."

I laugh softly, resting my forehead against his. "You really are a menace."

He shrugs. "Only for you."

My smile fades as his words trigger my memory.

"What is it?" he asks, instantly alert. And I can feel it in a way I never did before. His animal side rising up, ready to fight.

"At the church, when they took me away… You let them." The last part comes out a little strangled as I remember what it felt like to be carried away from my husband. To see him watching it unfold and do nothing to stop it. Even though I see now why he did it.

"I know. Fuck, I know." He runs a hand through his hair, the anguish in his eyes evident. "I'm sorry. It was the only way to make sure my father didn't get his hands on you or kill you before I had the chance to—"

"I know."

He blinks, clearly expecting me to be furious.

I lay a hand on his chest. "I know," I say again, watching the words sink in. "You did it for me. So that I'd be safe. I understand now."

He huffs. "I don't deserve your understanding. I let our enemy take you from me, and I stood there."

"You believed I could fight for myself long enough for us to find our way here," I tell him. And the conviction of that knowledge has me tearing up. "No one's ever believed in me like that. People have treated me like I'm stupid or helpless or defenseless my entire life. You're the first person to let me fight for myself—and to know I'm capable of surviving. Thank you."

"It was the hardest thing I've ever done," he says, his voice scraping my skin with its rawness.

I press my hand to his cheek, wanting only to assuage the guilt and torment in his eyes.

"I will always find my way back to you," he says.

Then he kisses me. And everything else fades away.

It starts soft. Gentle. Lips barely brushing, just enough to stir the edges of something waiting—something electric that buzzes beneath my skin.

But then he deepens it.

And whatever thing he's awakened between us comes fully alive.

The kiss turns greedy, open-mouthed, and consuming. His tongue sweeps into my mouth, claiming, coaxing, devouring. I moan, and he swallows it like it's his favorite sound.

My ears roar with the sensations. My skin feels like a live wire. And in my mind or my heart—I don't know which—I can sense him wanting me.

The mate bond.

What felt like a vague thought before suddenly flares to life between us. I feel the essence of him everywhere—*inside* me, like a second heartbeat. Like he's always been there, waiting for me to notice.

"I feel you," I gasp between kisses. "In a way I couldn't before. Like… like I *am* you."

He groans, pressing his forehead to mine. "That's the bond. It's real now. Fully awake."

"Is that what this is?" I whisper. "This heat? This ache?"

"Yes. And it'll only grow stronger when I bite you." He pauses. "But that doesn't have to be now. We can wait. We *should* wait."

I roll my hips against him slowly and feel the sharp intake of his breath as his erection presses against my thigh. "What if I don't want to wait?"

"Lexi..."

I reach between us and wrap my fingers around him, feeling the shudder that ripples through his entire body. "I want to belong to you in every way I can. Now. Here. Tonight."

He exhales a needy sound, and then he's kissing me again. His hands slide down my body, trailing reverent paths. Over my ribs. My hips. My thighs. His fingers part my folds, pushing inside me, and I gasp.

"I can feel how wet you are for me," he murmurs, stroking me slowly.

But it's not enough.

My wolf wants him—all of him. She wants to belong to him. At last, we agree on something.

"Grey," I breathe. "Please."

He slides his fingers out of me and lifts me up and over his erection. Slowly, he lowers me onto him, and I feel him sliding into me. Deep. Like we're falling into each other inch by delicious inch.

I gasp, clutching at his shoulders, and he stills.

"Too much?"

"No," I whisper. "It's perfect."

He moves inside me, his dark eyes locked on mine like he's memorizing the shape of my soul. Every thrust is unhurried, like we have all the time in the world. Like this moment is meant to stretch forever.

The sounds around us blur—the hum of insects, the rustle of leaves, the gurgle of the stream. All I know is his breath against my skin. His hands gripping my waist. His lips brushing my jaw, my neck, my shoulder.

The bond pulses with every movement we make. Every moan. Every whispered promise. My wolf stirs, snarling her approval in my mind.

Suddenly, the need building inside me is not a soft, slow thing. Soon, I'm rocking harder against him, whispering, pleading for him to go faster. His grip on my hips tightens. I hiss in pleasure at the roughness.

The wolf inside me preens and purrs at how he takes control. He's the only one we'll ever let hold power over us again. I close my eyes, lost to the way Grey feels inside me, against me.

He leans in, his teeth scraping over my throat. I buck against him, aching for his claiming bite. Nothing about that desire feels human, but I don't fight it. I don't even want to try.

"Do it," I urge him.

He presses his mouth against the soft flesh of my neck, and a moment later, his teeth puncture my skin. Pleasure spears through me, unlike anything I've ever known.

A snarl rips from me, more animal than human.

"That's it, baby," Grey says, leaning back to expose his neck to me.

Only ever to me.

I lean in and bite down, letting my wolf guide me. He shudders, loosing a deep groan I feel all the way through me. His blood hits my tongue, and I ignite.

Pleasure slams into me.

I cry out, driving faster, needing more.

Grey's hands are tight around my hips, squeezing with the possession of a mate's touch. His eyes on mine burn with a dark intensity that sears my heart to his.

"I love you," he murmurs into my hair. "So fucking much."

Tears slip down my cheeks, but they're not from pain. Not from grief.

They're from a feeling so foreign I'm surprised I know it. But even my wolf can't deny that this moment feels like finally *coming home.*

I fall apart around him with a cry, and he follows, groaning my name like a prayer. We cling to each other through it, shaking and breathless, undone and whole at the same time.

He lowers his back to the mossy ground, pulling me with him so I'm sprawled across his chest, both of us still slick with sweat and breathing hard. We lie there in silence for a long time, the stars twinkling lazily overhead. I roll over so I can stare up at the constellations, full of wonder at the new sensations swirling inside me.

I can feel Grey's presence—the mate bond—easily enough. Like a tether from my heart to his. It's incredible.

"Will it always feel like this?" I ask.

"The sex? God, I hope so."

I laugh. "The bond. I can feel you. I don't know how to explain it. Like, no matter how far away you are, I'll know whether you're happy or safe or sad."

"Yeah," he says in a hushed voice. Like he's just as in awe of it as I am. "I think it will." His hand reaches for mine, and he winds our fingers together.

We lie like that for a while longer, marveling at the connection we've just sealed between us. Eventually, Grey lifts himself up on his elbow and brushes his fingers through my hair.

"We should get going," he murmurs.

I blink lazily up at him, half-asleep. "Where?"

He frowns, and a tension fills the bond between us. It's the first jolt of reality that reminds me what we've left behind. His words are the second.

"I'm going to take you to stay with some friends outside the city. I'll come back and—"

"Without me?"

"Just for a few days. You need time to rest. To heal."

I stare at him, the weight of the past twenty-four hours crashing down all over again. My pack is waiting. My wolf is still pacing beneath my skin. Vincenzo Diavolo has his hooks into me deeper than ever. And yet, none of that is responsible for the emotion that catches in my throat.

"Grey?"

He blinks, softening instantly at my tone. "Yeah?"

"Are we… actually married?"

6

LEXI

Grey's brows pull together. "What?"

I look away, my uncertainty making me nervous. "I mean, the ceremony got interrupted, and I got accused of murder and then was basically kidnapped, and there was a lot of snarling and blood and murder today—so… did it count?"

The corner of his mouth lifts, and that one stupidly crooked smile somehow makes my heart squeeze harder than all the chaos ever could. Losing Grey would be the single worst thing that could ever happen to me. And the harder I fall for him, the more painfully aware of that fact I become. I need Grey Diavolo to love me like I love him: obsessively, unendingly—forever.

"You're seriously asking me this right now? After we've just claimed each other as mates?"

"I am," I say, trying to sound light, but I can't quite hide the nerves threading through my voice. "Claiming is between our wolves. But being married to you… I don't know. Maybe it's just me being a human, but it feels more like a public declaration. A different kind of promise. And I want to know if you actually want that. If it still means something, or if it was just part of the plan to keep me safe."

He's quiet for half a second; then he exhales like it physically hurts that I even have to ask. His fingers slide under my chin, lifting my face to his.

"You're my wife, Lexi. My mate. My alpha. You're not just part of the plan I have for the rest of my life—you *are* the plan. You and me. Forever. That's it."

My throat tightens, but he keeps going.

"And to be clear, human, wolf, I want every part of you. The Fast and Furious movie binges, the wolf who shreds her enemies to ribbons, the girl whose body I can't keep my hands off of. I want to spend the rest of my life being driven crazy by you and loving every second of it. So yeah. We're married. And no, I don't regret it for a second."

My lips part, but no words come out.

My wolf huffs softly in agreement.

Grey's hand trails along my own before he winds his fingers through mine. The touch reminds me—

"I lost the ring," I realize, looking down at my bare hand. "It must have fallen off when I shifted."

"We'll find it," he assures me with a shrug, but I have to blink back tears at how careless I've just been with the symbol of our commitment.

I shake my head. "I'm sorry."

"Don't apologize. I told you, my father picked that ring—"

"No, I know. I meant the twist-tie," I say softly. "The one *you* gave me."

I run my fingers over the bare spot on his hand, noting that the one I gave him during our ceremony is also gone.

"It's a hazard of shifting," he says. "Trust me, don't get attached to clothes or jewelry from here on out."

"I'm only attached to you," I tell him.

He leans in, brushing his mouth over mine like a vow. "That's a good fucking thing, *wife*. Because I'm never letting you go."

I smile, breathless and aching and stupidly, deliriously in love with this man. "I like hearing you call me that," I whisper.

His answering grin is pure hunger and heat and heart. "Then I'll say it every fucking day of forever."

"That sounds nice."

His answering kiss is light, playful. But I can't stop the heaviness from returning when I try to picture the "forever" he's just referred to. "Grey?"

He grins. "Yes, wife?"

"What happens next?"

His amusement fades to concern as he sees my expression. "What do you mean?"

"This whole alpha thing… I didn't kill Franco." His concern turns to guilt, and I have my confirmation of what I suspected from the moment Dutch interrupted our ceremony with the news. "But you already know that since you killed him."

His gaze snaps to mine. Whatever he sees there, he doesn't bother trying to soften it. Or pretend I don't already know. "Are you pissed?"

"I was at first," I admit quietly, "about telling them I had power that I didn't have."

"But not about me being the one who did it?" he asks warily.

"No." I sit up, still bare but not particularly shy about it. We've both seen too much of each other—good and bad—for modesty to matter anymore. "Franco was never going to change. And I don't think for a second you did it without a good reason."

His shoulders tense. He looks away.

"I had to," he says. "He threatened to hurt you."

The way he growls with each word spoken is more proof that, when it comes down to it, Grey will let a lot of things slide. Almost anything, really—except someone threatening me. It's the only thing he'll never show mercy for. I saw it with Dom. Even when Grey thought I'd betrayed him, he killed Dom for hurting me. I saw it with his father too. A man he'd never intended to go up against again—until Vincenzo tried to use me. And now, with Franco, there was never going to be another outcome once my safety became an issue.

And I can't possibly be angry at that. Not when he's the first person to ever protect me that way. And not when I'd do the same thing for him in a heartbeat. Hell, it's the whole reason I made the deal I did for my wolf. Not to protect myself, but to protect him.

Grey deserves someone to fight for him the way he's fighting for me. I'm determined to be that person.

"You could have just told them the truth," I say. "You'd be the high alpha by now."

But he shakes his head. "No, they wouldn't have voted me in unless I also killed my father. Too many questions of loyalty otherwise. They'd think my dad put me up to it as a consolidated power-grab." He grimaces.

I don't argue because he's right; that's exactly what his father wanted him to do from the start.

"Can I ask…what's stopping you from going after your dad?"

"Nothing, believe me." Murder swims in his eyes, a promise that he won't break for anything. "But this way—with you getting the credit—the pack sees you as strong. That's the only way you survive this. The only way they don't tear you apart. For you to be on the throne, calling the shots. I won't go to war with my father and his pack until I know you're safe."

He looks back at me, pain and regret reflected in his eyes. He didn't want to do this to me, but he saw no other way. And when he puts it like that, neither do I. Still….

I nod slowly. "I get it. But next time, don't make that decision for me."

"You were locked up. I was losing my fucking mind when my father took you, and I…" His tortured eyes meet mine again, and he blows out a breath. "I swear. No more playing savior behind your back."

"Thanks," I say.

A beat of silence passes, and then his tone changes as he says, "I'm glad you're not mad because that promise goes both ways."

"What do you mean?"

His expression shifts—sharp, wary. "Tell me the truth. How did you access your wolf?"

I freeze.

The moment stretches too long, and my silence is its own confession. But he gave me the courtesy of an explanation, so I do the same.

"Your father gave me a serum to trigger the change."

"A serum." He huffs, and I brace myself for anger, but his tone is gentle, and instead I feel guilty when he adds, "It could have killed you."

"You're right," I admit. "But he had files from when I was a baby. That fever I told you about… the records showed they gave me something called Aconitumex."

"Wolfsbane," he murmurs.

"My mom gave it to me to suppress the LAG gene Franco activated," I tell him. "But the dose was so high it suppressed my wolf."

"And the serum was the antidote," he says almost to himself.

"Wolf venom for the change, a gene booster to activate the LAG gene, and, yeah, the antidote." A beat of silence passes. "Are you pissed?" I ask, stealing his line.

He sighs, running a hand through his tousled hair. It's a move I recognize for when he's stressed. But he doesn't look angry as he says, "I'm disappointed you didn't wait for me so we could figure out your wolf together."

"I was so tired of being weak, Grey. I need to be able to fight, to protect myself."

"I would have—"

"Don't say you would have protected me."

His smile is rueful, but it vanishes quickly. "Okay, I get it. But I do have to wonder what exactly you promised him in exchange for such a thing?"

I wince. "Two things. He wants a blood sample from me so his researchers can access my wolf's gene code."

His cheeks flush, and I know he's doing his best to hold his temper. "And the second thing?"

"Relinquish my title to him."

He flushes red. Okay, definitely pissed now.

I rush to say, "At the time… my title was nothing more than an unnamed heir. It seemed like a small price to pay."

His brow lifts. "And now?"

I blow out a breath, despair and worry leaking in again. "I know it was only my first shift, but my wolf was so out of control. She feels… wild. And I think that's because of whatever Franco did to me. I worry she's too powerful. And if there's one person who shouldn't have access to more power, it's him."

"At the risk of sounding like a broken record, spending a few days out of town would—"

"No."

"I'd come with you," he counters. "We could use some time to ourselves."

"Jericho Grey Diavolo, are you using the idea of a honeymoon to manipulate me into running away from a war with your father?"

"Depends. Is it working?"

I punch him on the arm, and he grins, but we both sober quickly. "I can't run away," I say quietly. "I have to face this." I can't bring myself to say *my* pack, even though I think that's what it is now.

He frowns. "Lexi, you don't have to do this—"

"Yes, I do."

He looks pained. "If anyone finds out you don't have Franco's power—"

"I don't need it," I say.

Mostly because I can't imagine being much stronger than I already am. My wolf seems pretty capable already of taking out our enemies.

He looks like he wants to argue, but then he sighs. "You don't," he admits. "I felt it when I chased you here. You have more than a newly shifted wolf should. They must have felt it when they bowed to you."

Either that, or the triple murder convinced them.

"I will deal with my father. Later. Right now, all that matters is making you alpha."

"I thought you said I already was."

"The leadership voted you in. Now you have to convince the rest of the pack to pledge their loyalty to you. Then, it's official."

Shit.

No one said anything about pledges of loyalty.

"Will you help convince them?" I ask nervously.

"Wife," he says, pulling me to my feet and stroking a hand down my cheek. "I'll be by your side every step of the way."

An older model sedan is already parked on the side of the road when we finally make our way out of the woods. I squint through the darkness and am surprised to realize I can make out the figure inside. Enhanced eyesight. Endurance. Scent. I'm still trying to process all of the abilities my wolf has given me.

"Is that Crow's?" I ask, faltering. "How did he know we were here?"

Grey hesitates.

"What's wrong?" I ask, instantly on alert.

He blows out a breath. "Nothing. It's just… a pack thing."

"Pack?" I repeat, frowning. They've been in the same wolf pack since I met them, and he's never mentioned they can sense one another's location like this. I don't even think our mate bond will let me do that. "I don't understand."

"When my father took you, we knew we'd have to be ready to fight to get you back."

"What does that have to do with—"

"The night before the wedding, Dutch and the others pledged their loyalty to me, using a hex blade."

A pledge of loyalty. To him.

"Does that mean—?"

"I'm a full alpha now."

"Oh." I glance away, emotions swirling too fast for me to hang onto any single one.

An alpha. Of his own pack. A pack that doesn't include me. How can we be mates but belong to two different packs?

"Say something." His voice edges toward a plea.

"Is that how you were able to kill Franco? Because you had alpha power already?"

Honestly, discussing murder was preferred to the stupid hole in my heart his words caused. How could I still feel abandoned and alone after being married *and* mated to this man? Ugh.

"Yes. We'd taken the oath only hours before that. If we hadn't, I wouldn't have been strong enough."

I bite my lip, concentrating on that. Without the pack oath, he might have been hurt. Or worse. Franco might have—

I don't let myself go that far.

When I look up, Grey is still watching me warily. "I'm sorry I couldn't tell you sooner. I wanted to," he adds quickly. "But things have been moving fast, and I didn't want you to feel like you were—"

"What?" I snap harsher than intended. "On the outside?"

His jaw tightens. "You're not on the outside with me, ever."

"But I am," I say, quieter now. "You've got your pack. The ones who *chose* you. The ones who *belong* to you. I'm just an impostor demanding total strangers accept me or else, apparently, I'll rip them apart."

"You're not *just* anything," he says fiercely, closing the distance between us.

I don't move as his hands cup my cheeks. His touch isn't gentle, but it's not rough either. More…determined. Impassioned. Desperate.

"You're more than a pack member. You're my *mate.* My bonded. My heart. That's not some rank to hand out. Or a pledge to make, hex blade or not. That's everything."

My eyes sting. I hate that it still sounds like a consolation prize.

"But I'm not part of your pack," I whisper.

He looks at me like he's trying to will away my hurt.

"No," he says quietly. "You're not. Because I don't want you beneath me. Or behind me. I want you *beside* me."

"That sounds nice," I say. "But it's not the same as feeling it. Being in it. And it's not like I can just drop my own pack and join yours. If we do that, who will rule the city? Your father?"

He doesn't have a response for that.

I turn away before the ache in my chest makes my legs give out. This day feels centuries long.

"So, you have a pack bond. And that's how Crow knew where you were?"

He nods. "It doesn't happen to every pack. My father

doesn't... Anyway, it happened after Franco. After I inherited his power. We felt the boost in our bond immediately."

"So, you bonded to your pack," I say flatly. "And I didn't."

He flinches, and I hate that my reaction is hurting him—but not enough to take it back. It's the truth. But so is the bite mark I gave him. And our marriage. This is not me losing him. It's us building the next part of our future. That's what I tell myself, at least. And maybe if I repeat it enough, I'll start to believe it.

"I'm not angry," I say after a beat. "I'm just… I've spent my whole life not belonging to anyone. And now that I have a mate, and maybe a pack of my own, I still feel like I'm orbiting something I'll never quite land inside."

He steps closer again. This time, I let him. His hand brushes mine, fingers tentative.

"You're not orbiting, Lex. You're the *center*. They're circling *you*."

I blink hard, my eyes suddenly burning.

He grabs my hand and presses it over his heart. "Feel this. Feel me. Our mate bond. It means more to me than anything. *You* are my entire reason for existing. And that's how I know it's all going to work out. Because we have each other."

I nod once, swallowing around the lump in my throat.

"I hope you're right," I say.

He leans in, pressing a kiss to my forehead like a vow.

"I usually am," he murmurs.

And for the first time in a long time, I wish I could believe that without hesitation. Rather than let him see my worries, I change the subject as we begin walking toward the edge of the woods again.

"Can you tell through your connection whether Razor's okay? I think I might have nicked him on my way out of the meeting earlier."

"He's fine. Already healed," Grey assures me. At my worried expression, he holds my gaze and says, "I sent him with the others to find out what my father will do next, now that you've been crowned. Otherwise, they'd be here too."

At the mention of Grey's father, I tense all over again. It's only a matter of time before he calls in my end of the deal. And that's if Ramsey hasn't already told him I was a spy for Franco. But before I can think too hard about Vincenzo's wrath, we reach the edge of the tree cover, and I remember that I'm very, very naked right now.

When I hesitate, Grey tucks me behind a tree knowingly. "Wait here," he says and then jogs to the car.

He returns a moment later with a blanket and wraps it around my shoulders, pulling it tight. Then he leads me to the SUV and helps me inside. I marvel at how he seems to know what I need before I can say a word. He's always been driven to give me what he thinks will make me happy. But he hasn't always been good at knowing what that is.

Another perk of our bond.

"Hello, love birds. There's a pair of shorts on the seat for you, Grey. Lexi, sorry, my orders are to stay away from the penthouse, so I couldn't get you anything."

"It's fine," I tell him, drawing the blanket tighter around me while Grey slips on his shorts.

Where to?" Crow asks as Grey slides into the backseat next to me and shuts the door.

"Franco's," Grey says and then quickly corrects, "The Giovanni estate."

Crow twists in his seat. But he doesn't look at Grey.

Instead, he gives me the kind of direct look that only Crow can. I swear this guy sees so much more than he lets on.

"You good?" he asks me.

My heart swells. The concern means so much more than he'll ever know.

"Yeah," I say, trying for a smile.

I fail—miserably. But Crow must be convinced because he turns back to face the windshield and puts the car in gear.

"In that case, welcome to the family, Mrs. Grey," he says.

The title sends a jolt of surprise—and pleasure—through me.

I look over to see Grey watching me as if trying to read my reaction. I give him a soft smile and then press my lips to his quickly. "I think I like this title best," I whisper.

I watch as he lights up, his joy unmistakable through the mate bond, and then he kisses me back in the darkness for the rest of the car ride.

7

LEXI

We arrive at the Giovanni estate—*my* estate, apparently—just after midnight. The four armed guards manning the guardhouse at the gate give nothing away in their expressions as they look me over then wave us through. When we get close, the lights shining from inside the house cut through the darkness like watchful eyes. From the outside, it looks exactly the same as it did earlier today when I was dragged through these doors in my wedding gown. Only now, I'm not a prisoner.

Now, I'm the one calling the shots.

Hopefully, that makes up for the fact that I'm still naked and wrapped in a blanket.

The SUV rolls to a stop in front of the wide double front doors. Before I can reach for the handle, Grey is already out of the car and circling to my side. He opens my door and waits while I get to my feet, adjusting the blanket and tucking it in on itself so it's more like a dress. Then he holds out his hand like this is just another night, just another house.

It's not.

I take his hand anyway, using my other one to hold the blanket in place. Then, I do my best to walk with the kind of confidence an alpha would have—even a naked one.

The doors are already open when we reach them. A woman stands in the foyer, silhouetted by the soft gold glow of the chandelier behind her. Her brown hair is slicked into a low bun, and she's wearing a knee-length black dress that screams "practical" and "funeral" in equal measure. Her eyes are sharp, dark, and wholly unimpressed. She looks like she could poison a man with nothing more than a pointed glance.

"Ms. Giovanni," she says, not missing a beat. "You're late."

"And you are?" I ask, mustering all the fake courage I can find.

"Elena Vargas. House administrator. I ran the estate for your grandfather. I assume I now run it for you."

There's no sarcasm in her voice. No fear either. Just that cool, unnerving calm that tells me she's already assessed every variable in this moment—and found me lacking.

"That would be fine," I manage, hoping it's the appropriate response to learning you have a house administrator—whatever that is.

She doesn't bow, but the others behind her do.

Three figures who stand side by side in the foyer all dip their chins nearly to their chest. Two men who look vaguely familiar from my first visit here—security, maybe?—and a woman. Andy.

Oh shit. What does she think of me killing her husband?

Before I can catch her eye to find out, a second SUV

pulls up behind ours. Razor, Mia, and Dutch get out. I resist the urge to hug them, but I'm so damn glad to see them here. It feels like backup. Like friends.

I go straight to Razor first. "I'm so sorry about your arm," I tell him. "I wasn't in control. I hope you can—"

"Relax," he says, pulling up his sleeve to show me. "Already healed."

I exhale. "I really am sorry."

"I've had worse scratches," he says with a grin.

Mia winks at me as she and Crow step up behind us.

Dutch dips his chin at me and says with a mischievous smile, "Evening, High Alpha."

The title ripples through me, and my confidence surges.

More movement catches my eye, and I look to my left in time to see three strange men rounding the corner of the house. They stride toward us, wearing simple black clothing and earpieces. More security.

All of them belonged to Franco. Were loyal to him.

I tense at the sight of them, but they stop several yards away and fold their hands in front of them. They don't challenge me or seem surprised to find me wearing nothing but a blanket. They don't speak either. They just… stare. Not just at me but at Grey and the others too.

I knew this would be a risk, claiming my throne with former Diavolo pack beside me. But I refuse to do it any other way.

The air is tense. Charged. As if one wrong word will shatter the silence and spark a war inside these walls.

I can feel my wolf pressing against my skin. She doesn't like their eyes on us. Doesn't like the smell of uncertainty clinging to the air like smoke.

I take a breath and step inside the house.

No one moves to stop me.

"Summon the lieutenants," I tell Elena, following the instructions Grey gave me on the way over.

"Which ones?" she asks.

"All of them." I try not to make it sound like a question, but I honestly have no idea how many there are.

She nods once. "Would you like to address them here or in the atrium?"

"Here," I say.

I want them to see this is mine now. I want them to see I'm not hiding in the shadows of a dead man. But just in case they aren't convinced, dragging a dead body out the front door sounds a lot easier than cleaning up whatever the atrium is.

"As you wish." Elena turns and disappears down a hallway with a grace that feels more like a threat than a courtesy.

Razor exhales beside me. "She's charming."

"She's terrifying," Mia mutters.

"I like her," Dutch adds, smirking.

I ignore all of them and make my way farther into the house.

This time, I stop to notice the details I missed earlier. Granite floors and gilded artwork on the walls. A gleaming glass table with a crystal bowl that probably costs more than I've made in my lifetime. The grand staircase inlaid with ornamental details that continue up to the balustrade above.

It's all pristine. Not a speck of dust, not a thing out of place. If ghosts are real, I feel Franco's watching me from the walls, daring me to touch his things. But at least he'll see exactly what I do next.

I walk over to where Andy stands. The security guards beside her avert their eyes, refusing to meet mine without my permission, but Andy holds her chin high. If she wants to kill me, I can't sense it on her.

I try to think of the right thing to say. She showed me friendship earlier, and I returned it by killing her husband right in front of her.

"How are you?" I ask, feeling awkward.

"I'm okay. How are you?" she asks.

"I'm good."

She holds my gaze. It's still clear, but I know I can't bring this up here. Not now.

"Will you show me to one of the guest rooms?" I ask.

Confusion wrinkles her brow. "Why?"

"I'd like somewhere to sleep that's not—" I stop, unwilling to say his name. He deserves to be forgotten. To never be mentioned again.

"Of course," Andy says knowingly. "This way."

She takes the lead.

Grey is at my side instantly, and the others fall in behind us.

"Actually," I say, glancing at Razor and Dutch, "Can you guys wait here and make sure the only people who gain entry are the ones we invited?"

They look from me to Grey, who nods.

Different pack, I realize.

That's going to take some getting used to. Not just giving orders but remembering who follows whom. Wolf hierarchy is so weird. But I don't have time to adjust either. I'm already in the deep end. Now it's sink or swim.

"What can I do?" Mia asks.

I turn back, considering her offer. "We both need a change of clothes."

And I don't trust anyone else. I don't say it, but she nods as if she already knows.

"I'm on it." She's out the door without a glance at Grey, which makes me smile inwardly.

Mia is her own hierarchy.

To Crow, I ask, "Will you guard the stairs to make sure no one else comes up?"

His gaze flicks to Grey, but he doesn't hesitate. "Consider it done."

I exhale, relieved to know the people watching my back actually care whether I live or die. If the security guards are miffed that I didn't ask them for anything, they don't show it.

"Ma'am?" one of them calls when I'm halfway up the stairs. "What are your orders?"

I hesitate, considering. "What was your post before?"

"Patrolling the grounds," says the one who called out to me.

"Continue on your current schedule until further notice," I say.

They hesitate, their attention turning to Grey. "Word is you killed Albero. Is that true?" one of them asks.

I tense, remembering belatedly how I spilled those beans at the meeting earlier. And then completely forgot to tell Grey about it. But he stands tall, unflinching.

"It is," Grey says. "He attacked my mate, and I reacted accordingly."

I brace for some kind of fight, but they all nod. The one in the middle, the speaker, blows out a breath. "He assaulted my sister at a party last year. So, thanks for what you did, man."

"I'm sorry to hear that," Grey tells him.

"We'll see you around," the guard says, and they walk off, respect in their gazes.

It's a better outcome than I expected, but even so, I catch Razor's eye, and he nods then follows them out.

With Andy at the lead, Grey and I ascend the grand staircase. At the top, we take the corridor to the right—the opposite direction of Franco's suite. Good. I don't care if I'm High Alpha or Queen of the damned, I'm not sleeping where that monster laid his head.

Andy stops in front of a door at the end of the hall. She pushes it open and I peer inside to find a king-size bed, a dresser, and a sitting area, all done in neutral tones. There's a gas fireplace in the corner, unlit. Considering it's in Franco's home, the space feels surprisingly inviting. But just like the rest of the house, there is zero evidence my father ever lived here.

Grey slips past me and wanders inside. He moves to open the windows, letting in the night air.

I turn back to Andy, lowering my voice. "I'm sorry," I tell her, "About Toros."

"Don't be," she says. "He doesn't deserve your apology."

"Maybe not, but you do. You were nice to me, and I repaid you by killing your husband."

"This might sound cold to you, but I'd say I got the better end of our friendship already," she says, and I blink.

"Earlier, you seemed comfortable around him, and I thought…" I trail off, unsure how to describe it.

"Comfortable and love are not the same thing."

She has a point. I meet her eyes. "You're really not mad?"

"Lexi, you've taken out the four most toxic men this pack has ever been ruled by. Five if you count Dom. For the first time in my life, I'm hopeful."

I don't know what to say to that.

All I can think is that her count is wrong. I've only taken out three. Grey killed Franco. But I can't tell her that without unraveling this entire thing. And maybe even sparking a war. So, I keep my mouth shut and simply nod.

"I'll come get you when the lieutenants are assembled," she says. Her gaze flicks to the blanket I'm still wrapped in. "And I'll send Mia up the moment she arrives with your clothes."

"Thanks."

She strides away, and I close the door with a soft click.

I turn to find Grey already studying me.

"You okay?" he asks quietly.

No. Not even a little.

"I don't know what I'm doing," I admit.

"You're going to be great. And when in doubt, just rip out a throat or two," he jokes.

I wince.

"Too soon?" he asks.

I shake my head, padding into the room with the blanket still pulled snug around me. "I don't want to rule like Franco did."

"I know, bad joke," he says. "Hey." He catches my hand in his. "You're nothing like him."

"Thanks. It's just… I'm terrified I'm going to screw it up and they'll figure out I don't belong here."

"The fact that you want to do a good job means you're a leader who cares." He tucks a stray hair behind my ear then presses a calloused palm to my cheek. "And no one's going to question whether you belong. The power rolling off you is unmistakable."

I don't know whether to be relieved or worried at that.

There's a soft knock on the door. Elena doesn't wait for permission—she opens it and inclines her head just enough to show respect without deference.

"Clothing for you both." She hands a garment bag to Grey, who hangs it on the closet door for me. "I'm told more is being delivered soon. I'll make sure it's all put away."

"Thank you," I tell her.

"The guests are assembled in the foyer," she says. "Would you like me to announce you?"

I shake my head. "I'll do it myself."

She leaves, and Grey slips his hand around my waist, drawing me close. "Everything's going to work out," he says before I can find words.

"What if they don't pledge loyalty to me?"

"They will."

"But what if they don't?"

He shrugs. "Then we'll make rugs out of them."

I snort. Then I remember what he said when we were in the woods. "What about the hex blade?"

"What about it?"

"Should I use it to forge my pack? Like you did?"

He shakes his head. "The magic of the hex blade is an amplifier. It made my alpha stronger by speeding up my transition."

"So, why wouldn't it work the same for me?"

"It would, that's the problem." At my confusion, he asks softly, "Do you really want to offer your wolf more power than she already has?"

"Definitely not." I shudder.

His lips twitch. "I thought so." But then Grey's smile vanishes, and he says, "Pick a second in command."

"Like a general?"

He nods. "Someone you can trust to have your back." Regret flickers in his eye. "I know that's my job, and I'm not saying you can't count on me, but your pack needs a hierarchy. Establishing it sooner rather than later will put them at ease."

"Wait, you want me to pick one right now? Tonight?"

"It would help," he admits.

"I don't even know any of them— Wait. Who did you pick?" I ask suddenly, thinking of Mia and the others. Of their new hierarchy.

"I haven't," he admits, wincing a little. "And believe me, it's not any easier without one."

I don't say anything to that.

Grey unzips the bag of clothing and takes out a pair of slacks and a shirt. The pants look tactical more than dressy, and there are heavy black boots to match. It makes me wonder what Mia expects to happen at this meeting.

"I'm going to head down first and see if I can send word to Mia to get us new phones while she's at it," he says.

Right. I haven't seen mine since Vincenzo locked me away in his pool house days ago.

"What happened to yours?" I ask.

"Pretty sure it shattered when I shifted to go after you."

"Shit, I'm sorry," I say.

"Don't be. My father likely had a tracker in the damn thing anyway."

I blink, considering it.

When he's done getting changed, Grey kisses me. "Get dressed. I'll see you out there," he whispers, and then he's gone.

8

GREY

Inside the guest bedroom, the sounds of guests arriving downstairs are muted, thanks to thick walls and plush carpet. But the moment I near the top of the stairs, the walls echo with the murmur of voices, boots shuffling on polished marble, the metallic clink of weapons being forfeited into a container at the front door.

The Giovanni pack is assembling.

I descend the stairs, senses sharp, instincts on edge. Every breath carries the thick scent of tension. Outside, cars are arriving one by one. I can feel the presence of Giovanni wolves beating through the walls like a living thing.

If they don't accept Lexi, my wolf will destroy them all.

Elena is poised at the bottom of the stairs. She looks carved from marble—cold, composed, unreadable. She's always been like that. Even when I was a kid running through Franco's estate on forced visits, she ruled the staff like a general.

Now, she holds a phone in one hand, and her other one

rests at her side, fingers still and precise. She starts to push past me toward the stairs, but I stop her.

"What's wrong?" I ask.

Elena lifts her chin, dark eyes unblinking. "Alpha Diavolo is here. He's requesting to speak with Lexi."

The words are calm. Flat. Like she's announcing a wine delivery.

I descend the rest of the stairs in two strides. "I'll take care of it."

She doesn't blink. Doesn't argue. Just studies me for one long beat, like she's weighing whether this decision could end in bloodshed. And if it does, whether it'll stain the floors.

Finally, she nods once. "He's waiting out front. In the black SUV."

Of course he is.

My father is not one to wait outside, but even with Franco gone, Elena is still formidable as hell.

I step past her. "Lexi doesn't need to know he's here."

"You get one freebie, and this is it," Elena says, and then she turns on her heel and walks away.

Damn.

At least, I know she'll be loyal to Lexi.

Dutch appears just before I walk out the front door. "Heard the old man is outside."

"Did you find out anything about his next move?" I ask in a low voice.

Behind us, the foyer is filling up with Lexi's new pack, and I don't exactly want to include them in our conversation, so I keep my voice as quiet as possible and hope they're too busy talking amongst themselves to pay any attention to us.

Dutch shakes his head and says quietly, "After the vote, he went to the reception hall and tossed out the few wedding guests who dared to show up."

"I bet he's thrilled about paying for a party that never happened," I say wryly.

"Yeah, I'd look for a bill in the mail," Dutch snorts. "No way he'll cover it."

"Small price to pay," I murmur, glancing toward the open door and the night beyond. "Anything else?"

"No. Well, sort of, but it's probably nothing."

I tense. "I want to know everything."

"He stopped at the offices across from Altobello's for a second."

"Franco's restaurant? He doesn't have any businesses over there. What office did he go into?"

"Not sure. You said not to get too close."

I nod, torn between frustration and relief. I can't afford for my father to know we're watching him. "Then what?"

Dutch shrugs. "He drove back to his office and stayed there until Crow texted us to meet up here."

"And Ramsey?" I ask.

"Couldn't find a trace of that asshole," he says darkly. "But we will. Give it time."

I exhale. "Okay, thanks."

"Want some backup?" he asks as Razor and Crow appear from somewhere in the house.

"No," I say, shaking my head. "If we go out together, it'll look like a confrontation."

"Then it looks like what it is," Dutch says pointedly. "Maybe this is it. The moment we take him out."

I shake my head. "Believe me, I want that, but we can't move until Lexi's place is secure. Otherwise, we risk her safety, and I won't do that now when we've worked so hard for this."

Dutch scowls but backs off.

"So, then what? We keep letting him dictate how this goes?" Razor asks, always pushing for the fight.

"He asked for Lexi, and he's getting me instead. He came here to issue some kind of order, and instead, I'm going to tell him to fuck right off. So, no, he's not dictating anything," I say. Razor looks ready to argue. "But if you go out there with me, the minute he sees us together, he'll know we're not with his pack anymore. That puts us at five against…well, all of them. Even Lexi's pack might try to come at us if that happens. Have you seen how many guards are on this compound?"

"Shit," Razor grumbles. "We could take 'em."

Crow snorts loud enough that a few others glance our way. Razor notices and sighs. After another beat, they nod reluctantly and let me pass.

"We'll be here if you need us," Dutch says.

I hope I don't. Because once my father knows I've formed my own pack, it'll take more than just my four pack members to stop the chaos that will follow.

Outside, the sky is lit with stars and a sliver of a moon. The darkness isn't enough to hide a dozen of Franco's guards standing in a loose formation down by the gate. They watch the black car with tight expressions and weapons at the ready.

Good.

My boots scuff the concrete as I make my way over to where my former alpha is parked. Through the windshield, I see Rocco, Dutch's dad, in the driver's seat, grim as ever. His hands grip the wheel like he's trying not to snap it in half. Alvaro, Razor's and Crow's old man, sits shotgun, looking even more deranged.

Seeing them here is a stark reminder that it's not just my father we'll fight. Every one of my friends will have to face down their old man when we announce what we've become.

I hate that they'll have to live with something like that, but I'm done trying to keep the peace. This is the last remotely civil conversation I plan to have with this asshole. Next time, it'll end in bloodshed.

When I get close, the back passenger side window opens. My father sits in the backseat, eyes already locked on me like he knew I'd come instead of her.

I approach slowly, the scent of cut grass and asphalt mixing with the cologne he's always worn—sharp, synthetic, aggressive. I catch a whiff of blood too. Not fresh, but lingering. Maybe it's in my memory. Maybe it's always there when he is.

"Where's Lexi?" he asks, voice smooth as silk dragged over broken glass.

I plant my feet out of reach and shove my hands into my pockets. "She's not coming."

His gaze narrows. He doesn't raise his voice. Doesn't need to. Angry power rolls off him in waves. "She and I have a deal."

"I don't give a shit about your deal."

He leans forward slightly, forearms resting on his knees. Moonlight slices across the lower half of his face, shadowing his eyes. He's always been good at this—using stillness as a threat, using silence to make me feel like the one losing ground.

"She's your high alpha now," I say, refusing to be baited

by him. "That demands your respect. And at the very least, it means she doesn't have to come when you call."

"She can't even control her fucking wolf," he says. "And you expect me to believe she killed a high alpha?"

I stare him down, jaw locked tight. My fists itch to shatter his smug face.

He knows.

Or he suspects.

That *I* took Franco's life. That Lexi didn't kill anyone. That she just inherited the perks of my kill like a gift-wrapped curse.

Before I can answer, he frowns. "You smell like her," he says, voice low, and I freeze as I wait to see exactly what my scent tells him. "You claimed her, even after all this?"

"She's my fated mate."

He snorts. My father doesn't believe in mates for the sake of love—not even fated mates, not unless there's a benefit in it for him. He believes in leverage. In domination. In obedience.

"That alpha power coming off you in waves—it's hers. Through the bond."

His words land somewhere between a question and a statement. Like he's trying to process it for himself. I want so badly to tell him the truth in this moment. But I remember my pack members waiting inside. And every one of their fathers is sitting out here, ready to kill them for what we've become.

Let him believe whatever keeps him distracted.

"I never would have guessed that bitch had it in her," my father says to himself. "Smart of you to ally yourself with a high alpha, I'll give you that. But neither one of you will enjoy it for long."

I ball my hands into fists inside my pockets. My wolf strains against my skin. I take a step forward, blood pumping. "Lexi is my mate now. That means you don't touch her," I say, the softness in my tone a direct contradiction to the fury I'm barely leashing. "You don't look at her. You don't think about her. You don't say her name unless I give you permission."

He raises one brow. "Is that so?"

"You want to keep your tongue in your mouth, yeah, that's so."

He blinks like my threat surprises him.

A long pause stretches between us.

Somewhere behind me, a cicada clicks in the trees. One of Franco's—now Lexi's—guards shifts his weight. I clock every single movement and breath from the heartbeats in this place. And I map out how I'll kill every one of them if need be.

My father studies me like he's trying to decide whether I'm bluffing. He's looking for the boy he raised to be useful. The obedient son. The weapon he forged in back rooms and midnight meetings. That boy left the city years ago. Whatever was left of him died the moment I met Lexi.

And he knows it.

His expression twists into something colder. Crueler. "You've always been too emotional. A weakness inherited from your mother. It's why you were never going to lead our pack."

"No," I say, voice ice. "It's why I'll lead better than you ever did."

He chuckles—dry, humorless. "She's playing you if she told you that."

I lean closer to the open window, eyes narrowed. "You

want to talk about playing people? About forcing a wedding, drugging your future daughter-in-law, triggering her wolf without consent? You think I don't know what you did to her?"

His jaw tightens. "She consented and took that serum willingly. Now, I demand my price in return."

"You manipulated her just like you've done with everyone else," I say. "That's not strength. That's fear. You're terrified of what she is. Because if she's stronger than you, if *I* am—then all the blood you spilled, the games you've played—it would all be for nothing."

His expression stills. Rage burns behind his eyes.

"I built this city," he says.

"Maybe. But then you bled it dry."

"She's not ready for something like this."

"She's more ready than you ever were."

He leans back in the seat slowly, crossing one leg over the other. The utter calm in his expression makes him look like a king in exile. Dethroned but not yet buried.

"I'll give you one last chance," he says, staring straight ahead now. "Bring her to me. Let's do this the old way. A clean transfer of power. She steps down. Gives me the crown. We walk away civil."

I yank my hands from my pockets. My fingers flex at my sides.

Inside, my wolf stirs. There's a hunger in it that's never been there before. A thirst for a messy kill. Not just death and vengeance but carnage. Mayhem. Torture. And for the first time in my life, I can feel true temptation to give in to the darkness my father tried to instill in me.

"Fuck you," I say quietly but with the conviction of the emotion behind it.

His eyes narrow. "She steps down," he repeats, "or she gets taken out of the equation."

My vision goes red.

I step closer, voice razor-sharp but eerily calm. "If you ever—*ever*—touch my wife, I will peel your flesh from your fucking bones and keep you alive long enough to watch while I burn the pieces."

Rocco flinches in the front seat. Doesn't look back. Doesn't have to.

My father?

He just smiles.

Like he's been waiting for me to say that.

"There he is," he whispers, triumphant. "I've waited a long time for the monster to reveal himself. Unfortunately, you're too late."

I should walk away.

But I don't.

Not yet.

Because the words he says next lodge in my chest like splinters.

"This pack is mine," he says quietly. "To rule. To shape. To own. And I will have it in the end. Over her dead body if necessary. And yours."

I stare at him. Heart pounding. My wolf pressing against the edges of my control, snarling to be let loose. He wants me to break. To lose it. To give him proof that I'm too emotional, too unstable, too *much like her* to be trusted with power.

Instead, I breathe.

One breath.

Two.

Then I take a step back.

Let the silence stretch.

And I smile.

"You're right," I say softly. "You will have this pack."

His eyes narrow. He waits.

"As a memory," I finish. "Of what you tried and failed to control. A symbol of what you lost. Once the transfer of power is finished, I'm coming for you, old man. And there's not a single wolf in this city who can stop me from ripping you apart."

I don't give him a chance to respond before I turn on my heel and walk away.

The asphalt scuffs under my boots. The heat of his stare burns on the back of my neck like a brand. The moment I step back through Franco's front doors, the shadows swallow me whole.

Lexi is inside. Alive. Safe—for now.

But that safety is fragile.

Death is coming.

Just like he said.

But not on *his* terms.

On *mine.*

9

LEXI

Alone in my room, I pull the clothes out of the garment bag, relieved to find a one-piece with pants that Mia picked out. There are heels to match, but they aren't uncomfortably high. And the fabric is gentle against my skin.

My wolf approves, at least.

At the bottom of the bag, I also find a brush and some makeup, which a quick mirror check reveals are urgently necessary. After bathing in a river without soap or shampoo and then gallivanting around town in nothing but a blanket, I'm ready to feel some semblance of human again.

When I'm done, I've almost achieved the feeling.

Then I remember what I'm about to do.

Nerves grip me so hard that my breath turns shallow, and I have to practically drag myself out the bedroom door and down the hall. If I wait even one second more, I might run the other direction. And I refuse to run away ever again.

Not that my wolf would let me if I tried. She's bonded

to Grey in a way I don't think anything can break. Knowing that both settles and scares me. For the first time ever, it's no longer just me.

From now on, it'll always be me and Grey.

Like a family.

I haven't quite gotten used to that yet.

And now, I'm about to add dozens more to the list of people I'm promising never to leave behind. As long as they pledge the same to me.

Before I even reach the landing, the murmur of voices hits me, followed immediately by unfamiliar scents. My wolf stirs restlessly inside me, sniffing out the unease. The potential enemies in our midst. I do my best to shove her back. She's done enough to establish our dominance over these people. Losing control a second time in one day wouldn't help matters.

But I haven't been able to regain my sense of self since that first shift. Not fully. Not even claiming Grey steadied me like before. And I can't bring myself to tell him that.

When I get to the top of the stairs, I force myself to look out over the crowd gathered below. One by one, they look up at me until everyone is staring. The press of their eyes on me feels like a weight on my chest. I pause, drawing in a breath and gripping the banister. The railing is cool beneath my fingers, a small anchor to hold me steady.

I descend the stairs slowly, and the hush that falls over the crowd is deafening. Dozens of unfamiliar wolves gather in the foyer, the grand space now stifled with heat, tension, and too many bodies. Most are men—broad, lethal-looking, in leather jackets or tailored suits—but I clock a handful of women too. All of them radiate strength. All of them look up at me with the same expression: uncertainty laced with calculation.

They're sizing me up. Judging. Wondering if I'll break. Or maybe wondering if I'll be the same kind of cruel monster their previous alpha was.

My wolf urges me forward. Inside me, she's alert: ears up, ready to snarl, to assert. To take me over. But I force her back, grit my teeth, and walk into the crowd with slow, deliberate control. I don't rush. Instead, I let them feel the weight of my presence with each deliberate footfall.

They part to let me pass.

No one speaks.

No one challenges.

No one approaches.

Except Andy.

She steps forward just as I reach the center of the room. Her presence is cool and composed, her blue eyes meeting mine with something unreadable. Not doubt—but not blind faith, either.

"Alpha."

She bows her head.

A few other heads bow along with hers. No one breaks the silence.

It isn't loyalty. Not yet. But it's submission.

My wolf *purrs*, proud and pleased, pressing hard beneath my skin. She wants to throw her head back and *howl*. To stake her claim on this place, these people.

I inhale slowly, trying not to tremble at my attempt to control her.

They don't know me. Not really. But they're offering me a moment—an opening. And if I don't seize it, I'll lose them before I've even begun.

Near the front door, Grey stands, watching and supportive. But if I lean on him, they'll see it. This has to be all me.

I turn to Andy. "Step forward."

She lifts her head and meets my eyes, stepping toward me without hesitation.

"I need a second in command," I say, my voice steadier now. "Someone I trust. Someone who doesn't just know this pack, but can help me lead it. Will you accept the position?"

Andy raises an eyebrow, just slightly. "Me?" She glances around at the faces of those I suspect she thinks should have the role instead. "You're sure?"

"I'm not my grandfather," I say. "I won't rule through fear and blood alone. I don't want to be worshipped or feared—I want to be effective. And I need someone who knows how this machine runs but is willing to embrace the change that is necessary."

She swallows. The slightest flicker of emotion crosses her face—respect? Surprise? "Then I serve at your side. Whatever you need."

I step closer and place my hand on her shoulder. The moment my fingers touch her, something *clicks*. A low hum of magic spreads between us—vibrating in the air, threading into my bones. A spark of energy sizzles through my palm and races up my arm like electricity, wrapping around my spine.

The bond is forming.

Not fated. Not like Grey and I share. But *chosen*. Intentional. A different kind of connection. The kind shared by a pack.

I turn in place, scanning the faces. "I know you didn't choose me," I say to them. "Some of you were loyal to my grandfather. Others were afraid of him and are worried about having another Giovanni as your alpha. Maybe you liked the way he ruled. Maybe you didn't." My voice carries, firm but not hard. "But I'm not him. And I never will be."

They're watching closely now, the mood impossible to read.

"I won't promise perfection. Hell, I can't even promise I won't fuck up—a lot. But I *can* promise this: I will work to earn your respect. And until then…" I pause, breathe. "I will require your obedience."

A single heartbeat of silence follows. Then two.

"Or what?" someone calls. "You'll rip out our throats like you did to the generals? To Dom?"

I scan for whoever spoke, but they're lost in the crowd. Not that it matters. I have no doubt the sentiment is shared by many. But I don't back down or apologize. Grey told me I have to own this part, so I force myself to do just that.

"My wolf is new to me. She was threatened, and she acted accordingly," I say. "If you threaten me, it's only reasonable that I defend myself. But I won't attack without provocation if that's what you're asking."

No one argues it, and I only hope it's a promise I can keep.

My wolf sniffs as if she's not sure she can keep it either. But I can tell she wants this pack to belong to us just as much as I do, so I press on.

"My wolf chose this pack when she fought against those who threatened my right to lead it. And now I'm choosing it too," I add. "There are some who will challenge me. Challenge us. That's your right. But I won't give up or abandon you. I swear it. I'm going to rebuild this pack.

From the inside out. Starting with truth. Starting with no more backroom deals, no more forced matings, no more experimentation."

There's a stir among the crowd—unease, or maybe guilt. So they knew what Franco did to me. To my mother. To who knows how many others. Knew and did nothing. Maybe not all of them, but some.

"It's true that my wolf was suppressed after Franco experimented on me and my mother. I received the antidote a couple of days ago, which is why my wolf finally emerged today. But I also know he did the same to others—people who may have been hurt even worse than I was.

"I *will* find out who was complicit in forcing the women of this pack to participate. And when I do, I'll decide whether you have a future here or not."

Still silence. No one protests.

"Andy is my second now, which means she speaks for me. Starting tomorrow, she'll begin one-on-one interviews with each of you. No titles are permanent. If you've earned your role, you'll keep it. If you haven't, we'll find someone who has."

I glance at Andy.

She dips her head. "Understood."

I look over the crowd. "We are not who we were under Franco. And anyone who can't accept that should leave now."

No one moves.

But every breath in the room seems to grow heavier.

"What about him?" someone asks. A man I've never seen before with a short beard and hard, glittering eyes. He nods at Grey. "What's his place here?"

"What's your name?" I ask, heart thundering.

"Clifton Jones. Friends call me Cliff."

"Okay, Cliff—" I start.

His eyes flash. "As I said, my friends call me Cliff. You can call me Clifton. Or Mr. Jones."

My wolf seethes at that, but I hold my composure. A growl sounds from the back of the room, and I don't need to look over to know it's Grey. But I don't tear my gaze from the male in front of me.

My voice sharpens. "And you can address me as Alpha—or not at all," I tell him coolly. "As for Grey, he is my husband and will continue to be at my side, which is all you need to know about his loyalty—"

"If I may." Grey steps forward. "I'd like to answer his question."

I nod, still glaring at the asshole in front of me, despite my heart slamming against my ribs.

Grey pushes through the crowd, not sparing a single glance for Cliff as he drops to one knee in front of me.

The crowd murmurs, but I don't hear the words.

Grey looks up at me, the mate bond singing with the intensity of his feelings for me. The world narrows to just us.

"I pledge my loyalty and protection to you," he says. "Lexi Giovanni. My fated mate. My wife. My heart. Wherever you lead, I follow."

He doesn't say alpha, but every syllable he utters is steeped in devotion.

My chest twists. My throat tightens. For a moment, I can't breathe. The other faces around us blur at the edges of my vision. All I see is *him*—my anchor, my fire, my impossible choice that I keep choosing anyway.

One by one, the others kneel again.

But this time, it's not a formality.

"I pledge to my alpha," someone murmurs.

Then another. "To the alpha."

And another.

The sound swells like a wave, crashing against the walls of this house, reverberating through me like thunder.

Power slams into my chest.

Magic *howls* inside me.

It's a rush of heat and pressure and connection—so much that I stagger.

I *feel* them.

All of them.

A hundred threads snapping into place. Emotions that aren't mine, thoughts I didn't form. The press of lives against my mind, against my skin. Every heartbeat echoing like a drum inside me.

They're mine.

My pack.

My wolf *revels* in it. She throws her head back and howls with delight, her joy electric and wild.

I nearly lose myself in it.

But I can't.

I dig in my heels and push her down, grinding my molars together until the room comes back into focus.

Clifton Jones is still standing.

"The choice is yours," I tell him.

"This is bullshit," he mutters and then turns and makes his way out the door. "Franco is rolling over in his grave," he says as he walks out.

A few others follow him.

I don't let myself focus on the ones who choose to leave. Instead, I look out at all the faces who've stayed.

Knees bent, heads bowed. They chose me. So, I choose them too.

I draw a breath to steady my voice. "Rise."

They obey. My chest expands with hope.

Grey stands beside me, slipping his hand into mine.

"Nailed it," he whispers, and my shoulders lighten as some of the tension releases.

I turn to Andy. "I want a full list of departments and current leaders by morning. Start preparing the review schedule."

She nods. "You'll have it."

"Everyone is dismissed," I say—and then quieter to Andy, "Will you stay for a moment?"

She nods.

The room begins to empty, murmurs rising and fading as pack members file out the front door. Some glance back at me, some at Grey, but there are no more challenges.

I watch them go, my heartbeat finally slowing as the foyer empties out.

Through the thinning crowd, Grey motions at Dutch, Razor, Mia, and Crow, who are stationed around the room as subtle but formidable sentries. They make their way toward us against the tide of exiting pack members.

When the last stranger disappears around the corner, I exhale—and nearly collapse from the adrenaline release.

Grey presses in close. "You okay?"

"No," I whisper. "But I'm getting there."

He squeezes my hand.

Dutch winks at me. "Nice speech, boss."

I can't help but smile at the nickname he has only ever used on Grey. "Thanks for keeping an eye on things."

He shrugs. "You know we've got your back."

"I do," I say and realize it's the truth. I feel it now—deep in my marrow.

"You did well," Mia says, and the compliment ripples through me.

"Thanks."

Mia eyes Andy. "I don't think we've formally met. I'm Mia Reyes."

"Andy Balistrieri."

"Wait, but you're Toros' wife. Wasn't he a Campbell?" Razor asks.

Andy looks unfazed as she says, "Yes. But I'm not."

"Damn straight," Mia says.

Razor frowns like he doesn't get it.

Dutch simply stares at the blonde beauty like she's a puzzle he's trying to put together.

Andy ignores all of them, glancing between me and Grey.

"Did you need something else from me tonight?" she asks.

"No, I—" I start to tell her to get some rest.

"Wait." Grey interrupts.

"What is it?" I ask.

Dutch clears his throat, shooting a pointed look at Andy. "Maybe we should talk privately."

Andy crosses her arms. "If this is about the fact that Grey's an alpha and you're all members of his pack, don't worry about censoring yourselves in front of me."

We all stare at her, stunned.

"Well, it's not like I can't read his alpha power. It's practically yelling in my face," she says.

"You can't tell anyone," Dutch tells her with narrowing eyes.

Andy rolls her eyes. "Relax, I'm bonded to my own alpha, your *high alph*a in case you forgot, genius. I'm not going to spill anything she hasn't allowed me to."

I bite back a grin at the way Dutch stutters.

"We can trust Andy," Grey says.

"How do you know?" Razor asks.

"Because she's already risked her life for us once," Grey says.

Mia's eyes widen. "She's your source." She looks at Andy like she's seeing her in a new light.

"Source for what?" I ask.

"When you were brought in for your alpha vote," Andy explains, "I knew no one was going to bother texting Grey about the meeting, and I thought he deserved to know when it was happening so he could be there for you."

I blink at her. "You did that for me? You didn't even know me."

"No one deserved to go through that alone," she says, and while I can't feel her emotions through this new pack bond we share, something tells me she's speaking from experience. My heart aches for whatever she went through with Toros.

"In that case," Mia says, "I'll say it." Her gaze swings to Grey, and she's suddenly no-nonsense. "We need to know where we stand with you, and we need to know it tonight."

I glance at Grey, remembering what he said about pack hierarchy.

"Effective immediately," he says, "you're all generals. Dutch is my enforcer. Razor's my executioner. Mia is my strategist. Crow is recon. Now, I might be your alpha, but Lexi is your high alpha. You follow her orders like you would mine."

A new kind of connection snaps into place.

Not as strong as what I feel with Andy, but it's there.

Grey's pack is now my pack too.

"Fuck yeah," Dutch says, breaking the silence and earning an eye roll from Mia.

"So professional," she tells him. And then to me, with a smile, she says, "We're behind you both. All the way."

Razor claps Grey's shoulder. "Hell yeah."

I blink hard. The pressure behind my eyes builds, but I shove it down. Not here.

Dutch grins at me knowingly. "You good, alpha?"

"It means a lot," I admit. "Your friendship."

"We're family now," Mia says softly. "And get used to it."

She shoots me a smile that I manage to return.

"We'll plan our next steps tomorrow," Grey says. "Tonight, find a guest room. No one goes home until my father and the generals are dealt with."

I blink at him, but Mia nods. "He's right. If Andy sensed it on us, everyone else will too. We'll need to stay under the radar until we've dealt with"—her eyes flick to Grey—"everyone."

Despite the mention of the man who terrifies me even now, I stifle a yawn. I have no idea what time it is or how many hours I've been awake, but even my wolf isn't stirring anymore. We're both exhausted.

"Let's save that problem for daylight," Grey says, squeezing my hand knowingly.

"I can show you guys where you can sleep," Andy offers to the others.

"Thanks," I tell her. "And then feel free to head out and get some rest. Tomorrow will be a long day."

She leads the others up the stairs toward the guest wing where Grey and I are staying. We follow then slip past them when Andy points to the guest rooms along our hallways.

With one last murmured good night, we slip into our room and close the door. When we're alone, Grey reaches for me.

"How'd I do?" I ask.

"You were perfect," he whispers, brushing his lips over mine.

"I don't know about that, but at least, no one else tried to kill me."

He pulls me into his arms. I rest my head against Grey's chest for a beat, letting myself pretend—for just this moment—that everything is okay. That I'm safe. That this house isn't soaked in blood and betrayal.

But I know better.

This house is full of the pain of the past.

And some things don't stay buried.

10

GREY

Lexi stands just inside the room, frozen, like if she breathes too loud, the entire house will collapse under the weight of what she's been through today. I know the feeling. My skin's still buzzing, adrenaline high, and wolf pacing restlessly just beneath the surface. My beast doesn't like the silence that hangs inside these walls—not to mention the stench of Franco taking up every square inch. He wants to go back downstairs and circle the territory we just claimed. Stake it. Defend it.

But Lexi's my territory too.

And she needs me now.

"You were perfect," I say, ignoring the demons inside me as I kiss her softly.

"I don't know about that, but at least, no one else tried to kill me."

I pull her into my arms, holding her as long as she'll let me. As long as she needs. When she finally pulls away, she doesn't look at me. I can feel her utter exhaustion through our bond. I feel other things too. Darker things. I don't tell her that, though.

We've had enough darkness for one day.

She tugs on her clothing. A second later, her hands hover at the clasp on her shoulder, her fingers twitching like she can't quite remember how to undress.

"Here, let me." I step closer.

She lets me undo the clasp at her shoulder and then slide the fabric apart, peeling it down her torso where it pools at her waist. Wherever Mia found this thing, I need to tell her to get more of them. Watching the entire thing slide away from her skin is making it hard to concentrate. "The way you controlled your wolf tonight was impressive," I say, forcing myself to refocus, even as my dick twitches.

She shakes her head. "I'm not sure who controlled whom."

"Any other newly shifted wolf probably would have ripped out Cliff's throat for challenging you. Your self-control didn't go unnoticed by the rest of the pack. You should be proud."

Her laugh is dry. "If my wolf is so under control, then why does it feel like I'm going to puke?"

"Because you're human, too."

That gets a flicker of something in her expression. She finally lifts her eyes to meet mine, and I see it then: the fear. "And what if the wolf swallows the human whole?"

I shake my head. "It won't."

"You sound so sure."

"I am."

She stares at me for another beat, then lets out a breath and pulls the fabric so her one-piece outfit slides all the way to the floor at her feet.

My mouth goes dry.

It's not the first time I've seen her naked—not even close. But this time feels different. There's no performance here. No walls between us. Just Lexi, stripped down to nothing but her bare skin and the rawness still clinging to her bones from what happened today.

She unhooks her bra next, then steps out of her panties.

Following her lead, I peel off my shirt. The moment it hits the floor, I realize how tightly I'd been holding myself together. Waiting to see what Lexi's pack would do when she took control. Wondering if we'd have to fight our way out of this house before it was over.

I kick off my boots. Jeans next. Boxers. Until we're standing there, naked and exposed, just feet apart.

The room is dim, moonlight filtering through the curtains, painting her skin in silver and shadow.

She crawls into bed without a word.

I follow.

The sheets are cool, soft cotton against overheated skin. I pull them over us and stretch out beside her. For a few long seconds, we don't speak. Don't move.

Then my hand finds hers beneath the sheet.

Our fingers link.

She scoots closer, curling against me, her head on my chest.

Her breath is shaky.

"What if I can't keep their loyalty?"

"Rugs, remember?"

She tilts her face toward mine, lips parted.

In the back of my mind, I know I should tell her about the visit from my father earlier. The threats he made. But that doesn't feel nearly as important as putting my hands on the breathtaking creature before me. All I can think about is taking what Lexi offers me like the desperate, obsessed predator I am.

So, instead, I kiss her.

It starts gentle, just a brush of mouth on mouth. A whisper of heat. But it grows quickly, like a spark in dry grass. Her hands slide up my chest, fingertips tracing the line of my collarbone, the dip of my throat. She's not trembling anymore.

She's hungry.

So am I.

I roll her onto her back, sliding between her legs. My cock is already hard, pressed against the inside of her thigh. She arches beneath me as I kiss down her throat, over her collarbone, down to the swell of her breast.

Her body is fire beneath mine—soft and strong and hot enough to melt steel. I slide a hand down her stomach, fingers teasing between her thighs. She gasps, hips lifting.

"Grey—"

"I've got you."

I slide two fingers inside her, curling them until she moans. Her walls clench tight around me, and the sound she makes is almost enough to undo me completely.

I kiss her again, deeper this time. Our teeth clash. Her nails dig into my shoulders.

Her hips rock up to meet mine, and I groan. My cock rubs against her entrance, and it's all I can do to hold back.

I shift, line us up, and slide into her.

She lets out a strangled cry—half pleasure, half something more desperate—and clutches me tighter.

The world narrows to this.

Her. Me. The rhythm of our bodies. The sound of skin

on skin. The way my name sounds as she moans it against my throat. I want to memorize every piece of her all over again. I want to feel her come undone around me, and then put her back together with my hands, my mouth, my body.

She moves faster, rocking into me like she can't get close enough.

And then—she freezes.

Her breath catches.

Her body tightens in a way that has nothing to do with pleasure.

"Lexi?"

She doesn't answer.

She jerks beneath me, her back arching off the mattress, her mouth open in a silent scream. Her nails rake down my back—

Only they're not nails anymore.

They're claws.

My skin burns as it's peeled open.

"Lex—fuck—I need you to stop, you're—"

With a groan, she shoves me off her with more strength than she's ever had before. I land hard on the mattress beside her and scramble up just in time to see her glowing. Her eyes. Her fingertips. Her entire body pulsing with barely leashed power. She's not shifting completely, but she's close. Her fingers are elongating again. Her teeth have sharpened. Her chest rises and falls like she can't get enough air.

She clutches the sheets to her chest, panicked. "No, no, oh my God—I didn't mean to—"

"It's okay," I say, hands up. "You're okay."

"I could've hurt you."

"You didn't."

She looks at my back. At the blood I can feel trickling down my spine.

She shakes her head, eyes wild. "I did."

"You stopped," I say. "That's what matters."

"I almost couldn't stop it." She chokes on the words. "I didn't even feel it coming—just this… pressure. And then I was gone, and *she* was in control."

I climb onto the bed and sit beside her, reaching for her hand. Her claws have retracted, but her skin is still flushed and hot, like the magic hasn't fully faded.

"I'm losing myself," she whispers.

"No," I say, and this time I grab her chin and make her look at me. "You're waking up. And yeah—it's messy. But we can figure this out."

Her eyes search mine. "How?"

"We find Franco's lab and go look for answers."

A beat of silence.

Then she nods. "Okay," she whispers.

I pull her into my arms again. This time, she doesn't resist. Her head tucks under my chin, her breath hot against my chest.

"I'm scared," she says so quietly I barely hear it.

"I know."

"Don't let me become him."

She doesn't have to say Franco's name, but I know who she means. And how she feels.

"I won't," I promise.

She exhales and slowly—finally—sleeps.

But I can't.

Not tonight.

~

THE AIR IS cold against my skin as I stand on the rooftop patio. I didn't bother putting on a shirt when I left Lexi in our bed and slipped up here. I needed to breathe. To feel the night against my skin.

Below me, the sprawling lawn of Franco's estate stretches out like a blanket. Lights glimmer from the guardhouse down by the road, twinkling through the tree branches that offer privacy for the front of the house. Along the northern perimeter, I can sense guards patrolling. Can almost make out their murmur of voices as they chat while they walk. Life continues, ignorant of the storm brewing inside this house. Inside me.

Franco's dead.

Lexi's the high alpha now.

And I'm… something else entirely.

I grip the edge of the concrete railing until my knuckles go white.

My wolf is snarling just beneath the surface, pacing like a caged animal. There's no peace in him. No calm. Only this constant, gnawing heat—like I'm being boiled alive from the inside out.

I feel stronger. But not better.

Feral. Unstable. Like if I breathe too hard, I'll shift. Like if someone looks at me the wrong way, I'll snap their neck. Even my own pack bond isn't enough to settle the darkness.

Franco's power is inside me.

I can feel it. Crawling through my blood. Whispering in my ears. It started as a nudge, but since the declaration of war my father made earlier, it's been growing louder. More insistent. And now, it has a voice.

Franco's voice.

Control is for the weak. Take what you want. Kill what stands in your way.

I shudder and shove the voice away, but it comes back louder.

She'll never be strong enough. You'll always have to protect her. You'll always be the one bleeding. Dying. Breaking. Take her place. Rule them all. Make them bow.

"Shut the fuck up," I snarl.

I slam my fist into the wall beside me. The stone cracks. A few pieces come loose, raining down at my feet.

"Whoa," Dutch says behind me. "Didn't realize we were remodeling."

I don't turn around. "What do you want?" I snarl, harsher than I intend.

"I couldn't sleep," he says, his voice placatingly calm. "Thought I'd check on the rest of the insomniacs."

I round on him, glaring. "I don't need to be checked on."

"Your anxious pacing and resting bitch face would suggest otherwise." I open my mouth to spew curses and threats, but he cuts me off. "Bro, you're lit up like a fucking Christmas tree."

I look down at my hands. My veins are glowing neon blue beneath my skin, like they're filled with something other than blood. My stomach turns as I realize what it is: magic.

"It's been like this since I killed him," I say in a ragged voice.

"And you're just now telling me?"

"I'd hoped it would go away when Lexi became alpha," I admit.

Dutch crosses his arms. "And how's that working out for you?"

"Not fucking great as you can see."

He sighs like my outburst only confirmed what he already knows. "You're scared."

I glare at him. "I'm dangerous."

"Those things aren't mutually exclusive," he says. "Look, man. We've seen power gone wrong before. Packs who lose their mind when they bond. But this… this seems different."

"Because it is," I say, hoarse with the reality of it. "I didn't just kill an alpha. I took his magic. His legacy. Including whatever synthetic shit he pumped into his own veins inside that lab. And now it's inside me, mixing with the magic of the hex blade, crawling around like it wants to tear me apart from the inside out." I bite back the fury that rises as my next words tumble out. "It's doing the same to her."

"Who, Lexi?" He waves my words away. "She just needs time. First shifts are always hard."

I turn so he can see the wounds on my back. They've begun to close already, but not by much.

"What the fuck," Dutch says, gaping.

"This is more than a first shift," I say. "She almost couldn't stop it. Her control keeps slipping. Like at the meeting."

"Maybe the synthetic alpha magic Franco used on her is mixing with her own alpha power—just like yours is doing."

"Maybe." I stare bleakly out at the night. "And she doesn't have two decades of being a wolf to ground her against it."

Dutch is silent for a moment. "You think she's gonna lose it?"

"I think she's holding herself together with string and duct tape. And I think, if I don't hold it together too, we're both going to implode."

I can feel it inside both of us. The pressure building.

The rage.

The grief.

The power.

I want to burn the world down just to quiet the storm inside me.

I shake my head. "Sometimes, I swear I hear his voice. Like he's still here. Laughing at me. Waiting for me to become him."

"Your dad?"

"Franco."

Dutch looks over at me like I've lost my mind. Maybe I have.

"You won't," he says at last.

"You don't know that."

"I do. Because I've seen what you're willing to do to *not* be him. Or your old man, for that matter. And I've seen what you have that neither of them ever did." I look at him. He shrugs. "Lexi. She's your anchor. Neither one of those bastards has love like that. They only ever ruled with fear."

I exhale, closing my eyes.

"I want that to be enough," I say.

"It is," Dutch says.

He sounds so certain that I let it convince me for a moment.

But when he finally leaves, and I'm alone again, the voice comes back.

Only this time, it sounds like my father.

You think you're strong enough to protect her? You couldn't even keep her from turning into a monster.

I clench my fist. Drive it into the wall again. It crumbles a little more. My knuckles come away bloody.

I stare at the red staining my skin, weirdly relieved that it looks normal now that it's escaped my veins. It's a sign of normalcy—one I need desperately right now. Almost as desperately as I need answers. For Lexi. For me. For our future.

As soon as we can, we go to the lab.

And if there are still monsters inside it—anything that represents the horrors that were done to Lexi or anyone else—I'll kill every last one of them. Maybe then the voice in my head will die too.

11

LEXI

I wake up cold.

Not physically. Grey's body is still warm against mine, his breath steady at my shoulder, his arm a heavy comfort around my waist. No. This is the kind of cold that comes from the inside. The kind that seeps into your bones and whispers, *What if you hurt him? What if, next time, you can't stop?*

The memory of last night's close call is still vividly clear in my brain. My wolf clawing to the surface while Grey's mouth was on mine, my nails digging too deep against his back, a snarl rising in my throat.

I hurt him. And the worst part is that I'm not sure how to keep myself from doing it again. Even now, I can feel that uncontrollable monster inside me, lurking in the shadows.

I shift under the covers, trying not to wake him. But he stirs anyway, instinctively tightening his hold. "Stop worrying," he murmurs against my neck.

"I'm not."

"Liar." His voice is still scratchy with sleep, but his hand slides up my ribs, slow and grounding. "You've been tense all night."

Because I almost killed you. On our wedding night, no less.

"I can't lose you," I whisper.

He pulls back just enough to look me in the eye. "You will never lose me."

"You don't know that."

"I do." He strokes my cheek, his thumb gentle on my skin. "You're mine. All of you. Even the parts you think I can't handle."

I want to believe that. I do. But I can still feel the pulse of the monster, raw and restless beneath my skin. I'm not sure whether to be relieved or worried that we're headed to the one place that might tell me why the beast inside me is trying to take me over.

"Come on, gorgeous." Grey kisses my cheek loudly then yanks the covers off us both. "If we don't get out of this bed right now, I'm never letting you put clothes on again."

"If that's supposed to be a threat, can I just say you suck at them?"

He laughs, and it soothes my soul to hear that sound. "Noted, Princess. I'll remember that."

Capo Research Institute is carved into the side of a mountain an hour outside city limits and less than a mile from the ward line that encases Indigo Hills in hexerei magic. According to Franco's records, which Elena delivered to me this morning literally ten minutes after I made my request—*damn, she's scary*—it's shielded by ancient wards and enough glamours to hide a small army. It's not on any map, and if Crow hadn't already done the legwork to find out about the place, I wouldn't have been sure it even existed.

Now I'm not sure we should've found it at all.

"This looks like something out of a James Bond villain's fever dream," Mia mutters from the passenger seat. "Ten bucks says there's a dungeon inside full of the bones of children. Or a cryo-chamber. Or a portal to another world."

"Twenty says it's booby trapped," Crow says from the driver's seat where he's scanning the opposing tree line with sharp eyes. The gun my security team issued to him is holstered but within reach.

Andy found us before we could slip out this morning and requested that I meet the grounds security team to decide whether they can all be trusted. No one challenged me like Cliff did last night, so I greenlit them all and then requested weapons for Grey's pack so they could act as our personal guard on today's outing.

Guarding the grounds is one thing. Watching our backs out in the field is another. And even though my wolf offers an added layer of protection, I'm still not sure I want to give in to her after yesterday.

Now, Grey sits next to me in the backseat, silent but steady. I can feel the hum of tension in him, the way his alpha power coils just beneath the surface. It's still new. Not just that Franco's power is now his, but the fact that I can feel it through our bond. It pulses out of him like a living, breathing entity.

I shake off how menacing that sounds.

We pull onto the narrow drive, the SUV crunching over gravel and pine cones until the trees give way to a steel door barring entry inside the place. Before we're fully out of the car, two armed guards step forward, rifles slung over their shoulders, their movements sharp and precise.

The man on the left is lean, late thirties, eyes sharp. The other is bulkier, younger, but both of them wear matching uniforms—navy blue with silver trim and a silver emblem on the left breast that looks like a strand of DNA. Definitely not the tactical all-black clothing I've seen Franco's security teams use.

They eye us with outright hostility.

"Stop right there," says the older one.

"And show us your credentials," the other adds.

"You know who we are. Open the door," Grey orders.

"You're not cleared for entry," the first one says. "Only authorized personnel beyond this point."

"We're not tourists," Grey snaps, already moving to step between me and the barrels of their rifles. "She's Lexi Giovanni. Franco's granddaughter. Your new alpha as of yesterday. Let us through."

The second guard flicks a nervous glance at me then checks something on a data pad. "I know you who are, ma'am. But as of the last registry update, no other names are on the access list except Franco and his generals." He gives me a pointed look.

Right. The generals I just murdered.

"Then update it," Grey growls.

The first guard squares up, eyes narrowing. "Can't. Only the high alpha can issue access approvals."

I blink. "I *am* the high alpha."

"Thumbprints must be registered from the secure workstation inside."

Grey glares. "Let me get this straight. We have to go

inside in order to register our thumbprint so we can be let inside. Do you know how stupid that sounds?"

The guard starts to answer, and from the look on his face, it's not going to be the response Grey wants.

Before the man can get a word out, Grey closes the distance between them and wraps his hand around the guard's throat. The man struggles, but he's no match for Grey, even with both hands free.

The second guard starts to intervene, but Mia cuts him off. A wicked-looking blade glints in her hand before she buries it in the man's thigh. He makes a sound of pain as she shoves him against the steel door.

"I don't think you want to fuck with us." Mia lowers her voice, eyes flashing. "Or maybe you do. Try me. Please. It's been a really boring month. I've barely been able to kill anyone."

The first guard, whose face is now purple, claws at Grey's arm, but he might as well be clawing at a wall.

Grey doesn't flinch or break his grip as he leans close to the guard's face and snarls, "You will obey a direct order from your alpha, or you won't like what happens next."

Both men sputter, struggling to break free, but there's zero chance of that happening for either one. The one Mia stabbed flicks a glance at me and then, when I don't move to help him, he glances past me to where Crow lounges lazily against the hood of the car.

When he realizes no one's going to stop this, he waves at us, still wincing in pain. "Go," he manages. "Franco coded his heir's thumbprint as a secondary access. That will get you in."

Still, Grey doesn't release the first guard.

The man's face is purple, and his eyes are bulging.

"Grey," I say, sensing that pulsing darkness inside him from before. Except now, it's the only thing I feel. Like it's all there is of Grey's essence.

"Grey," I repeat, more forcefully this time.

I touch his elbow, and he snaps to attention.

"We have what we need."

In the next instant, he releases the guard, who collapses to the ground, choking and drooling as he sucks in air.

"Come on." Grey's hand lands on the small of my back, and he propels me forward. There's not a trace of emotion in those two words.

Mia yanks her knife out of the second guard and then yanks him aside. He stumbles then hurries into the woods where he vanishes into the trees, leaving his friend to his own fate.

Mia wipes her blade on her pants before tucking it back into her belt. She catches me watching and says, "What? I didn't even hit an artery. He'll be healed in half an hour."

I shake my head.

Grey takes my hand, and I look over to find his expression still somehow both dark and devoid of feeling. "There," he says, nodding.

I look over. And just ahead, a silver panel is embedded into the rock, disguised as part of the hillside. My stomach clenches as I step forward. There's a biometric scanner embedded in the wall.

I hesitate.

Franco never acknowledged me as his blood relation. He killed my parents and then let me rot in foster care. Forced me to spy on Grey and the others. Used me like a pawn. I expected nothing from him. Certainly not…

I press my thumb to the glass.

It flashes red.

Then green.

A low hiss escapes as the steel door begins to open with an ominous groan.

"Well," Mia mutters. "That's not creepy at all."

I shake my head. "Franco never acknowledged me," I say, staring at the now-open door.

"Doesn't mean he didn't see you as his heir," Grey says quietly. "Maybe he meant for you to have his title in the end after all."

The idea makes me want to throw up.

Having a monster like Franco's blessing is almost worse than not having it.

We step into a dim hallway that smells like bleach and wet earth and, beneath it all, something older—a scent I can't name but somehow know is magic. The lights flicker overhead, casting everything in a sterile, lifeless glow. The air feels thinner here, like the mountain itself is built too tightly to let even oxygen inside. Like, once you go in, you don't come out.

When the door slides shut, I jump.

"This place gives me the creeps," Mia mutters.

"Just wait," Crow says. "I'm sure it gets worse."

We pass sealed rooms with windows offering glimpses into the tiny space. Inside are tables with leather restraints, monitors that sit blankly, refrigerated cabinets filled with labeled vials. I can't help imagining that some of them could be marked with my name.

I force myself not to look.

Then Grey goes still beside me.

I catch the shift in scent too—ozone, body odor, a touch of blood. Someone else is here.

A door slides open just ahead.

A man steps out, tall and sharp like a scalpel. White lab coat. Salt-and-pepper hair. A smile that belongs in nightmares. If he's a wolf, I can't sense it. Not like I can with the others.

"Ah," he says. "The prodigal subject returns."

The name on his jacket lapel says Severin.

"Hello," Grey greets coolly. "I'm Grey Diavolo. This is Lexi Giovani, the high alpha of Indigo Hills. These are our friends." He gestures to Mia and Crow, who don't look inclined to offer their names or any other bit of manners.

I stiffen. Charlie told me he'd seen the name Severin in Franco's research files. *Lead researcher. High clearance. Ruthless.*

"You're Dr. Severin," I say, ice settling in my spine. "The one who experimented on me."

He smiles without warmth. "I see my reputation precedes me."

"I read your name in a file," I say, my shock slowly turning to fury. "Didn't expect to meet the monster in person."

"Monster is a bit dramatic," he says, bemused. "I prefer architect."

"And psychopath," Mia mutters. "But hey, tomato, tomahto."

Before I can say anything else, a second figure appears beside him.

She's young. Early twenties, maybe. Long dark braid, confident smirk, eyes like a storm. She wears a white lab coat too, but there's something less intimidating about hers. Maybe it's the stain that looks a lot like ketchup near the third button.

"Hi, I'm Davina," she says before I can ask. "Hex

witch. Technically, Severin's lab assistant." She leans in and drops her voice to a whisper as she adds, "Not his biggest fan."

Severin doesn't react despite the fact that she said it loud enough that he clearly heard her.

"You're a hex witch?" Mia asks, not bothering to hide her surprise.

"What are you doing here?" Crow chimes in.

He makes it sound like hex witches are scarce in Indigo Hills, and from everything Grey has told me about them, he's not wrong. Witches might have created this city—and especially the magic that hides it from the human world—but they didn't stick around to live in it. And the wolves don't seem particularly mad about that last part either.

"Franco got me out of a bit of a clusterfuck with a coven I'd rather not name," Davina explains. "In return, I have to work off my debt here."

Mia's expression turns mildly suspicious. "Work—as in manual labor or…?"

"Magic," Davina says, and Grey tenses at that.

"What sort of magic?" he asks gruffly.

"The kind that powers this place," she says as matter-of-factly as if she were explaining how a light switch works.

But I can't help but gawk. "Your magic powers this entire facility?"

She nods warily, and I note the others looking less impressed and more unsettled.

"What else do you do for him?" Grey asks her.

I can't help but feel that this interrogation has now become about Davina rather than Severin.

"It's classified," she says, apparently also realizing her answers aren't going well for her.

Grey scowls and starts to respond, but I cut him off, not ready to make an enemy of someone with enough magic to power an entire science lab for years on end.

"How much do you owe him?" I ask. "For the debt, I mean."

"My life," she says with a shrug, "Which is ambiguous, I know, and my fault for not being specific in the terms of our deal." Her expression darkens, and I wonder just how much Franco took advantage of this girl and what he's made her do in the name of that debt. Does powering this place hurt her at all?

"Well, in case you haven't heard," Mia says, "let me be the one to tell you the good news: Franco's dead. I think it's safe to say your debt is paid."

"Yeah, you don't have to keep this place going," I tell her.

"Thanks." She glances away. "But I still have a few loose ends to tie up."

Severin clears his throat. "If Davina left, we'd need another way to power the lab."

I start to tell him that won't be necessary, but Grey stops me with a subtle shake of his head. "Let's look around," he says pointedly. "Before making any final decisions."

He's right. We came for answers.

I blow out a breath. "Fine."

Grey looks at Severin. "How about a tour?"

"Certainly. The doctor gestures at the sliding door Davina came through. "The main lab is just through there."

"Lead the way," Grey says in a tone ominous enough that I certainly wouldn't have turned my back on him. But

Dr. Severin is clearly used to dealing with murdery alphas because he turns around and does as Grey asks.

On the other side of the sliding door, the lab opens into a wide, high-ceiling chamber filled with softly-glowing screens and enough circuitry and screens to make my head ache just looking at them all. In the center, a holographic image of what looks like a strand of DNA rotates in the air —twisting, pulsing red and blue.

"What is that?" Mia asks.

"This," Severin says, "is the LAG gene sequence."

Mia wrinkles her brow. "Is that a gamer term or…?"

I fold my arms, trying to brace myself against the horrors of my past. "It stands for Lupine Alpha Gene."

"Very good." He taps a few keys on a computer in the center of the room. "The Lupine Alpha Gene was discovered decades ago in rare shifter bloodlines—most often dormant or operating at a much lower level than what you see here. Franco had the vision to activate it. Enhance it."

"You mean he experimented on people without their consent," Grey says in a hard voice.

Severin doesn't even have the decency to look ashamed as he says, "Sacrifice is always necessary for progress."

Mia glares at that. I can see her toying with the handle of her knife again. "This is what Ramsey was talking about," she says, looking back and forth between me and Grey. "The experiments Franco did."

"Yes," Grey says.

I blink, startled. "Ramsey told you?"

"We were basically interrogating him at that point, but yes. He said Franco experimented on you and your parents, trying to activate the gene."

I take a wobbly breath, refusing to look at Severin in

case my wolf decides to rip his throat out. "He didn't just try," I say quietly.

Mia snarls at that and turns back to face the doctor, her knife gripped in a white-knuckled hand.

My stomach churns, and I'm not sure I'll stop her if she tries to take the asshole out right now. The more I think about what was done to me—not just the experimenting but the way my wolf was stolen from me all these years—the wilder my wolf becomes. She wants out. To take her vengeance on this place, these people.

I flick a glance at Davina, who hovers near the back, watching and listening with arms crossed. Her participation here was technically forced. I can't let my wolf hurt her for something she didn't have a choice about. Still, I'm getting the feeling her magic did more than keep the lights on.

"The research you did," Grey says to Severin, and I try to breathe deeply, to calm the fire in my veins. "Do you have a list of names of the people you experimented on?"

"I'm afraid access to those records isn't part of the tour," Dr. Severin says.

This time, it's Crow who takes a step forward with his fists balled, but Grey holds up a hand to stop him.

"If that's what you think, then I'm afraid you've misunderstood our presence here," Grey tells the doctor in a voice that's deceivingly calm compared to what I feel through our bond right now. "Lexi is your new high alpha and you—"

"I'm human," Dr. Severin interrupts with a note of smugness, and I can't help but snort at the way he obviously thinks that will somehow protect him now. "Which means I don't answer to any alpha."

"You are alive at the mercy of my wolf," Grey snarls.

My feet are moving before I realize it, and I step

between them, snagging Mia's knife from her hand as I go. Pressing the tip into Dr. Severin's throat, I meet his eyes, letting him see the fury I'm barely leashing. He flinches, but then goes utterly still when the knife's tip threatens to puncture his skin.

"And mine," I tell him quietly.

At that, Severin swallows audibly.

"We'll take those records now," Mia says with fake sweetness.

"I'll get them." Davina makes her way to the central computer where she starts typing in a flurry of keystrokes.

I turn my attention back to Severin. "You used me against my will. And my parents before that. For years, you injected poisons and drugs into people, leaving them broken or worse. How can you still think that's okay?"

"I gave you purpose," he says, triumph shining in his cold eyes. "You were the key to the next phase of evolution. And from what I hear, your wolf is the most powerful and lethal this pack has seen in generations. You should be thanking me."

Fury rises like bile in my chest. Baring my teeth, I press hard enough with the knife to draw blood. Through the bond, I feel the darkness pulse, egging me on, and it's impossible to tell whether that darkness belongs to me or Grey or both.

"Listen, dude's a prick," Mia says from behind me. "But are we really doing this?"

I don't answer her. Neither does Grey.

"I thought we were doing things different than the old man did," she points out.

I don't answer, my voice lost to the beast hovering just beneath my skin.

Crow says something I can't hear over the roar in my ears.

A moment later, Mia appears at my side. "Lex, he's not worth it," she says quietly. "Or if he is, this is not the way. I don't want you to lose yourself just to end this piece of shit."

Maybe it's the fact that it's coming from her, a girl who, not ten minutes ago, casually stabbed a guard in the leg for me, but her words reach the part of me that my wolf's fury is trying to bury.

I blink.

Some of my humanity leaks back in.

The wolf snarls as I shove it back. My pressure on the knife's tip against Severin's throat eases a little. Bright red blood trickles from the tiny wound, and I have to turn away from the sight of it before my wolf takes control in her thirst for more to spill. My veins burn with what feels like some kind of chain threatening to snap.

Mia gently covers my hand with hers and slips the knife out of my grasp. Severin stumbles aside, pressing a hand to his bleeding neck.

I meet Mia's eyes, my hands shaking with the effort of leashing my beast.

To my relief, there's no judgment or pity in her expression. Only understanding. "He's done hurting people," she says. "Done hurting *you*."

I nod, not trusting my voice.

"Are you okay?" Davina's voice cuts through the silence.

I look over, half-expecting to find her worrying over Severin. But she's looking at Grey.

"I'm fine," he says, folding his arms behind his back.

Behind him, Crow frowns but says nothing.

"What did I miss?" Mia asks sharply.

Davina stares steadily at Grey, and I swear the air around us begins to thicken.

"Nothing," Grey says, and the pressure dissipates as suddenly as it came.

Davina returns to the computer and hits a few keystrokes. Then she pulls a thumb drive free and holds it out.

"These are the names of the people they experimented on. And the medical outcomes. Tests, notes, stuff like that. There's more about the LAG gene itself in the deeper files. You're welcome to them, but it's pretty science-heavy with lots of medical jargon."

"Thanks," I tell her.

Before I can reach for it, Mia steps in front of me and snags it out of her hand.

Davina doesn't look insulted. In fact, she barely looks at Mia at all. Instead, I feel the full weight of her stare. And whatever secrets are locked behind it.

"Will it tell me how to reverse it?" I ask.

She hesitates, her brow furrowing.

"It's a gene activation," I say, my voice pitching high as fear spikes. "There has to be a way to turn it off again."

"I'm afraid that's not possible," she says.

I tense, the fury from earlier rising swiftly. Grey steps up beside me, pressing his hand to the small of my back. Unlike before, he's now calm. As if he anticipated the answer already.

Dammit.

He already knew there was no cure.

"We came here for answers," I say bleakly. "You're telling me nothing can be done."

"I'm telling you nothing can reverse it," she says, glancing between Grey and me. "Whatever you can do to harness the power of your wolf… I don't know. I'm not a shifter."

"We'll look through the files," Grey says, but I can't summon much hope in that. Not when Davina's looking at me like she already knows it won't yield what I'm looking for.

"Did you infuse magic into the drugs they gave us?" I ask.

Silence follows, so heavy that I immediately know the answer is yes. I realize belatedly the others already knew it too.

Rather than give me a confirmation, Davina says, "Franco didn't just see you as an heir, you know. He saw you as a weapon. You're the evolution of the alpha line. The first of a new kind."

She glances from me to Grey, but I don't look at him. I can't. My stomach roils with the thought of what Franco intended to use me for. What I'm capable of. Suddenly, injecting myself with the serum Vincenzo gave me feels like a terrible idea.

"Let me guess, there's no way to remove the magic either," I snap.

Davina doesn't answer.

"I want it shut down," I rasp, not looking at anyone in particular. "Everything."

Severin makes a noise of alarm.

His nostrils flare. "You don't have the authority."

"She has all the authority," Grey says.

"I spent my life on this work," Severin hisses. "Stopping now would be a waste."

"No," I say, stepping forward. "It would be justice."

Severin's mouth opens, but I'm already turning away.

"You know, if you really wanted to secure your position as the strongest wolf pack in the world, this lab could give you the tools to build a superpack," Davina says carefully. "It's what Franco was going to do."

"The LAG gene isn't what makes us strong," I tell her. "And I don't want a superpack; I want a pack who takes care of each other. Who uses kindness rather than fear to inspire loyalty. And we will not be testing or experimenting on anyone ever again."

Severin scoffs. "Idealism is a poor substitute for power."

"Sounds like something Franco would say," Mia mutters darkly.

"How do I shut down the power in this place?" I ask Davina.

Her brows furrow. "I'm not sure," she says. "But I think I would have to disengage the spell I wrote."

"That's it?" I ask.

"Davina, don't you fucking dare," Severin warns.

"And then you activate the shutdown command," Davina says, ignoring the warning.

"You little bitch," Severin hisses from where he hovers against the far wall.

Davina glares at him, the first sign of temper she's shown. "Did you expect anything else after the way you treated me here?"

She stalks over to the main computer and hits a few keystrokes. There's an audible click from somewhere in the room. Davina strides over to the wall beside the door we came through and yanks open what looks like a normal electrical box.

"Don't you fucking dare," Severin warns.

Ignoring him, she presses her palm to the breakers and whispers a few words in a language I don't understand.

There's a strange pressure in the air again, like earlier. Then, nothing.

She steps back. "It's done."

"Useless fucking witch," Severin spits.

Crow, who's been moving steadily closer to where Severin hovers against the wall, sends his fist into the doctor's face. Severin crumples, unmoving.

"Fuck, I couldn't take any more of that," Crow says.

With my wolf hearing, I note Severin's heartbeat still going at a steady rhythm. Just knocked out, not dead then.

"When he comes to, let him know he's under house arrest until further notice," I tell Crow.

He nods. "With pleasure."

I exchange a look with Grey.

He nods at me to keep going.

"Um, does that whole house arrest thing include me?" Davina asks.

I wince, feeling bad for everything she's been through. "It's just until everything is sorted out."

She swallows. "I guess it's better than whatever Franco would have done to me in the end."

"I'm sorry," I tell her and mean it.

She looks back at the screen. "Now, the shutdown command. You'll need your thumbprint. It won't take mine. Not for this."

I step to the center console. My thumb unlocks some kind of access panel with several options. One of them is labeled Emergency Shutdown.

I take a deep breath and press the button.

Around us, the hum of machines begins to die. Then, the lights go too, along with the holographic image of the DNA flickering out like a bad dream.

But even in the dark stillness, the nightmare doesn't end. It lingers. Burrows deep.

I thought shutting this place down would give me peace. Or clarity.

All I feel is the weight of what we didn't find… and the creeping sense that we're already too late.

12

GREY

The warehouse feels colder than usual, the air metallic and sharp with an edge that creeps beneath my skin. Maybe it's just Lexi's absence that has me so tense. I don't want to be away from her, especially this soon after sealing our mate bond, but Andy needed her at the house for pack business, and none of us wants to wait on combing through these files. Not after the way Severin acted about them earlier. Or the way Lexi reacted to learning there's no cure for her gene activation.

Besides, between Razor, Mia, and Andy, along with the two dozen armed guards roaming the place, Lexi's safe where she is.

So, even though I believe Davina—Franco wouldn't have wanted a cure for something that he saw as the ultimate transformation, so I'm not surprised he would have essentially prevented one from being possible. I'm determined to find something helpful, not just for her but for me too. The strange glowing in my veins is getting worse. Not to mention the crazy bastard's voice in my head, urging me to kill everything in sight.

The warehouse is the only secure place we've got. And not just for these files either. For me. Just in case.

The lights overhead cast grim shadows across the table cluttered with the research we printed out from the thumb drive on the way over. Page after page of Dr. Severin's clinical notes and lab reports—words like *forced evolution* and *gene activation* staring back at me.

Next to me, Dutch sits hunched, head bowed, as he flips through pages. Crow, usually calm and detached, radiates a restless energy where he sits at his computer, scanning the patient files that we didn't bother to print yet. His fingers tap impatient rhythms against the metal table, eyes narrowed in laser-sharp concentration.

"What the hell," Dutch mutters, frowning as he flips through a file for the third time.

"What is it?" I ask, tensing.

"I found more gaps in the protocol data," he says.

"Again?"

I set aside my own stack of files and peer over Dutch's shoulder. This makes the fourth set of lab reports with missing protocol information.

"Look." He holds up the pages to show me. "There are at least three sections missing from this batch alone. Someone deleted files."

"And they aren't on the thumb drive either," Crow pipes up, fingers flying over the keyboard. "Whoever did this, they knew what they were doing to make sure I can't recover them."

"Protocol data on what, exactly?"

"Subject trials," Dutch answers, mouth tightening.

"Lexi's?" I ask, straightening.

Dutch shakes his head. "Not that I've seen yet. From the looks of it, these are his earlier experiments, though. A couple of pregnancies. From twenty years ago. Someone named Sofia and—hey!"

Crow grabs the binder out of Dutch's hands.

"What the fuck," Dutch says.

"Switch me." Crow shoves the computer at him.

Dutch takes it, shooting me a glance with brows raised. I shrug and look over at Crow again. His brow furrows, and he turns pages with a slow intensity that feels personal. Something's off, but I have no idea what.

My eyes drift back to Dutch as he speeds through security footage Crow pulled from the lab's camera feed. "There's not much recent footage here," he says.

I glance over to see grainy images flickering across his screen, distorted angles of sterile hallways and darkened labs.

Suddenly, Dutch pauses abruptly, fingers tightening over the mouse, his knuckles white.

"What?" My voice comes out sharper than intended.

"I don't fucking believe it." Dutch shakes his head slowly. "Fucker got there before us."

"Who?" I ask.

He turns the screen so I can see. "Look."

Crow sets the binder aside. We all lean closer to the grainy image. Dutch hits play, and the video resumes. The figure onscreen moves quickly, face hidden beneath a hood. But even with the bad angle and grainy darkness, there's something distinctly familiar about the way the figure moves.

My gut tightens.

Dutch's jaw works silently; then he lets out a breath. "That gait. Look how he favors the left side. Fuck. It's Ramsey."

"How the hell did he get past their security?" I wonder.

"Umm. Guys, look at the date." Crow's voice is quiet but weighted.

"Fuck," Dutch says as I squint to make it out in the bottom left.

"Yesterday?" I snarl.

The knowledge hits like a fist to the gut.

"He must be the one who took the missing files," Dutch growls, voice dark with barely-contained violence.

"I don't think so," Crow says. Dutch looks ready to argue, but Crow adds, "I'm not saying he wouldn't try, but I've seen him around tech, and there's no way he'd be able to get all the way inside the lab with all that security they've got and access their files. I watched Davina, and she entered two encrypted passwords to get passed all their firewalls."

"Okay, but then what the hell was he doing there?" Dutch asks, frustration etched in every tense line of his face.

"Play the rest of the video," I say. "See where he goes."

"It ends there," Dutch says.

Crow leans in and types a few commands.

We wait in silence to see what he can pull up. But a moment later, he scowls and shoves away from the computer. "No, it's fucking deleted. Just like the other files. And I can't retrieve it."

Crow's gaze flicks to mine, dark eyes blazing. "I think it's safe to say the Ramsey we thought we knew doesn't exist. Which means we need to consider he *is* capable of accessing those files."

Dutch is right, and we all know it.

An uneasy silence settles around us. My chest burns with rage, thick and suffocating. Ramsey has haunted our every step since his betrayal. Knowing he's back, stealing the research we desperately need—it's too much.

I clench my fists, the wolf inside me howling for violence. "We need to find out what he took."

"Maybe we should interrogate the doc and the hex witch," Dutch says. "Instead of just putting them on house arrest."

"As much as Lexi hates the guy, I don't think she'll green light torturing him." Dutch scowls. "Crow, look deeper. Find out who the subjects were."

Crow hesitates.

"You okay?" Dutch asks him.

"That's the thing, I already know who the subject is. Was." He swallows hard.

"Who?" Dutch asks, leaning closer.

When Crow finally lifts his gaze, pain shines stark and raw in his eyes, like a wound torn wide open. He swallows hard, fighting for composure.

"My mother." He reaches for the binder, setting it between Dutch and me. "Her name's here. Sofia."

I stare at the name, the revelation hitting me like ice water. Crow doesn't talk about his mother, but I know for a fact he's always blamed Alvaro for her having a mental break that ultimately led to her ending her own life. "Are you sure?"

He shoves the page toward me, jaw clenched so tight the veins in his neck bulge. There, typed neatly at the top of the lab note: Sofia Solano.

Crow's mother.

Beside her name, a line of text stands out: Consent for treatment given by Alvaro Martinez.

Crow's father.

Dutch lets out a low whistle, disbelief coloring his expression. Crow's eyes glitter with fury and grief. I know exactly what he's feeling—the betrayal from someone meant to protect you. The helplessness that claws at your sanity. It reminds me of the helplessness I felt over my mother's abuse. The way I tried and failed to protect her for years before I did the only thing I could: tried to kill him myself.

I still feel the guilt over failing at it. Failing her.

Something tells me Crow feels that way now.

"The date is two years before you were born," Dutch says quietly.

Crow's fists tremble.

"There's no end date listed, so…" Dutch trails off, opting to shut up.

Probably a good idea.

Crow's not processing anything right now from the lost look on his face.

"You want to talk about it?" I ask quietly.

Crow shakes his head sharply, his voice strained. "About the fact that he took it upon himself to sign her life away? To commit her as nothing more than a lab rat in between using her for—"

He doesn't finish, but he doesn't have to.

Alvaro's a fucking monster.

Dutch rubs his jaw, staring at Crow sympathetically. "Uh, I don't mean to… I mean, shit, I don't want to make it worse, but… If they experimented on your mom during her pregnancy... does that mean you have the LAG gene too?"

I send him a look, trying to convey SHUT UP.

Crow's fists curl tighter, his voice a deadly rasp. "I don't know. Some of the files are missing." He looks at me, his eyes shining with violence. Urgent, desperate violence. "He needs to answer for what he did."

The raw agony in his voice sends a stab through my heart. "Those answers won't bring her back," I warn.

He shakes his head, the movements jerky, unsettled. "He let them experiment on her, and it killed her in the end. I need to know why. I need to hear him admit what he's done."

I can smell his wolf on him from here. Crow's rarely out of control, but right now, the rage simmering beneath his skin is a tangible thing, threatening to consume him.

"Listen to me," I say, pushing to my feet and leveling him with a steady gaze. "We will confront him, I promise you. But we can't afford rash moves. My father will come for us the moment we move on your father. It would be war."

Crow's breathing is uneven, nostrils flaring as he fights for control. "You can't expect me to do nothing, Grey. Not after this."

"I'm not asking for nothing," I reply carefully. "I'm asking you to trust me. We'll handle it together. Smart. Precise. Controlled."

The tension stretches, brittle and electric. Crow's eyes flicker with indecision, pain written plainly across his face. Finally, he exhales, a ragged, defeated sound. "Fine. But when the time comes, that fucker is mine."

"Agreed," I say firmly.

Crow gives a sharp nod, retreating into silence. The hurt etched deep into his features lingers like smoke after a fire, raw and choking.

Dutch clears his throat. "We need to track Ramsey down. Whatever he stole—it matters enough to risk coming back here. And if I had to guess, I'd say it involves the experiments on Lexi since I don't see anything about her in the files we have."

"A lot of my mom's records are missing too," Crow adds.

"Do you think he plans to sell the info to Vincenzo in exchange for his place at the table?" Dutch asks.

"Fuck," I say because, yeah, I do think that.

"It's all he cared about when Franco shot his old man," Dutch adds.

"I know."

It all comes back to my father—the puppet master pulling strings from the shadows, determined to control the pack through Lexi. Through Ramsey. Through me. Anger boils beneath my skin, a familiar burn.

Before I can speak, my phone buzzes loudly. Mia's name flashes on the screen.

"What is it?" I ask immediately.

"Do you know anything about a meeting between Lexi and your old man?" Mia's voice is clipped.

Alarm bells go off at the urgency in her tone.

"No. Why?"

"Because he just arrived, and Lexi allowed him through the gate."

The idea of my father alone with Lexi right now sends

ice rushing through my veins. Lexi's powerful, but her wolf is unstable. If anything happens to her—

Dutch stands immediately. Crow tosses the binder down and heads for the door.

"We're coming," I tell Mia, voice raw with restrained rage. "Don't let her out of your sight."

"Wasn't planning on it," Mia mutters darkly. "But hurry."

She hangs up.

Crow meets my gaze, his own pain momentarily set aside. "I'll drive."

I nod tightly, forgetting about the research and Ramsey and everything else. All that matters now is getting to Lexi.

We rush from the warehouse, the heat of the afternoon sun leaving a layer of sweat on my brow. The streets blur past in a haze as Crow drives, my heart hammering relentlessly. Lexi's face fills my mind, her haunted eyes and stubborn pride. I promised to keep her safe. It's why I claimed her, married her, moved in with her at Franco's fucking house of all places.

Yet, despite everything, she's still vulnerable.

Still at the mercy of my father. A man I can't seem to protect the women I love from, no matter how hard I try.

"Grey?" Crow glances at me from the driver's seat, his eyes dark with worry.

I look down to see my veins practically glowing beneath my skin. My wolf is writhing inside me, and the voice—the one that sounds a lot like Franco—whispers at me that I'll never make it in time to save her.

My jaw clenches, my voice scraping out harshly. "Drive faster."

I stare out the window, fists tight in my lap.

If my father hurts her, he won't have to come for me. Losing her will rip out my fucking heart and render me lifeless the moment she leaves this world. The only piece that has ever mattered on this board is the queen.

13

LEXI

I pace in front of Franco's old desk, polished wood glinting sharply beneath the overhead lights in the study. The vaulted ceilings echo my every move, amplifying every step I take, every breath I force myself to draw. The grandeur of this place feels oppressive, like it's still fighting against me, still whispering that I don't belong.

No one else has challenged me or spoken against me since that first meeting, but the house is constantly full of people coming and going. Security changing over their shifts or doing patrols. Lieutenants reporting in. Andy meeting with various leaders or city officials. The house feels more like an office than a place to live. And I'm on display the entire time. I've already shaken more hands and made more small talk than I've done in my entire life combined. And that's just since returning from the lab.

I immediately shove aside thoughts of what happened there. It'll only upset my wolf, and I'm barely leashing her as it is. She feels suffocated inside these walls. She wants the forest again. Freedom. She wants me to shift.

Later, I promise her.

She snarls back at me.

From a chair near the fireplace, Andy flips through the pages in front of her, scribbling quick notes with narrowed eyes and tight lips. All morning, she's been grilling the pack leadership—interviewing them, determining who stays loyal and who needs to be culled. Whoever doesn't pledge their loyalty—and prove it—will be banished from Indigo Hills.

It's brutal and cold but necessary.

I still can't decide if I admire or fear how easily she slips into the role I've given her. Sentencing her pack—her people—to banishment can't be pleasant, and yet she hasn't questioned it. Or me.

"You're pacing again," Andy remarks dryly, without looking up. She flips a page, sighing heavily. "You're also making me dizzy."

"Sorry," I mutter, forcing myself to stop and drop into the chair opposite her.

I glance at Razor, standing silent and stoic against the wall by the door. His eyes dart to mine briefly, assessing, reassuring, before returning to his careful watch. Knowing Razor is here, guarding me, should be comforting, especially considering I don't know who I can trust in my own pack yet. At the same time, it reminds me how vulnerable I am—how much I still need protection from others, even after everything I've gone through to access my wolf.

I need to get her under control.

Before she gets me under *her* control instead.

"You look like someone waiting for the firing squad," Andy says quietly, finally setting down her pen.

I sigh, bracing my hands on the back of Franco's chair—my chair. Ugh. "Maybe I am."

She tilts her head, giving me a considering look. "Want to talk about it?"

I open my mouth to answer but am cut off when a pack member appears in the doorway. He's in a security uniform, but I can't remember his name. I need to work on that. "Alpha," he says, offering me a respectful dip of his head. "We're finished with the shift change. Do you need anything else before my team and I head out?"

"No, we're fine," I say a little more sharply than I intend.

Razor snorts.

The guard glances at Andy then Razor. Neither one offers any kind of explanation, so he clears his throat and says, "Right. I'll, uh, see you tomorrow."

When he's gone, I find Andy looking at me with an arched brow.

"This house is just so freaking crowded," I snarl.

She offers a tiny smile like she gets it. "They're more scared of you than you are of them, Lexi."

"I doubt that."

Andy shrugs. "Believe what you want, but I see it in their eyes when I interview them. You killed Franco. And then you executed his generals in front of the entire pack. Some might resent you, but most are smart enough to respect your power."

Right. Franco.

They all think I killed him, including Andy.

Guilt tugs at me for lying to her, but I shove it aside. As for the generals…

"I didn't exactly do it on purpose," I admit, my words more vulnerable than I like.

Andy's gaze softens slightly. "Intent doesn't matter to these wolves. Only outcome."

"Is that why no one's even batted an eye about finding out Dom's dead?" I ask.

Her gaze flashes with an intensity I haven't seen often from her. "Dom had no friends among us. He burned every bridge and left hate and violence in his wake wherever he went. No one's sorry to see him go."

"So, no big fancy funeral for him, then?"

"Elena suggested a simple memorial stone in the pack cemetery to appease any family. I approved it," she says wryly.

"Wow. Okay. Thanks for taking care of that."

"Elena did most of the legwork. She's really good at what she does."

"Scarily good," I agree.

Andy grins.

The silence hangs between us, growing warmer, less tense.

"How do you handle it so easily? The violence, the having to be on your guard constantly—the pressure of it all?"

Andy glances at Razor, and I realize I'm asking a personal question in front of someone she probably considers her enemy. But she doesn't brush off the question, and when she speaks, there's a surprising amount of openness in her tone.

"Franco recruited my dad before I was born, so I grew up with violence and power games as the norm. My father used to take me to work with him. Said it would bring us closer. Make me stronger."

Razor snarls at that.

Andy gives him a look. "Yeah, we're a lot alike."

"It's fucked up," he says.

"It was," she agrees.

I shake my head, thinking of Grey. His dad did the same thing. So did all Vincenzo's generals. It's horrible.

"Did it?" I ask. "Make you stronger?"

"Sort of. Believe it or not, my dad was a good guy, all things considered. Better than any of the current regime—on both sides. I came to realize he did bad things for what he considered good reasons. When he died, Toros took his place, and Franco decided a marriage between us would unite those divided about Toros' quick promotion to general."

"Toros led the Bane though," Razor says. "He fought against Franco. I still don't get why he gave that up and joined the fucker."

"Power is a heady thing to dangle in front of someone. Regardless of their principles or morals. Although, I think Toros was always in it for power more than he was in it for the cause."

Razor scowls.

"You didn't have a choice?" I ask. "About marrying Toros?"

She shrugs. "I wouldn't have said no despite not wanting it."

"Why not?"

"This pack has always been my world, brutal as it is."

I watch her, waiting, sensing there's more. After a pause, she adds quietly, "I remember watching my father come home bloody one night after carrying out Franco's orders against someone he deemed a threat. My mother started crying, telling him to leave, to run, so we could start a new life somewhere else. But he knew that wouldn't work. We'd seen it." She flicked a glance at me. "Your parents' death sent a message to anyone who'd considered trying to get away. And my mother died feeling like a prisoner here."

"I'm so sorry," I tell her, my heart breaking a little at what it must have been like to grow up that way.

"I decided early on that I would never be weak like that. I wouldn't be made to feel like a victim or a pawn." Her voice is steady, but beneath it, the pain is evident, old wounds reopened just slightly.

I nod slowly, understanding more clearly why Andy acts so hard, so controlled. Survival. Just like me.

"I grew up in foster care," I tell her. "Never had a real home. Never belonged anywhere. I got into some bad homes, bad situations, and did what I had to so I could stay safe. But families saw my file, saw a troubled kid, and sent me packing or passed me over entirely. I learned early that no one was coming to save me."

Andy meets my eyes, something flickering in her expression. Respect. Understanding. "We both learned that lesson early, then."

"Yeah," I breathe out, relaxing slightly. "Guess we did."

She leans forward, offering me a slight smile. "Maybe now we get to rewrite those rules for someone else."

The unexpected kindness catches me off guard, warms a place inside my chest I usually keep locked down tight. "Maybe," I agree softly.

When I catch Razor's eye, there's sorrow and fury reflecting back at me. "You're both fucking badasses, you know that."

"Thanks," I tell him, his words healing a few more of those wounds I still carry.

Before I can say anything else, Elena bursts through the office door. Razor stiffens, instantly alert.

"Alpha." Elena bows her head only slightly. "You have a guest," she announces.

"Another interview?" I ask, glancing at Andy.

Andy shakes her head sharply, lips pressed tight. "There's nothing else scheduled until tomorrow."

"Who is it?" I ask.

"It's Vincenzo Diavolo," Elena says. "Here to give his update."

"What update?" I ask carefully, heart thudding now. There's only one thing that man wants an update about. But they don't know that.

Elena sniffs. "Mr. Diavolo had a standing monthly appointment with Franco to report in on pack business and financials. I expect he's here to do that with you."

Razor snorts.

A second later, Mia appears behind Elena. She's breathless, and I wonder if she ran here all the way from the guardhouse where she was auditing the patrol schedules by shadowing the guards.

Our eyes meet.

There's no way Vincenzo is here to resume anything he had with Franco. Not when he'd rather kill me than pledge his loyalty to his new alpha. The deal we made hangs like a noose around my neck. The alpha title he wants, the blood sample I promised. Both things I refuse to hand over now.

"Send him away," Mia says.

I take a deep breath, steadying myself. "Let him in."

"Lexi—" Razor protests sharply, stepping closer.

"I'll handle it," I say firmly, cutting him off.

Mia turns away, sliding her phone out and speaking in a

low, clipped tone. Grey. Fuck. I don't have much time before the cavalry shows up.

Razor hesitates, wincing as he says, "If he looks closely at me, he'll know I'm not his pack anymore. Same with Mia."

"Stay in the hall. Don't let him see you when he comes in. Be ready if I call for you, but do not come in unless I say."

Razor's jaw tightens, indicating he's clearly unhappy, but he nods sharply. "Fine."

Mia returns just in time to say, "The fuck I am. I'm staying in here with you."

"Mia, this is an order—from your high alpha," I tell her. "Round up the closest guards, and send two of them in here with me."

She glares at me, and I wonder if she's going to refuse. "I'll send six. And I'll be in the hall with Razor. If you so much as breathe heavy, I'm coming in."

I nod. "Fine."

She disappears.

Andy rises, gathering her papers.

"Will you stay?" I ask her.

"Of course." She remains standing near the window, her expression stony and blank.

A second later, exactly as Mia warned, six guards file into the room and fan out behind me, feet planted, hands clasped. They don't say a word, but I can't deny their presence is comforting.

I turn to face the door again and wait.

The silence amplifies my heartbeat, pounding loud and chaotic in my ears. My palms sweat, and my breath feels too shallow. I force myself to straighten my spine, lifting my chin defiantly.

The door opens slowly, deliberately, like he's savoring my anxiety. Vincenzo Diavolo steps inside, shutting it carefully behind him. He's impeccably dressed, polished in every way that's designed to intimidate. He glances over the other occupants. Andy. The guards. Then me. The faint smile curving his lips sends chills down my spine.

"Hello, Lexi," he drawls smoothly, eyes cold and calculating.

I stand firm, meeting his gaze without wavering. "You can call me Alpha."

His smile tightens slightly, eyes narrowing. For a heartbeat, the air thickens, charged and dangerous.

"You look well," he says, ignoring my title. "Not quite as bloody as the last time I saw you."

"What do you want?" My voice is cold, hard, even as my pulse hammers in my throat. Every nerve is on high alert, waiting for the trap he's surely about to spring.

"Just what I was promised," he says calmly, hands clasped in front of him. "You do remember our deal, don't you?"

My fingers curl into fists beneath the desk. "I remember."

He steps closer, lowering his voice conspiratorially. "Good. Then you also recall the terms. I'll take your title now. And the blood sample."

My heart kicks painfully in my chest. My wolf snarls in my mind, protective and fierce. "I changed my mind."

A brief flash of rage crosses his expression before he masks it with practiced ease. "Careful, Lexi. Changing your mind could have dire consequences."

I meet his gaze, holding steady despite the ice sliding down my spine. "Threatening me won't change my decision."

He smiles slowly, darkly amused. "You forget your place. You're not ready for this role. I can help you—protect you from your own inexperience. From the rejection of your pack."

"I don't need your help," I snap sharply, anger lending me strength. "And I won't be handing anything over."

His eyes darken dangerously, a predator's stare that pierces straight through me. "You're playing a dangerous game. Do you really think Grey will protect you from the consequences?"

My chest aches fiercely at the mention of Grey's name. "I'm not involving *my husband*."

He arches an eyebrow skeptically. "We both know that's a lie. Grey is involved, whether you want him to be or not. And if you refuse to honor our agreement, he'll pay the price first."

"Any threat against Grey is a threat against me."

He flicks a glance at the guards behind me but doesn't look nearly as worried as I'd hoped. "Your pack can't be happy about you being married to a member of another pack. I doubt they'd fight to protect him."

Fear stabs deep, sharp, and painful. My mind races with images of Grey—injured, captured, killed. My wolf strains to act, to defend and protect. "Touch Grey, and I'll rip you apart myself."

He chuckles softly, eyes glittering with cruel amusement. "Such loyalty. Such foolishness."

My wolf snarls, pushing to the surface, urging violence. I fist my hands, fighting for control. If I shift now, I'll likely kill him where he stands. But there's no telling who else I'll go after once my wolf takes me over. "You underestimate me."

"And you underestimate the enemy you've just made," Vincenzo murmurs coldly. "You're making a mistake."

"I don't think so," I snap back, heart racing, adrenaline flooding my veins.

"Very well." Vincenzo inclines his head mockingly. "Have it your way. But when the walls come crashing down, remember this conversation. Remember your choice."

He turns smoothly, heading for the door. Pausing, he glances back, eyes chillingly calm. "Tell Grey we'll see each other very soon."

The door shuts behind him with a quiet finality, leaving me standing in trembling silence. I let out a shaky breath, my legs finally giving out as I sink back into the chair, heart thundering.

I know I've just declared war by refusing his demands.

Vincenzo will retaliate. He'll target Grey, Mia, Dutch, Crow, Razor—all of them just to hurt me and make me give in. I squeeze my eyes shut against the panic clawing at my throat. But beneath the fear, there's determination.

I won't let him hurt the people I love.

If I have to lose myself to my wolf forever, it will be worth it.

14

GREY

The second I pull into the driveway, I know I'm too late.

My father's striding out the front doors like he owns the place, dressed like a fucking politician and smiling like a snake who just swallowed the mouse. He's buttoning his suit jacket slowly, like he has all the time in the goddamn world, and when he sees me leap out of the passenger seat of Crow's car, his grin sharpens.

"The knight in shining armor here at last," he calls across the gravel, tone slick with malice. "Too fucking late. Meeting's over. You missed all the fun."

I stop cold, realizing I don't see a single member of my pack. Or Lexi.

My vision tunnels.

The beast inside me roars.

If he hurt Lexi, I'd know. I'd feel it. Still… I need to know she's okay. To see her with my own eyes.

A figure moves in the door behind him.

Lexi stops short at the sight of me facing off with my

father. But I don't care that she looks stricken with fear. She's unharmed from what I can tell. That's what matters.

"Did he touch you?" I demand.

"No," she says, and I nearly sag at the relief in that single word.

"Not yet," my father adds, and I snarl, my skin hot with the effort of holding my human form.

Whatever darkness that's been gathering inside me is threatening to unleash itself here and now. I've never felt so unbound to my wolf before.

"Security, hold your positions," Lexi commands sharply, not even flinching as half a dozen of her guards pour out of the house behind her and surround us all. Elena comes to stand in the doorway, guarding Lexi's back.

Seeing her pack surround her helps ease the raging inside me just a little, and for a moment, I think I can let him walk out of here.

My father stalks closer to me, undeterred, eyes glinting as he snarls, "Tell that bitch you're all going to pay for double-crossing me."

My fists tighten, and any hope of letting him walk evaporates with the words he just spoke.

"She's your high alpha now," I growl. "Watch your fucking mouth."

He laughs—sharp and humorless—and shoves me.

Hard.

I don't think. I slam both hands into his chest and send him flying back into the hood of his black SUV with enough force to dent the grill. The satisfying crunch his body makes barely registers before I'm closing the distance to rip him apart.

My wolf surges to the surface, and I barely manage to

yank it back into my skin when I see Lexi running toward us, barefoot, hair flowing out wild behind her, eyes wide with panic.

I move to position myself between her and him, but my father is a split second faster. He peels himself off the grill of the car and stands. His gaze shifts from me to her. And then—

He lunges.

"Lexi!" I shout, but she's already reacting.

She spins to meet him head-on, arms up.

Except that she doesn't shift. Doesn't call on the wolf I know must be clawing beneath her skin. She fights him as a human.

Thanks to the strength and speed of her wolf, she gets a few hits in—one solid punch to his jaw that would've dropped any human. But my father's not human.

He's fast. Strong. Not just a wolf but an alpha.

Before I can get between them, he backhands her so hard she stumbles sideways and then hits the ground with a choked sound that punches the air out of my lungs.

"Shift!" I scream. "Lexi, shift—"

She pushes up on her palms, blood leaking from her mouth and pure defiance burning in her gaze. "No."

She's trying to win on her own terms.

But she's losing.

I launch myself at him with a roar, but he's ready for that and sidesteps rather than facing me head-on. Lexi's security surges forward, shifting as they come. Out of the corner of my eye, I see Rocco and Alvaro rush to block them.

In the second I split my focus, my father slips past me.

He yanks Lexi up by the throat, her feet barely touching the ground, and I snap.

My wolf surges.

Control shatters.

I crash into him like a freight train, but not before he tosses Lexi so hard through the air that her back slams into the marble column behind me. My fists find bone. His ribs, his face. I don't hold back. Not this time. Not with Lexi bleeding on the ground, brutalized by this monster.

I hit him again.

And again.

And again.

His blood splashes across the gravel, and still I want more.

The darkness inside me is a living, breathing thing. It's managed to shove even my wolf aside, filling me with this obsession for death.

When I've all but lost myself in it, my father shoves me off with a burst of strength. Then he climbs to his feet and stumbles back, lip split, eye swelling, blood streaked across his shirt and face.

"Grey." Dutch's voice is sharp enough to break through the haze, and I glance over to see every single guard lying dead on the pavement. Rocco and Alvaro are covered in blood, but one whiff of the scent tells me it's not their own. "Are we doing this?"

He's tense. I know what he's asking.

If we fight now, it'll mean Dutch against his father. Razor and Crow against theirs. And their pack will come. My father will call them, and they'll come, and they'll destroy us.

Lexi refuses to shift. I don't know where that leaves us in a fight like that.

I hesitate, breathing heavy and blood dripping from my knuckles.

Rather than answer, I reach down and help Andy pull Lexi to her feet.

My father's eyes lock on mine—and something clicks behind them.

Realization.

He staggers, spitting blood, and looks from me to Lexi and back again. "It wasn't her," he breathes. "It was you. You killed Franco."

I don't answer.

I don't need to.

He sees it.

Sees the truth in every drop of alpha power radiating off me, in every inch of my stance as I step between him and Lexi, chest heaving, ready for round two.

"You're an alpha now," he says, wonder and hatred twisted into one low snarl. "And still, you tied yourself to her. Let her take the credit. You're hiding behind her. Like a fucking coward."

Despite her injuries, Lexi snarls.

He wipes his face with the back of his hand, blood smearing across his cheek. "I should've known. Should've seen it sooner."

Lexi leans into me. She's limping, but she's upright. And her eyes are pure fire. "You would have seen if you'd bothered to look at him. You never saw Grey for who he really was," she snarls at him.

But my father is long past pretending to care about me.

His eyes narrow as he says, "It looks like I'll be coming for both your titles then."

"You won't get either one," I tell him.

He laughs, low and bitter.

"So be it. If you won't give me this city…" He looks around, taking in the sight of all of us gathering now—Dutch on his left just behind Alvaro, Razor flanking Lexi silently, Crow stalking toward where Rocco stands beside the SUV, Mia striding through the courtyard with purpose in her eyes, more of Lexi's guards behind her. "…I'll burn it down with all of you inside it."

His confidence confuses me, considering how outnumbered he is. But then I catch movement at the tree line and realize what he already knows.

Wolves—dozens at least—emerge from the woods that border the back of the property. Not Giovanni pack.

Diavolo pack wolves.

My father has used his alpha power to call his pack.

And even with my newfound alpha power and my pack at my side, there's no way we can win against this many wolves. Not today.

My father smirks like he knows what I'm thinking.

Before I can say anything, Lexi steps forward so that she stands on her own rather than leaning against me. Her shoulders are squared. Lips bloodied. But she's standing. And her expression is set with ferocity.

"You can threaten us," she says coldly. "You can throw your tantrum, call your wolves, bring your wrath—but it won't change anything. And if you let your pack kill us rather than taking that victory for yourself, you won't get our alpha power—and you won't be crowned king."

A flicker of irritation passes over his expression. He

knows she's right, and he's pissed about it. But rather than give that away, he merely straightens his jacket like he's about to walk into a board meeting. "Looks like we'll save our war for another day."

"Looks like," I growl, stepping up beside her. My hand finds hers, and she laces her fingers through mine without looking away from him.

I watch as my father's gaze flicks between us.

He sees it now.

What we are.

What we've become.

Those cold, hollow eyes gleam with something dangerous, but he says nothing more. He turns, climbs into his car with his generals, and peels away in a spray of gravel and smoke. Along the tree line, his wolves fade slowly back into the forest and disappear.

The moment they're all gone, Lexi's knees buckle. I catch her before she can hit the ground.

"Lex," I whisper, sinking down with her, cupping her face.

"I'm okay," she breathes, but her voice trembles. "I just… I couldn't let myself lose control to her. I know it sounds crazy, but…I don't know if she'd give it back."

"I know," I whisper, brushing hair from her face. "I know, baby."

Her fingers curl into my shirt.

Everyone else stays back, silent and still.

We sit there in the center of the driveway—Alpha and High Alpha, bloodied and breathless—and I feel the weight of everything that's coming settle on our shoulders.

War with my father and his pack is no longer a possibility.

It's a guarantee.

I look over at Crow, whose frame still trembles from the rage he's trying to hold back. "Okay," I rasp. "No more waiting."

"Are you saying what I think you're saying?" he asks warily.

Rocco and Dutch take a step forward. Dutch looks hungry; Razor looks hopeful, which probably means they've filled him in on what we found out at the lab. Then again, Razor always wants a fight, so maybe not.

"Go get your answers," I tell him. And with a glance at Razor, I add, "Together as brothers. Tell me when it's done."

"What are you…?" Mia looks back and forth between us. She might not have been there for our conversation earlier, but she knows what I mean. They all do. They've been waiting for me to give the order all along.

"There's no coming back from this," she warns, but it's not a reproach, only a reminder. "If you do what I think you're going to do—"

"There was never any going back," I say, and then I pull Lexi into my arms and carry her inside.

15

LEXI

Breathing hurts.

Every inhale is a reminder of the marble column Vincenzo threw me against like I weighed nothing. I'm bruised, battered, probably cracked somewhere inside—and I haven't slept. Not really.

Not since I looked Vincenzo Diavolo in the eye and declared war.

The morning after the attack, I lean against the kitchen island, munching on toast. A security guard passes through on his rounds, and I can feel her eyes on me. It's not unfriendly, but the sorrow in her gaze guts me. We lost seven guards yesterday, thanks to Rocco and Alvaro.

Seven Giovanni pack members who did nothing except try to protect me.

I owe them everything. A debt I can't possibly repay.

Andy sits at the breakfast bar across from me, sipping her coffee. She hasn't said much this morning, but it's a comfortable silence. I'm beginning to feel myself wanting to trust her. I can only hope that trust won't prove misplaced—like it did with Ramsey.

The thought of him sends a wave of anxiety through me. Grey didn't leave my side after his father left, and after he'd patched up all the cuts left behind by the fight, he filled me in on seeing Ramsey on the video feed at the lab. Then he told me about the creepy phone call Ramsey made to Grey the day of the pack vote. Ramsey's up to something, and I doubt it's going to be good for any of us when he reveals what it is.

I've stopped worrying that he's going to out me to Vincenzo for spying. Even if he did, Vincenzo's determination to come for us is already absolute. And Ramsey doesn't do anything that won't serve himself first.

I asked Grey what he thought about all of the lab findings. Not just Ramsey but Crow's mom's files. The experiments. Maybe shutting it down wasn't enough. Maybe we should have burned the fucking place to the ground. But Grey assured me we'd stopped them from hurting anyone else. Now, all we can do is move forward. Starting with apprehending Vincenzo so we can stop the bloodshed before it starts.

Every day he remains free is another threat to the people I love.

This might all be so much easier if I could make peace with my wolf. Not shifting yesterday could have killed me. But deep down, I'm still constantly fighting her for control. I haven't admitted it to Grey since that moment in the driveway, and he hasn't asked.

I'm just downing my last bite when Dutch comes in, phone in hand, eyes stormy.

"They've got him."

My pulse skips. "Alvaro?"

Grey told me what Crow asked for. The order he gave to let them loose on the general, who consented to allow Severin to experiment on Crow's mother. And how she eventually took her own life. My heart aches for Crow—and for Razor. Having a father like that is just as bad as not having one at all. But now that Crow and Razor have unleashed their rage on the man, I'm not sure he'll live much longer anyway.

Dutch nods at my question. "Razor said they have him at the warehouse. Told us to come soon if we want to try to get our own questions answered."

I straighten. My ribs hate me for it. "So, he's alive.?"

Dutch's smile is grim. "For now."

I nod, grabbing the hoodie I left slung over the back of a chair.

Grey walks in just as I'm pulling it over my head. There's something different about him today. He hasn't touched me since he rolled out of bed alone this morning when he thought I was still sleeping. Hasn't looked at anyone too long.

Something's off with him. Worse than the expected Daddy issues, which no one would even blame him for anyway. But there's no time to unravel him now.

Mia would probably know, but she's gone to look for a way to check on Charlie. He wasn't with the other generals yesterday, and I can tell she's not sure whether to deem that a good thing or a cause for worry. I can't quite give him the benefit of the doubt, but I understand needing to know he's safe.

"I'm going with you," I tell Grey defiantly, bracing myself for a fight, but he just nods.

"Okay."

"I'll hold down the fort," Andy says.

"Actually," I hesitate, hating that it's come to this. "I need you to call a meeting with the lieutenants we decided to keep."

"What do you want me to tell them?" she asks.

"They can each handpick a team and start running patrols of the city. Vincenzo Diavolo should be arrested on sight."

Andy nods. "Understood."

"And for the funeral arrangements for the guards," I say haltingly, but Andy waves me off.

"I'm taking care of it. Along with Franco's and the generals," she adds a bit quieter.

"You don't have to do it alone," I say, but she snorts.

"Believe me, Elena wouldn't allow that for a second."

I exhale. "Thank you."

"Go take care of business," she says.

I follow Grey and Dutch out as fast as my injured ribs will allow, my stomach full of both determination and dread.

THE DRIVE to the warehouse is quiet; the only sound is the swish of the windshield wipers as they clear away the drizzle that's falling. We take a navy blue Rolls-Royce Dutch found in Franco's garage. Any other day, I'd be enjoying my first time in a car like this one, but today I'm distracted by what waits for us at the warehouse. Dutch drives, leaving Grey and me in the backseat. He holds my hand, but his face is turned toward the window, and he looks pensive. I want to ask him what's wrong, but even without wolf hearing, there's zero chance for privacy. So, I settle for squeezing his hand and sending as much comfort through our mate bond as I can muster around my own anxiety.

Just before we park, he leans in, wrapping his hand around the back of my neck and pressing his lips to mine in a chaste kiss that feels like a promise of love and violence all rolled into one. I try not to overthink the fact that it comforts me more than any words could.

Crow meets us at the warehouse door, his face and knuckles streaked with dirt and blood. His hair is disheveled, and his gaze is wilder than I've ever seen it. Somehow raw and closed off at the same time.

He doesn't speak. Just nods and leads the way.

Inside, the space is dim, barely lit by the overheads. In the large open bay, we pass a table stacked with files from the lab records they printed and went through yesterday. Dust swirls in the shafts of light as we make our way through the halls toward the back room where I already know they keep their prisoners.

Sure enough, it's the same room I visited the night I first arrived in Indigo Hills. The room where Grey questioned and then killed Trucker—a vile man who betrayed his pack and preyed on young women.

I can't help noting how I view Alvaro as no better than Trucker—and no less deserving of that same fate. How far I've come from that shocked and traumatized girl from just a few weeks ago.

When we finally reach the small room, Razor's standing beside a folding chair placed in the center of the space, sleeves rolled up, blood on his knuckles. Crow slips by and moves to stand on the other side of the chair.

Alvaro is tied to the chair, his white shirt stained brown and red, his face and arms bruised and bleeding. Even so, there's something smug about his expression that makes my stomach twist. Like he still thinks he's in control.

"Looks like you've already started," Grey says, toneless. "Learn anything interesting?"

Crow's voice is low, wrecked. "He didn't deny any of it." He finally glances back at us. His eyes are hollow. "If anything, the bastard seemed proud that he served my mom up like a fucking lab rat for Franco's whims."

Silence.

My throat tightens. "Was she…? Are you…?" I can't seem to get the words out, but we all know what I mean.

If Crow has the LAG gene, his wolf could become just as unpredictable as mine.

Crow turns fully now, expression unreadable. "He said the experiments happened *after* I was born. So, I wouldn't have inherited whatever the hell gene they were testing. It was just about her. And her wolf."

"Against her fucking will," Razor says the words like he's delivering a verdict.

Alvaro merely snorts.

"He says it caused changes in her wolf. Lack of control. A darkness that—" Crow swallows hard. "That's probably what drove her to do what she did."

Horror blooms inside me like an inkblot across my chest. How can a person do something like that and laugh about it all these years later?

I don't realize I've asked the question out loud until Alvaro lets out a ragged laugh, wet with blood. "She knew what she was signing up for when she married into this life."

"That's the thing. She wasn't married," Crow snarls. "You used her like she was nothing. And then you locked her away so you wouldn't have to acknowledge what you'd done."

"Not that your wife had it any better," Razor puts in darkly.

"Gloria knows her place," Alvaro mutters, but some of the cruel humor has gone out of his expression.

I don't know the details of Gloria's relationship with Alvaro, but judging from the look Razor wears, it's not good.

"Yes, and you always knew your place, didn't you?" Crow asks, the words more like a taunt.

"Generals make hard choices for the good of the pack." Alvaro sneers. "Not that you'd know anything about being one."

Crow's fist cracks across Alvaro's jaw. The general's head snaps to the side. Blood sprays from his mouth, but he merely laughs then juts his chin at me.

"You gonna let the bitch watch?" he sneers through blood-stained teeth. "Show her how to take a beating like a fucking wolf? Or was yesterday lesson enough?" When I don't answer, he says, "You look worse than I do, *alpha*."

My title drips with sarcasm.

Crow's fist answers that. Then Razor's.

For the first time since meeting them all, I see an uncanny resemblance between the three of them. It exists mostly in the expressions twisted with rage that each of them wears.

Razor and Crow don't let up either. They take turns. Fists. Claws. Curses. This isn't justice. It's a reckoning.

They make him feel it. Every bruise. Every betrayal.

Every scream Crow's mother ever swallowed while Alvaro signed the forms that put her in a cage.

I don't flinch. Maybe I'm past that now. Numb to the shock of the code these wolves live by. A code that's mine now. A code I command. Although, this particular moment is Grey's to command. It's his orders that allowed it, and as much as I might hate the sight of so much bloodshed, I won't intervene. Not when they're all unleashing a lifetime of trauma that I wasn't present to witness.

Grey stands behind me, silent. Despite his eyes locked on the scene, there's a disconnect in the bond, like he's drifted somewhere far away. I want to reach for him, but I don't.

Not yet.

Footsteps sound in the hall.

A second later, Mia rounds the corner into the room. She stops at the sight of Alvaro being beaten to a pulp. Her eyes widen, and she looks from him to Grey and then to me.

When she takes in my bruises and swollen face, her gaze softens, and she slips into the room wordlessly to stand on my other side. Her hand slides into mine, and she squeezes.

It's touching, her reassurance.

After a few more blows, Mia says, "That's enough."

Her words are loud and sharp enough that Razor steps back, breathing hard. Crow drops his arms, blood dripping from his fists.

"You want to go soft on him?" Razor asks her.

"Absolutely fucking not," she says. "I want to let him recover before you go again. If that's what you need to put this asshole out of your head for good. He doesn't deserve your energy—not even your hate. Not after this."

"Mia's right," Dutch chimes in. "Besides, he has other uses…" Dutch's eyes gleam. I wonder if he's thinking of using our hostage to draw Vincenzo out. We talked about it back at the house, and while it's probably the smartest play, Grey already gave Crow and Razor lead on this. They get to call the shots on whether Alvaro lives long enough to act as bait.

Besides, dropping a dead general on Vincenzo's doorstep is almost just as good as dropping a live one.

"Whatever," Razor mutters. He looks at Crow. "I'm done. He's all yours."

Crow nods and steps in front of his father. The words—and Crow's stance—have a finality that Alvaro clearly misses.

"You think this makes you strong?" Alvaro spits blood onto the floor then glares up at his second son. "You think she'd be proud of you for this?"

Crow stares at him. And then he says, "No. But she'd understand."

His hands shift just enough that his fingernails lengthen into wolf claws. He reaches out and slits Alvaro's throat.

The general's eyes widen as he realizes what's just happened. Blood pours from his open flesh. Life drains from him quickly.

And that's when Grey moves.

It happens too fast to stop.

One second, he's standing behind me. The next, he's across the room, slamming into Alvaro so hard the chair topples. They crash to the floor in a tangle of limbs, and Grey's *on him*—teeth bared, claws out, growling like something unholy.

The sound he makes is like nothing I've ever heard from

him—beast or man. Darkness pours into the bond, so thick that I can't sense anything beyond it.

I can't sense *him*.

"Grey!" I scream, but he doesn't hear me. Or he doesn't care.

Some creature between human and wolf, he tears into Alvaro's throat like a beast. There's a gurgle, a gasp, and then nothing from the general.

His blood soaks the concrete floor.

"Grey," Dutch calls, and the creature turns suddenly, glowing yellow eyes locking on Dutch as if he's the enemy now too. "Oh, fuck."

"What the hell," Mia breathes.

Razor moves first, but Grey snarls and swipes at him with claws—close enough to split skin if Razor hadn't ducked.

"Grey, stop!" I scream.

The creature lifts his head, blood dripping from his mouth, eyes *blazing*. But they're not focused. Not *human*.

And then he turns toward me.

The world freezes.

I don't breathe. I don't blink.

He stalks toward me slowly, every movement controlled but *charged*. A predator with no logic left.

Dutch steps between us. "Back the fuck off."

Grey growls—a warning. Not a request.

"Why is he acting like this?" Crow asks.

"What the fuck *is* he?" Razor adds.

"Lexi, move!" Dutch barks over his shoulder.

But I can't. I'm stuck.

All I can think about is the first night Grey and I ever met. I'd run from him then too, and even as a wolf whom he fully controlled, Grey hadn't been able to resist chasing me. Hunting me.

Now, standing before this monster, I'm not sure he wouldn't stop with just catching me this time.

Behind him, I see Crow and Razor close in, flanking him.

Grey lunges for me, and I brace, calling my wolf in a moment of panic.

They tackle him before he has a chance to reach me, dragging him down, pinning him.

He thrashes like a demon. Teeth snapping. Claws flailing.

"Get her out of here!" Dutch yells.

My skin itches as my wolf surges, and I try to shove her back again.

Mia grabs me hard, yanking me back toward the wall. My breathing's coming too fast. Pain spikes in my ribs, but I don't care.

All I can do is watch as the man I love snarls and claws at the people trying to save him. Or trying to save me from him.

Grey's voice rips out of him—distorted, strangled. "Let me go—LET ME GO—!"

"No fucking way," Razor grunts, holding down his arm.

Crow's face is pale but focused, blood running down his temple. "He's not there. It's not *him*."

"Yes, it is," Grey howls. "I am—I *am*—"

Then suddenly, he goes limp.

Chest heaving. Bloody. Broken.

Still.

Dutch doesn't release him. Neither does Razor or Crow.

Mia stops trying to shove me out the door. I can feel fur sprouted along my arms. My nails have extended into claws. My wolf strains to be let free. I swallow hard, begging her to recede.

Grey's head turns slowly. His eyes find mine.

And I see it.

He's back.

Tears track down his cheeks, unnoticed.

His voice cracks. "I don't…I don't know what happened."

"You were something I've never seen before," Razor says roughly. His grip on Grey is tight as ever.

Grey swallows, still restrained. "I felt it snap. Something in me. When he started talking about her—about your mom," he says to Crow, his voice barely audible. "And then all that fucking blood." He looks at me, guilt swimming in his gaze. "It wasn't just rage. It was instinct. *Franco's* instinct. That power... it doesn't belong to me."

"Yeah, it does." Dutch eases off first, crouching beside him. "The problem is you've been fighting it ever since you inherited it."

"You have?" Shock ripples through me, followed by realization. I've been so wrapped up in my own struggle with my wolf that I totally missed his. The darkness lurking in our bond—I'd assumed it was my fault. Or part of his worry over his father. Over my alpha vote. But now, I realize it's so much more than that.

Grey looks at me, and I see it clear as day.

He's terrified.

"I need help," he rasps. "Before I hurt someone else."

My chest aches, but I nod. "We'll figure it out."

At that, Razor and Crow finally ease off Grey, and they

all get to their feet. Apparently satisfied Grey is back to normal, Mia releases me. Her gaze flicks to Alvaro's mangled corpse.

"We'll clean this up," she says. "Make it look like he skipped town. He's got a rep for disappearing on benders, right?"

Dutch nods. "We'll find some Diavolo pack members who are loyal to spread the story."

"What if we don't cover it up?" Razor asks. "Fuck him and Vincenzo. He already declared war. This is just us making the first move."

"Because," Mia says, "once Vincenzo finds out about this, he'll retaliate. You saw the way he called the pack yesterday."

"So we call Lexi's pack to fight against them," Razor says.

"I'm not going to order that," I say, "Not after yesterday's losses. They need time to mourn."

"Lexi's right," Mia says. "An order from Lexi to fight now might just turn them against her. She needs more time to win them over. And we need time to get more of our old pack to come over to our side."

Not to mention finding answers for my wolf—and Grey's.

"Yeah, fine," Razor grumbles.

"You should talk to Gloria," Crow tells him quietly. "See if she'll join us."

Razor frowns, but he nods. "It's a risk, but yeah. She deserves to choose a different side."

"Yours too," Crow tells Dutch.

I look at Grey. "You should talk to your mom, too."

The flicker in him tells me he's already thought of it.

"Yeah. She hasn't been answering my calls." His worry is palpable, but I can't bring myself to offer reassurance.

"Andy's preparing my pack for round-the-clock patrols," I tell them. "If they see Vincenzo, they have orders to detain him."

Mia's quiet for a second. Then—"I think we should bring my dad into this."

Everyone turns to her.

Razor blinks. "Charlie?"

She nods once. "I talked to him earlier. He's still working for Vincenzo, but he's loyal to me. To us. If we're going to survive what's coming... we need someone on the inside."

"I don't know," Crow begins, and I know he's thinking of Alvaro and how he sold out those he loved without a second thought.

"My dad isn't like yours," Mia says, and even though her tone is gentle, I can feel the way Crow's hackles raise at that. But in the end, his shoulders sag.

"Maybe you're right."

"He did help me," I say, "at the party that night Dom tried to... And then again before the wedding, he tried to warn me not to trust Vincenzo."

Everyone looks from me to Grey.

Grey nods. "Call him."

Mia's already pulling out her phone. "It's time we start stacking our side of the board," she says, and then, "Hey, Dad? We need to meet."

16

LEXI

Even after we return to Franco's and I've showered and changed, I still smell the blood. It's there every time I inhale. Or blink. Or lick my lips. My wolf revels in it, but the human me is a little sick over the smell of copper that lingers or the grisly scene I see every time I close my eyes.

Grey hasn't left our room since we got back. He's not hiding exactly. More like—he's isolating. A predator caged in silence. He says we're safer if he stays away from us for now, and after seeing what he became earlier, I can't argue with him. Not until we have some answers. Dutch has positioned himself outside the door, keeping watch like a sentry. I hate to admit that I feel better knowing someone will be there to stop Grey if he tries to attack again.

I check in when I can—offer a touch, a kiss, a whisper through the door. Sometimes he answers. Sometimes the silence growls back.

He's not gone. But he's fighting with whatever inside him is threatening to break free.

And I don't know how much longer he can hold it in.

Mia returns from her meeting with Charlie as I'm sitting down to lunch. Elena is like a drill sergeant about making sure I eat. "It'll help you heal faster," she insists in a voice that I don't dare argue with.

Mia smirks as she sits down across from me, but her smirk vanishes when Elena points a finger in her direction. "You too, missy. You're too skinny for a general."

She stalks out with a threatening, "I'll be back with your plate in a minute," tossed over her shoulder.

"That woman scares even me," Mia admits when we're alone.

I snort, silently admitting the food is helping. Not that I'll ever tell Elena that. But I can finally feel my wounds from yesterday beginning to ease slightly.

"How'd it go?" I ask Mia when Elena has delivered her food and left again.

"He's in," she says just as Andy walks in.

Mia goes silent at the sight of my second, but I wave her to go on. "Andy's caught up," I say. And she's trustworthy, I don't say. Because even I sometimes waver, but I know that's only my own insecurities coming out.

"What do you think about getting information from my father?" Mia asks her warily.

"I don't know him, so I can't vouch for his loyalty, but I know you wouldn't endanger your pack for anything. I think it's smart," Andy says with a shrug. "We have to play offense. The sooner the better, especially with an enemy like Vincenzo."

Mia nods like Andy's just passed some kind of test. "I agree."

"So, did he give us any insight into where to hit first?" Andy asks.

"Well, yes, but to be fair, we've already hit first, technically speaking."

Mia's voice drops low, and I know she's aware that Razor and Crow are somewhere inside the house. They've been subdued since they got back from disposing of Alvaro. I've been giving them space, but only because I don't know what to say.

What do you say to someone who just killed their father in cold blood, knowing he deserved it?

"Until Vincenzo knows about it, I don't think we're going to count it," Andy points out.

"Yeah." Mia sighs and sets her fork aside.

I noticed she didn't do much more than push the food around. I, on the other hand, cleaned my plate. I make a mental note to ask Elena about the recipe—at some point when I'm not terrified of her. The food here has been delicious so far.

"I have intel about Vincenzo's plans, but you're not going to like it," Mia warns.

I can't help arching a brow at that. "The asshole's trying to kill me and the people I love. I didn't expect to like it."

"Fair," she says. "I guess what I'm saying is we can't handle this on our own. We need your pack to step up." I start to respond, but she rushes on. "I know you wanted to wait until their loyalty was more certain." She glances between me and Andy now. "But we don't have that kind of time."

"Yeah." My shoulders sag, but I know she's right. "We'll call a meeting for this afternoon with the patrol leaders and lieutenants."

I glance at Andy, who nods and pulls her phone out. "I'm on it."

She's not even out of the room when I hear her start talking to whoever's on the phone.

Mia looks at me, softening. "How are you?"

"My ribs don't feel like they're stabbing my organs quite as badly," I say.

She grins. "That's always a plus." But her smile vanishes quickly. "I meant about Grey. About earlier."

My stomach tightens. "That wasn't a normal wolf thing, was it?"

"No."

"It has something to do with killing Franco, doesn't it?"

"I think he took in too much alpha power," Mia says.

"Dutch said it was because he was resisting fully accepting it."

"Could be that. Or maybe Franco's power has the same boost yours does."

"The LAG gene," I realize.

She nods. "I think Franco would have experimented on himself."

"Even though he thought it didn't work on me?"

"The bastard was aging. He would have hated that."

I focus again on the dark energy pulsing through our bond. It's a constant now. A shadow that eclipses the connection I felt the night we claimed each other. My wolf doesn't like it and has been snarling about it all day.

"Severin couldn't help us," I say, defeat creeping in. "Or wouldn't help us. Unless there's another gene expert in the city, I'm not sure where that leaves us."

"Unfortunately, there isn't."

"You say that like you've checked already," I half-joke.

The look she gives me says it all. I lean forward. "You have?"

"Of course. We don't have time to waste."

"But you didn't find anyone?"

"Not in Indigo Hills." She sounds just as deflated as I feel. "I'm going to do some research and see if I can find any other packs who've done gene research or have a pack doctor that might be able to help shed some light."

"How can I help?"

"You can start by leading this meeting," she says pointedly.

"Actually," I say slowly, "I was thinking you should do that."

"Me?"

"You're the strategist," I point out.

She shakes her head. "But they're not my pack. They aren't going to listen to me, much less trust me."

"And they never will if we don't show them what it looks like."

She meets my gaze, and I can see her considering it from all angles that I'm sure even I haven't thought of yet.

"Okay," she says finally. "But be warned, I'm not taking anyone's shit."

"I would never expect you to."

Pack members begin to arrive within the hour. Grey still hasn't come down, though when I go up to check on him, he seems much better. He reassures me he's feeling more like himself again and will be down soon.

I take my place in the foyer just like Andy and Elena did

when I first arrived as alpha. Beside me, Andy is a steady presence, greeting our visitors with me while whispering the names of pack members as they arrive. Donahue and Camila, two top lieutenants who also happen to be mates, are the friendliest and actually offer their help "in any capacity you need." It's a pleasant surprise and one that makes me hope today's meeting topic won't be met with resistance after all.

As the last few pack members find their seats, Dutch saunters in, hair damp from a shower, rolling his shoulder like he's trying to shake off tension. His shirt says Ask Me About Real Estate.

"Nice shirt," I say.

He glares. "I don't know why Mia got you nice clothes but sent me thrift-store cast-offs."

My smirk fades. When Grey's pack pledged themselves to him, they lost their homes, their belongings, and their families in one swoop. It sucks.

"Hey, how are the ribs?" he asks, standing against the wall with me. It's more comfortable than sitting for my aching body.

"I'll live," I tell him.

"And your wolf?"

"She's pissed I didn't let her participate."

"Can't say I disagree. Maybe next time let her participate a little more, okay? You gave me a fucking heart attack, you know."

I glance over and find his expression more serious than I've seen. No humor. Only genuine concern.

I nod. "Okay." I turn to face the room again.

"Shouldn't you be up there?" He nods at the table in the center of the room where Mia sits at the head.

"We need to learn to trust each other," I explain. "Besides, I want to be able to observe. To see what they really think of this new regime."

He gives me an approving look. "You're not so bad at strategy either."

"Thanks. How's Grey?"

"Getting dressed." He glances over the assembled faces as he adds, "He'll be okay."

"How do you know?"

He shrugs like it's a foregone conclusion that we'll all be fine. "Because he has you."

I don't bother to remind him that I'm not exactly fit to be someone's anchor in the storm right now.

His eyes flick toward Andy. Then to me.

"So," he says under his breath. "What's her story?"

I give him a look. "You mean the woman who didn't flinch when I slaughtered her husband right in front of her and thinks emotions are just the thing that get in the way of doing her duty?"

He lifts a brow, intrigued. "She sounds like my fucking dream girl."

"Be careful, Dutch," I murmur. "If you break her heart, I'll break your jaw."

He grins, but there's a flicker of something more serious behind his eyes. I shake my head, biting down on a smile I shouldn't have time for, and focus on the table.

Everyone's here—well, almost everyone. Grey's absence is one I can feel like a sore rib. But we can't wait any longer.

When I give her the nod to begin, Mia doesn't waste time.

"We're here because Vincenzo has officially declared war on both our packs."

No preamble. No pleasantries.

"And you're here because your pack isn't big enough to ride in the HOV lane together," one of the lieutenants calls out. I don't remember his name, but his taunting expression suggests he's not exactly an ally just yet.

At his comment, a few others snicker.

Mia's head snaps toward the one who spoke up. Her eyes narrow.

I can feel a few people glance at me, but I don't intervene. This is Mia's to handle. As I have no doubt she will.

"Broderick, you're still the same pimple you were in middle school, who doesn't know when to shut up."

The snickers are louder this time as Broderick's face flushes. "I could shut you up," he says, the words dripping with innuendo.

Irritation flares through me at the disrespect.

"Welp, he's fucking dead," Dutch mutters.

"You're welcome to challenge me and try," Mia tells Broderick, eyes glittering as she pins him with a look of pure invitation.

The unconcealed hunger in her gaze hits me, and I wonder if she's been itching for a fight with this guy for a long time. Or maybe Mia just likes the unexpected adventure of it all. The unpredictability of a moment, like when she stabbed that guard in the thigh yesterday.

Because then she winks and says, "But we all know you won't proposition me with anything else after I turned you down in that bar the summer after senior year."

Broderick mutters something, ducking his head, and the snickers turn to hoots.

Mia turns back to the rest of the group, and her smile

fades. "Now, Vincenzo Diavolo might be a piece of shit, but he's not a threat to ignore."

"So, this is a meeting for battle strategy?" someone asks.

"Not directly," Mia says. "We don't believe he'll come with force. Not right away."

"What makes you say that?" another of my pack asks.

Donahue. His tone is curious rather than dismissive.

Mia eyes him but answers evenly. "Because he already tried that yesterday with our high alpha and failed. He won't make that mistake twice."

Everyone looks at me. The bruises on my face have faded into a lovely purple, and my face burns red beneath them as they all scan my body as if they can see my aching ribs and sore muscles.

Dutch slings an arm around my shoulders and squeezes lightly. "Don't fuck with our girl here, am I right?"

His comment earns a few murmurs of agreement. I don't know how to feel about it. Their respect. Dutch's affection. The fact that these two feuding packs are suddenly working together—and no one's tried to kill each other yet.

It gives me hope.

And I've learned from experience that is a very dangerous thing to have.

"As a result," Mia says, drawing everyone's attention away from me. I exhale. Dutch's arm falls away. "Vincenzo knows Grey is an alpha. He might be an asshole, but he's not as stupid as he looks. He knows he's up against two alphas and two strong packs, which means he'll come at us another way."

"You think he'll fuck with our families?" Camila asks.

She glances nervously at her mate. Donahue covers her hand with his own.

"I won't rule anything out," Mia says. "But Vincenzo's style has always been grabbing for power. Our source on the inside tells us he's moving to call a vote." She looks at me. "He wants the pack leaders to formally reject your claim to the Giovanni seat and install him as regent while they assess stability."

My jaw tightens. He's going to tell everyone Grey killed Franco. That I'm a fraud.

"Those same leaders just voted her in," Donahue points out.

"He'll use their fear of her," Mia explains, glancing at me almost apologetically. "Point to the way you took out Franco's generals. Call it public violence. Reckless. Say you're unstable."

"He's not wrong," Broderick mutters, then quickly adds, "I mean, that's what they'll say."

Mia glares at him but otherwise stays calm as she says, "Donahue is right. It likely won't be enough to get the pack leaders to back him since they just voted Lexi in for those same reasons. Especially when most of yours have already sworn loyalty to you. He'll have to get the public on his side too."

"The public loves Lexi and Grey," Razor says with a snort.

"They don't love power plays. Corruption. Vincenzo has already begun to spin it so that Grey and Lexi look like they've been secretly planning this takeover." She tosses a newspaper onto the table.

I look over the heads of those sitting and read the headline: Pack Princess or Puppet Master? Con Woman Exposed."

"This article claims you're using your alpha status for your own nefarious purposes," Mia says.

My eyes widen at the absurdity. "That's a lie."

She shakes her head. "The truth doesn't matter as much as perception."

"I get that he fed the media this shit," Dutch says, "But how the hell can they just take his word for it? He has no proof."

"He has the LAG gene." Mia glances at me, her expression once again reflecting an apology. Like she hates to be the one to deliver this news. No wonder she said I wasn't going to like her intel. "He gave them your medical record. Or the parts he'd already gotten his hands on. He says you have motive for revenge. That you're trying to destroy the city for what Franco did to you and your mother."

Dutch curses vehemently.

Razor echoes it.

A few others look over at me, clearly speculating whether that might be true.

I lift my chin and cross my arms over my chest. "So how do we counter it?"

"We do exactly what we've been doing all along," she says. "We beat him at his own game."

Razor groans. "We're back to politics and parties, aren't we?"

Crow whispers something in his ear, and he shuts up. I swallow hard, thinking of Alvaro. We've done enough with violence already. Apparently, Razor agrees.

"What's the mission then?" Donahue asks. "If we're not going to attack him outright—which I'm starting to think plays right into his hands if we do—then how do we stop him?"

"We'll need to find a way to spin this story," Mia says. "It would help to know which media members he has in his pocket so we can try to flip them."

"I say we just drive over there and take him out," Broderick says. "Show this fucker who he's messing with."

"If we do that, he'll use his alpha power to call every wolf in the Diavolo pack to fight for him," Mia says. "We saw evidence of that yesterday."

Broderick shrugs. "So? We'll call all of ours. Giovanni pack has always been the strongest."

"A lot of his pack are innocents," Mia says. "People who only remain part of his pack through generational loyalty. Not to mention women and children."

"So, we give them a chance to switch sides," Broderick argues.

"Actually, that's a good idea," Donahue puts in. He looks at me. "Shouldn't we offer them a chance to defect before we attack them?"

I glance between Donahue and Broderick. "Yes. But that takes time. Which is why we can't afford to attack today."

Broderick scowls but lets it go.

"He has the numbers to make this a very messy war if he wants to," Mia says. "If we want to protect the people of this city, we need to alert them to what's coming and let them choose."

"I'm all for this plan, but it's not like we can go door to door," Dutch points out. "How do we plan to get the word out?"

"I'm working on that. In the meantime, we need round-the-clock patrols of the grounds so we aren't caught off guard if and when Vincenzo does show up here again—" Mia halts when the door slams open hard enough to rattle the windows.

Grey stalks inside, chest heaving like he ran down here. His clothes are rumpled, the first few buttons of his shirt undone like he couldn't be bothered to finish dressing. His eyes—storm-grey and wild—lock onto mine, then swing around the room, sharp and searching.

I tense, panicked that he's lost to the darkness of that creature again. But then he focuses on the computer on the table, and when he speaks, his voice is his own.

"Turn on the news," he says.

Crow is the fastest to react. He leans over the laptop perched near Mia and jabs a few keys. The screen flickers from the spreadsheet of patrol schedules to a live news feed.

"...a statement today from Vincenzo Diavolo," the anchor says, her voice smooth and polished like this is just another day's gossip.

The screen cuts to Vincenzo.

Standing at a podium in front of a sea of reporters, he wears a mournful expression so convincing it makes my stomach turn. Behind him, the glass walls of The Tower reflect wealth and corruption; a portal to the underworld he rules.

"My heart is heavy as I stand before you today with such grave information," Vincenzo begins, "but I have a duty to the citizens of Indigo Hills. And that duty to protect goes beyond even my allegiance to the alpha."

Grey appears on my left. He leans forward to grip the chair in front of him, one hand dropping to the back of it like he needs something to hold him up. With his other hand, he brushes the nape of my neck. I can feel his fingers trembling.

"I have become aware of a very serious crime committed by our late alpha," Vincenzo says solemnly. "I had hoped these acts would end when he died, but I have learned our new alpha continues in her grandfather's footsteps. And I can no longer, in good conscience, allow the truth to remain hidden."

Vincenzo pauses dramatically, and the effect isn't lost on me. My stomach tightens, and my wolf snarls in protest of the fear that builds inside me. "Proof has come to light that Lexi Giovanni—who many of you have accepted as your high alpha—is not what she claims to be."

The words hit like a slap.

The screen flashes to a copy of my medical chart—a file Grey and the others said was missing from the records we retrieved from Capo. Vincenzo's voice continues while the screen shows dates of injections and the scientific names for the drugs they apparently gave me.

"She is, according to these medical records, the product of illegal genetic tampering," Vincenzo says, his voice brimming with false regret. "An experiment conducted by Franco Giovanni and his corrupt scientists, altering her very nature before she could even walk. Altering her wolf itself. Permanently."

He pauses as if to let the viewer take it all in.

"In recent days," Vincenzo continues, and the screen returns to him at the podium, "Lexi Giovanni visited the very laboratory where these atrocities occurred. Not to shut it down. Not to bring justice. But to continue the work."

The screen shifts to video footage of Capo. Grainy, but clear enough.

There I am. Walking beside Grey into the lab. Mia and Crow following.

No context. No sound. Just the visual of us stepping willingly into a building dripping in horror stories and criminal behavior.

My stomach pitches.

"I also have records and personal statements belonging to other women. Citizens of Indigo Hills who were forced to undergo similar experiments. It started with Franco, but I'm afraid it hasn't ended with him. Lexi Giovanni carries the same bloodthirst, the same ambition, the same corruption, as a man who desecrated his own kind," Vincenzo says. "And now, she seeks to use her newfound power to make you all into an abomination just like herself."

He looks straight into the camera. "To make matters worse, I have borne witness to my own son committing treasonous acts nearly as damning. He attacked and killed Dominic Albero without provocation and has yet to report it to the pack leadership. This is a direct violation of our pack law and should be treated accordingly."

Grey snarls, but I don't make a sound, rooted to the spot where I stand and riveted to the screen.

Vincenzo finishes with, "I will not stand by and watch this city fall into darkness."

I shudder at the last word and the way it reminds me of whatever unleashed itself from inside Grey today.

Onscreen, the broadcast cuts back to the newsroom, but nobody's listening to the anchor.

The room is silent.

Not a breath.

Not a shuffle.

Just everything we've been building tilting dangerously, cracks spiderwebbing through the foundation.

I stare at the frozen image of my own face on the screen.

At the monster Vincenzo just painted me to be.

Grey's hand tightens so hard on the back of the chair that the wood cracks. I flinch as a chunk splinters off in his hand. When I turn and walk out of the meeting room, no one stops me. Not even Grey.

17

LEXI

Behind me, voices sound as the meeting abruptly breaks up. Even though I'm striding through the house, I still feel trapped in that room, still staring at the screen where Vincenzo took everything I am and turned it into something dirty.

Something broken.

Something I might never be able to fix.

I don't remember deciding to leave the house. Or slipping the guards and losing myself in the woods. I just know I'm moving. Fast. Like, if I stop, I'll shatter into a thousand pieces I can't put back together.

Vincenzo twisted my greatest fear into a blade and used it to carve me right out of the place I'd made for myself in this world. And the worst part? I believed him. For one long, gutting moment, I believed that I didn't belong here.

But not anymore.

It's time to fight for my place in Indigo Hills. Not just taking what's offered but really stepping up and using my voice to claim this place as my home.

Home.

The word doesn't sound quite as foreign as it used to. Instead, it sounds like I suddenly have a lot to lose if Vincenzo has his way. But I survived too many nights alone to give up now. Foster homes. Empty apartments. Self-reliance is written into my bones. I've always been the only one who saved me.

The only difference now is that I'm saving more than just myself. I'm saving my pack. I promised them I wouldn't abandon them, and I intend to keep that promise.

I run faster.

At some point, I become aware that I'm not human.

The realization that I've shifted into my wolf stops me short. Sensations slam into me then. Four legs. Powerful strides. A snout that can scent anything that moves in my vicinity. Instead of feeling possessed by something "other" like before, I feel as if I've just come back into my body after a long time away from it. A ghost returned to corporeal form.

It's somehow both disturbing and grounding all at once.

My wolf whines at me.

She thinks I'm being dramatic.

I snort at her, and then, I let her run.

She takes off like a whip, trees blurring past. Scents filling our nose. Sound muted, thanks to the wind in my ears.

Moving this way is freeing. Giving over to my wolf, letting her take charge—for the first time since I felt her presence inside me, I welcome her. And some of the overwhelm recedes.

Finally, I near the city and recognize the need to be human again. My wolf argues that point. I think she'd happily walk right into the heart of downtown in her four-legged form without a qualm. But I know better than to draw that kind of attention to myself—especially considering the news report.

After struggling for what feels like an interminable amount of time, I shove my wolf down and shift back to two legs. Then I spend another hour creeping naked through hedges until I manage to find a towel hanging over someone's fence and wrap it around myself.

How do shifters manage to stay clothed, anyway?

On the outskirts of downtown, I find a faded, aged thrift store in a small strip shopping center. Forcing my chin up, I walk inside, holding the towel tightly around my body.

The cashier does a double-take.

The two shoppers inside stop and stare at me. One of them drops the macrame dream catcher she's holding. Her jaw falls open. I step toward the cashier and whisper, "Do you have anything in the back that you're tossing out? Something I might borrow?"

"You're…you're Lexi—I mean High Alpha."

I wince. "Just Lexi is fine."

She nods emphatically.

"Um, the clothes," I begin.

Her eyes widen. "Right. Yes. Come with me."

She rounds the counter and leads me toward the back, walking on my right to shield me from the shoppers' nosy view. I keep my head down, letting my long hair fall across my face like a curtain. But not before I see one of the shoppers raise her phone and take a picture of me. Or video. Ugh. So much for anonymity.

I whisper a silent plea that these women are Giovanni pack and not Diavolo.

In the back, the cashier winds past piles of boxes and bins full of people's donations. She stops at a hanging rack and thumbs through the clothing there.

"Here," she says, holding out a dress that someone's grandmother probably wore. It's not in bad shape though, and I can't imagine they're going to throw it out. "This looks like your size."

"It's pretty nice. Are you sure you can't sell it? Don't you have a trash pile I could—"

"Absolutely not." She softens. "No one deserves to wear trash, honey. Least of all you." She leans in and says, "My cousin's best friend lives next door to Gina."

"Gina?"

"Conrad's wife. Or widow, I should say."

"Oh." Conrad. Franco's general. Or he was before I killed him. Shit. "I'm sorry—"

"Don't you dare apologize. I've heard stories of what kind of monster he was. How he treated Gina. You saved her life doing what you did. Thank you."

She looks at me like I'm a hero rather than the villain. It's weird. No one's ever looked at me like that before.

"Anyway, the dress is the least I can do," she adds.

I blink, remembering the garment she's offering. "Thanks." I take it gratefully and then hesitate when she doesn't move. "Is there somewhere I can change?"

"Oh, yes." She jumps and then shuffles past me to a scuffed gray door along the wall. "Bathroom's here. Take your time, and help yourself to anything else you need."

"I will."

"I'm Becky, by the way."

"Thanks, Becky."

She smiles and then leaves me alone.

In the bathroom, I pull the dress over my head. Becky was right. It's close to my size. The fabric is thick and not very breathable. But it's better than a towel. After rummaging through a few bins, I manage to snag a pair of worn sandals and a floppy hat that I shove onto my head. The last thing I need is someone reporting back to Vincenzo that I've been spotted alone.

When I'm done, I find a scrap of paper and a pen and scrawl a note to Becky, thanking her again. Then I slip out the back door into the sunshine and make my way downtown.

Through the mate bond, I feel Grey's worry like a steady heartbeat. It's not urgent like I expected, which means he senses that I'm okay. Maybe even that I need this alone time. I send back what I hope is gratitude and reassurance that I'm safe.

As I walk, the city unfolds around me, bright and busy, oblivious to the war brewing in its veins. I slip through it like a ghost until I find what I'm looking for.

Polished glass. Gold lettering. A memory tucked into the edges.

The salon Mia brought me to that first time she tried to dress me up and teach me how to move in this glittering world.

Inside, I walk up to the receptionist at the desk. Her smile falters when she sees me—wrinkled clothes, fraying shoes, hair wild from the wind—but I don't care.

"Can I help you?" she asks.

"Is Alejandro here?" I ask, knowing it's a long shot that the same stylist I met before is even here and has an opening.

Sure enough, there's a beat of hesitation.

Then she nods. "Right this way, miss."

~

ALEJANDRO IS EXCITED to the point of exuberance when he sees me. He hugs me and air kisses my cheeks and holds onto me long enough to whisper, "Long live the queen."

When I pull away, there's genuine affection in his brown eyes and a hint of connection that takes me a beat to realize comes from a pack bond. He's Giovanni pack. And he's clearly pledged his loyalty to me already.

I relax, realizing I can trust him.

"Thanks for fitting me in," I tell him gratefully.

"Anytime. Darling, you look…" His expression contorts as he takes in my outfit.

"I know," I say hastily. "I need a transformation. Can you help?"

"Hah! Can I help? It's what I do."

I'm pressed into a chair and covered in plastic, which I think relieves him since it hides my dress. Then, he starts picking at my hair and eyeing me in the mirror as he peppers me with questions.

When he manages to pry out of me what I intend to do after this, my outfit is deemed "absolutely disgraceful." My shoes and hat are thrown in the trash.

Alejandro says something to the receptionist, who gets on the phone.

Several minutes later, a woman arrives with a handful of outfit choices from the boutique down the block. While my color sets, I'm tucked into and out of a dozen different outfits until both Alejandro and the boutique clerk deem one of them "truly exquisite."

Two hours later, I stare at my reflection and barely recognize myself. The girl looking back at me has sleek, styled hair that hangs in perfect waves. A deep emerald dress that hugs her body in a classy, subtly sexy way. Heels sharp enough to command attention.

I look like someone worth listening to.

I look like a leader.

A knock sounds at the door to the private dressing room Alejandro provided. Whoever it is doesn't wait for me to answer before pushing the door open. I turn as Mia sweeps inside, followed by Andy, both of them looking a mixture of amused and impressed.

"What are you doing here?" I ask, bracing myself for a rant about safety and allowing myself to be guarded at all times.

"What the hell does it look like?" Mia replies. "We're watching your back."

"But…how did you know where to find me?"

"Find you?" Mia shares a look with Andy that suggests I'm being slow. "We've been following you since you left the house."

"And we've had enough of guarding the exits," Andy puts in.

I blink. Since I left the house? "I didn't sense you."

"Okay, maybe not since you left," Mia amends. "But close."

"We picked up your trail at the thrift store," Andy explains.

"But how—" I stop as realization dawns. "Grey."

"He was going to make us leave you alone as long as you were in wolf form and away from the city. But when you shifted back and came here, he said we should find you and keep a closer eye on you," Andy says.

"He didn't come himself," I say, glancing past them toward the front doors.

"He said he had something else to take care of," Andy says, and worry spears through me. I search the bond to make sure Grey is okay. He was targeted with that interview too.

"Is he all right?" I ask.

"He's fine," Mia says, but I shake my head.

"His dad outed him about Dom. Maybe I should have stayed."

"You should know that not a single pack member said a word about Dom's death after you left," Andy says.

"Literally no one," Mia adds wryly. "Vincenzo only tossed it in to upset you."

I blow out a breath, remembering the way the guards practically thanked Grey for doing it.

"I hope it's okay that we're here," Andy adds.

"It's fine," I assure her. "I just… didn't expect it."

"Yeah, well, I didn't expect you to come to my favorite salon without me," Mia pouts. "If anyone's going to be pissed, it's me."

My lips curve upward. "I'm sorry. Forgive me?"

"You're a pain in the ass," Mia scowls, hands on her hips.

Andy grins, gaze sweeping the length of me now. "But a gorgeous one."

I don't answer. Even with their swift forgiveness and easy jokes, I still half-expect anger. A lecture.

Instead, Mia closes the space and pulls me into a tight

hug. "Next time," she murmurs, "we make appointments and come together like besties."

When she pulls away, I blink hard, throat burning with emotion.

"Deal," I manage.

"Now, are you going to tell us the plan, or do we have to keep stalking you to figure it out?" Mia demands.

I clear my throat. "How do you know there's a plan?"

"Please," Andy snorts. "I just met you, and even I know your trauma response is not retail therapy."

Mia laughs. "Yeah, that sounds more like me."

"So," Andy prompts, eyes glittering now. "What are we doing with this weapon you've made yourself into?" She gestures to the dress, makeup, and hair. "Because whatever it is, we want in."

"Really?" I ask, my surprise slipping out before I can stop it.

Andy softens. "You don't have to do everything alone anymore, Lexi," she says gently. "That's what friends are for."

For a second, the scrappy orphan inside me recoils, suspicious. But their warmth is real. And their loyalty is absolute. It reminds me of my friend Violet. How she used to constantly push me to open up to her. And how I never quite let myself do it.

But in this moment, with two badass friends standing in front of me, offering to fight at my side, I'm tired of surviving by myself. So, I hold my hands out, and they each take one.

"Thanks," I whisper, my voice wobbling as I start to tell them my plan.

To my surprise, they both love it and offer to help put the gears into motion. By the time I'm finished explaining, Mia has made a couple of phone calls and set everything in motion.

They help me finish getting ready—adjusting the matching jacket, fixing my necklace, smoothing invisible wrinkles—and when we're done, Mia pulls back and gives me a once-over.

"You're going to knock 'em dead," she says.

"Preferably not literally," Andy adds, and we all laugh.

I can't help but think it's such a healing sound.

Outside, for once, there's no black SUV waiting to take me somewhere. Instead, Mia calls us an Uber, and we pile into something tiny and electric and head toward the business district.

A couple of minutes later, we pull to a stop at the curb and climb out again. Mia and Andy both sweep their gazes up and down the street, scanning for threats. I turn my attention to the building before me. Directly across the street from where I stand, the Indigo Press office looms, stark against the cloudy sky.

"Ready?" Andy asks, coming up beside me.

"Ready," I murmur and hold my head up high as I walk inside.

18

LEXI

The click of my heels echoes in the empty lobby. But when the elevator opens on the second-floor news office, we step into a scene completely opposite. Noisy, chaotic, and smelling of stale coffee, the scene brings me up short. For a moment, I don't know where to look.

"Oh, there's Savannah," Mia says, waving at a brunette in a deep blue business suit, who smiles as she approaches us.

"You made it." Savannah extends her hand first to Mia and Andy and then finally to me.

"Hi, I'm Lexi," I tell her.

"Oh, I know." She smiles at that, but it's friendly.

She looks familiar, and it's not until I'm shaking her hand that I place where I've seen her before.

"We've met," I say, remembering the night Grey took me to dinner. The paparazzi had been lying in wait outside, though we'd known they would be. The same night Grey's mother had told me that my parents had run from Franco only after they'd failed to change things here for the better.

Something I'm determined to do in their memory. Even if it means coming here.

Mia assured me Savannah has a reputation for kindness rather than exploitation like some reporters in this city. I hope she's right.

"It was a big crowd," Savannah says. "I'm surprised you remember."

"Of course I remember. You asked me what Franco thought of my engagement."

She tilts her head. "Sharp memory. You'd make a good reporter."

"Oh." The compliment throws me off. "Thanks."

"Then again, you have a more important job now." She grins at that and motions for us to follow her. "Come on back; I'll show you where we've set up."

We turn away from the maze of cubicles that fill the center aisles. A few people give me curious looks as we pass them, but most ignore us. At the end of the hallway, Savannah shows us into a room that feels a lot like what I pictured for a TV studio. Two oversized chairs face one another, each with a side table set with staged books and decor, and several bright lights on tripods are pointed at the sitting area.

"Take a seat," Savannah says. "My producer will be in the room to your right. Your friends can wait there too." I glance over and note what must be one-way glass on the opposite wall. "As requested, the only other person in the room with us will be the cameraman," she finishes.

Andy and Mia linger, both giving me a look that makes it clear they won't leave until I say it's okay. My chest fills at that, but I nod at them, ignoring the roiling in my stomach at what I'm about to do.

"I'll be fine," I tell them.

"You're going to be great," Mia corrects.

"Break a leg," Andy says as they file out. "But not someone else's," she adds, and I hear them both snicker before the door shuts behind them.

When I'm alone with Savannah, she takes a seat. I do the same, settling into the chair opposite her, careful to keep my ankles crossed demurely. I can only hope I don't forget myself and pull my knees up to my chest halfway through the interview.

"Nervous?"

I look up to find Savannah watching me, amusement shining in her eyes. "Is it that obvious?"

Her expression fills with understanding. "Pro tip: Pause before you answer my questions so you can catch your breath."

"Do you get nervous too?"

"Sometimes." She winks. "Also, it just makes the whole thing feel more dramatic, which is good for ratings."

My expression must reflect my anxiety at that because she hurries to add, "Sorry, newsroom humor. I don't mean to imply I only care about the ratings."

"I know, I just… I want this to be honest and genuine. No manipulation."

"You mean the opposite of what Vincenzo Diavolo did today?" she asks wryly.

"Basically, yes."

"You can relax. I don't do business like that."

I exhale, letting her words reassure me. Though my nerves are still sending adrenaline coursing through me. I've never been much for the spotlight, and now I'm about to shine a light on every dark corner of my past for the entire city to see.

I make myself a deal to not throw up until after it's over.

"You tell me when you're ready, and we'll start rolling," Savannah says.

I tense. "Are we live?"

"We will be. Just like you asked."

Right. I exhale shakily, reminding myself this was my idea. And when it comes to Vincenzo, it's the best one I have. I'm fighting fire with fire.

"Okay." I inhale, letting my breath fill all the scared, lonely places inside me. And even though it's a lie, I say. "I'm ready."

Savannah nods at the one-way glass.

A moment later, a scruffy-faced guy in a stained shirt slips into the room and pushes a few buttons on the giant camera aimed at us. With the bright lights aimed at my face, it's hard to even notice him there. I focus instead on Savannah, whose open, relaxed posture reassures me.

"Rolling," the camera guy says.

Savannah doesn't acknowledge him. She just starts talking. "Welcome, everyone, and thank you for joining us. I have with me today in the studio none other than Lexi Giovanni herself, the new high alpha of Indigo Hills and heir to Franco Giovanni's legacy and empire. Thank you for agreeing to this interview," she says. Her eyes are sharp but not unkind.

"Thank you for giving me a chance to speak," I reply.

No turning back now.

"Ms. Giovanni," she begins.

"Please call me Lexi," I say quickly.

Savannah smiles almost ruefully. "Lexi, I'd be lying if I said I wasn't surprised that you called. Apart from doing this live interview with me, you've already had quite the week."

I smile faintly. "You could say that."

"Is it safe to say the events of this week are the reason you're here to talk to us?"

"It is."

"There are so many events to choose from. Let's see, you got married, took out an alpha—" I try not to flinch at that part. "—and were voted in as the city's newest high alpha. Goodness, is that everything, or did I miss something?"

"I think that pretty much sums it up," I say, feeling my cheeks heat as I think about what happened after that vote. With Grey. Claiming him. Fucking him out in the open. Are the rumors saying that part? I really hope not.

"Wow, where do we start?"

"Well." I follow Savannah's advice and pause to catch my breath. It really does help me collect myself a little before I say, "I think I'd like to aim straight for the elephant in the room. The statements Mr. Diavolo made about me earlier this morning."

"Ah. Yes, his interview has stirred up some speculation about you."

"Yes, I imagine it has raised some concerns."

"Some," she agrees, "But I think people just really want to know more about you. Are you up for that?"

"It's why I'm here."

"Great. Let's start with your background. Can you tell us about your upbringing?"

I nod. "My parents moved away from Indigo Hills when

I was very young. They died shortly after, and social services couldn't find any other living relatives, so I grew up in the foster care system. I didn't know about my family legacy or being a shifter. I didn't know anything except that the world can be a very lonely place when you don't have anyone."

Her brows knit with genuine confusion. "You didn't know you were a wolf? How is that possible?"

"I've recently learned that my wolf was suppressed when I was a child." I hesitate and then say the truth that has to come from me for this to work. "I recently took an antidote to the suppressant I was given as a baby. The first time I shifted was in the council meeting that named me as High Alpha."

"Wait. That was the very first time you ever shifted?" Savannah's wide-eyed shock is genuine. "How is that possible?"

"When Mr. Diavolo brought me here, he told me about the experiments Franco—my grandfather—had performed on me. He offered to help trigger my wolf, but in exchange, I had to promise to give him access to my blood so he could use the research on himself."

"Are you saying Mr. Diavolo knew about the lab and was complicit in its methods?"

"I am."

"And your wolf… it was made in a lab?"

"No. I was born a shifter. The gene mutation my grandfather triggered in me was an attempt to make my wolf stronger and faster."

"He wanted to make you a stronger alpha than he was."

"No. He intended to use the winning research on himself."

"So that he would remain unchallenged?" she asks.

"Yes, but more than that, I think he wanted to find a way to live forever."

"I see." Savannah's frown tells me she sees it all. And her thoughts are racing to sift through and find the best questions.

I'm glad Mia chose her.

There's no judgment in her tone. Only curiosity. And concern.

"How did you know to come here?" Savannah asks suddenly, and I realize I was right about her finding the best question to ask. "To Indigo Hills, I mean. If you didn't know you were a Giovanni or even a wolf...what made you come to this city?"

I hesitate for only half a breath before I say, "Mr. Diavolo kidnapped me."

Savannah's shock is almost comical.

She recovers quickly, though her expression darkens as she warns, "That's a strong word to use here."

"Is there another word for being thrown in a trunk and driven here then locked in a tower?"

Savannah shakes her head. "No, I guess there isn't. But there's clearly more to the story if you're sitting before me today, not only a free woman but the most powerful one in the city."

"Yes, I suppose to tell every detail would be a very long story," I say, "But the gist is that I fell for Grey. And he fell for me. And we decided to fight for each other. We could have run—more than once actually—but we decided to stay and fight for the people of this city too. That's what I came here today to say."

I look at the camera, even though it's nerve-wracking. "I've never had a home before. Not a single structure and definitely not a city or a town I felt like I belonged in. But Indigo Hills is that place for me. The friends I've made here, the man I fell in love with here, the people who've shown me kindness, who've accepted me without reservation or judgment—those are what made me feel it. And I refuse to let what Vincenzo said about me change that."

Savannah's eyes are glassy as she says, "It sounds like you got a lot more than you bargained for in Indigo Hills."

I breathe through the ache. "Honestly, I didn't expect anything good. When Grey took me, I—"

"Wait. Grey kidnapped you? Jericho Grey Diavolo? And you still married him?"

Her tone is intimate now. And for a second, it's easy to forget the camera. To pretend we're just having girl talk.

I smile ruefully. "I know how it sounds. But... Grey was the first person who saw me as something more than a bargaining chip."

"And he literally killed to protect you from what I understand," she adds.

I force myself not to wince as I nod. "Dominic Albero attacked me. He would have killed me if Grey hadn't stepped in to defend me."

Savannah leans in, a romantic light in her brown eyes. "You really love him, don't you?"

"Yes. And not just him. I care about the people of Indigo Hills." I smile, real and bittersweet. "The protestors. The shopkeepers. The everyday citizens. Becky at the thrift store on Poplar Hill. Alejandro at the salon downtown. They all deserve an end to the violence and corruption this city has suffered through."

"And what are your plans for this city now, Ms. Alpha?"

"Change," I say simply, my heart aching over the word

—and how much my parents gave up to pursue it once. "Starting with full transparency. No more leaders appointed by bloodlines alone. I want to hold elections. I want to return the money stolen by corruption to the schools, the neighborhoods, the people."

Savannah's eyes widen slightly. Even the cameraman gapes at me. This isn't just damage control. This is revolution.

"And the experiments?" Savannah asks carefully.

My throat tightens, but I nod.

"Vincenzo was right. I was experimented on as a child, but I wasn't the only one. For years, Franco forced other women to undergo those same experiments. They were lied to and manipulated, and I wish I could go back and change it. But the next thing is to go forward and change it instead. I visited the lab to shut it down. But that's not enough. I want to fund a support center. Medical, mental health—all of it. A place where people who were affected by that lab can go for treatment and help."

"That's very generous of you."

"It's the least of what this city deserves."

"And you? What will you do now?"

I hold her gaze. Because I know what she's asking. What Vincenzo will demand—has already demanded of me.

"Even as a human, I became a fighter. And now that I have my wolf back, I'll use every ounce of strength—every scar, every flaw—to protect the people of this city. I will not be stepping down or relinquishing my title, and I will not hide from hard conversations. If Vincenzo wants to debate the merits of my wolf, he's welcome to do so the way our pack has always done it. By challenging my wolf to a fight."

A beat of silence.

"Wow, well, you heard it here, folks. Our new high alpha is putting the people first. And she's not afraid to throw down the gauntlet against Vincenzo Diavolo while she does it. I, for one, am very interested to see what happens next."

Savannah smiles—not the press smile but something genuine.

"Thank you," she says softly. "For your honesty."

The camera light blinks off.

Mia and Andy are already walking through the door when I manage to stand up. The relief that crashes into me is so intense I sway on my heels for a second. Then they're both grabbing me in a tight hug and telling me what a great job I did.

When they finally step back again, a figure catches my eye from the doorway.

Grey.

Looking dangerous and wild-eyed and absolutely magnificent in his black tee and dark-wash denim. His gaze locks onto mine, and in that moment, it's like the whole world falls away.

He smiles. "Hello, wife."

Mia and Andy vanish. Or I just can't look away from Grey as he walks toward me.

"You were absolutely fucking perfect," he murmurs.

Emotion chokes me. I can't speak. I just nod.

He crosses the space between us and yanks me into his arms, crushing me against him. I bury my face in his shoulder and let myself be held. It was only an interview. Not a war. But it feels like I've been beaten down and still somehow come out victorious in the end.

"You look good enough to eat," he says, his breath hot against my ear, and I shudder.

"You're not mad?" I whisper when I can find my voice.

He releases me just enough to look down at me, confused. "Why would I be mad?"

"I told them…the first time I shifted was the meeting. Soon, they'll figure out I couldn't have killed Franco."

"I don't care," he whispers fiercely. "Let them."

Something in me unwinds. I exhale as he presses his lips to mine.

"Come home with me," he says, voice low and rough.

I hesitate.

"What is it?" he asks.

"Franco's house will never be home," I admit.

He squeezes my hand, his thumb brushing over my knuckles.

"Good," he says. "Because that's not where I meant."

I blink up at him, confused. "Then where?"

He grins—boyish and secretive. "I have something to show you."

19

GREY

The drive takes longer than I want it to. Not because of traffic but because I'm impatient. Lexi sits beside me in the passenger seat, quiet and tense. I see her worry in how she fidgets with her hands, the way her eyes dart to mine like she's making sure I'm real, like maybe she's still convincing herself she didn't just risk her life and mine on a live stream.

I'm proud of her. So fucking proud. But I'm also aware of how much this cost us. What my father tried to do… what she just did in return… How fragile the future feels. Her energy is fraying at the edges, like a candle burning at both ends. I can feel it in the tether that connects us. I can feel it in my wolf too—how he paces, alert, even though danger isn't imminent in this very moment. Like he knows what comes next is just as important as the war we'll fight eventually.

The dark creature that rose in me at the warehouse hasn't been back. I have no idea what it was or how it took me over like that. I was my wolf…but not. And the theories

I've been wrestling with about how to explain the foreign feeling of it all would make me sound crazy if I said them out loud. So, I've kept them to myself. Haven't even told Dutch or the others. Because what I felt like in that moment was Franco.

"Where are we going?" she asks, finally breaking the silence.

"You'll see."

She rolls her eyes and looks damn cute about it. "That's not an answer."

I smirk. "I know."

She huffs, but it's affectionate. She's used to my evasions by now.

I spend a few miles making sure we aren't followed. Then, I head for the highway. Just before we exit the city limits, I turn off the main road and wind down a narrow two-lane drive flanked by old-growth trees. Spanish moss dangles from the limbs like nature's curtains, and late-afternoon sunlight flickers through in soft, golden patches. There's no street sign. No mailbox. Just a barely-there gravel path tucked behind a rusted gate that blends so well into the underbrush, you'd miss it if you didn't know where to look.

Lexi leans forward in her seat then shoots me a dubious look. "This looks like a murder road."

I laugh. "I think you'll change your mind in a minute."

I pull up to the gate and type in the code. A second later, it swings open with a low creak. The gravel crunches beneath the tires as we make the slow climb up a wooded incline. At the top, the trees open to reveal a small, stone-front cottage with blue shutters and a porch swing that moves in the breeze. Faint smoke curls from the chimney like the place is already waiting for us. Thanks to Dutch, who better fucking be long gone now.

Lexi stares at the house.

"What is this place?" she whispers.

I kill the engine.

"It's ours," I say, turning toward her. "I bought it under a fake name, paid cash. No one knows it's here. Not Vincenzo. Not our packs. Not even Dutch—well, until today."

Her eyes widen. "You've had this… how long?"

"A few weeks. I found it right after the engagement party."

When I knew I'd fallen in love with her.

Emotion flickers in her eyes, but she pushes the door open and climbs out without a word. I follow.

Inside, the house is all honey wood floors and creamy walls. Low beams cross the ceiling, and the living room has a plush sectional sofa big enough for both of us to sprawl out together. There's a fireplace. A real one. And a kitchen with copper pans and stone counters and light streaming in through windows that look out into the wooded backyard.

Lexi runs her fingers over the back of the couch like she's not sure any of this is real.

"What are you thinking?" I ask when I can't wait any longer.

She looks up at me, her lips curving. "This couch is a lot nicer than the one we met on."

I grin. "Thought about going back to Shady's and making him an offer."

"Is that why you brought me here? Hoping for another lap dance?"

Her question, and more specifically, my answer, sobers

me. "I brought you here because you deserve to feel safe somewhere in the world."

She blinks then looks away, but not before I glimpse tears brimming in her eyes.

"You don't have to decide anything tonight," I tell her softly. "You don't even have to move in. I just wanted you to know it's here. A place that's yours. Ours."

A place we call home.

I don't say the last part. Mostly because Lexi *is* my home, and that has nothing to do with walls or a roof. But I know she doesn't feel comfortable at Franco's, and truth be told, neither do I.

She turns to me slowly. "Show me the rest?"

I nod and lead her through the house.

There are two bedrooms, both already furnished. The one I've mentally marked as ours has a king-sized bed covered in bright throw pillows (a nod to how much Lexi seemed to light up at Mia's bright-ass apartment) and a bay window seat overlooking the side yard. White curtains frame the French doors that lead straight out to the backyard.

She arches a brow at me. "Is this the guest room?"

"I thought this might be our room."

She gives a mock gasp. "No monotones this time? How will you manage to sleep in here?"

"Smartass," I say wryly, swatting her ass. "Besides, I don't plan to do much sleeping in this bed."

She grins and goes back to exploring the room.

A few books line the shelves—I stocked them with titles she's talked about, ones I remembered her mentioning as being better than the movies. Her black duffel sits on the bench at the foot of the bed.

I don't mention it.

She notices, though.

She reaches out and gently touches the bag. "Is this…?" She looks up at me sharply. "You said we couldn't go back to the penthouse now that— I thought I'd never see this stuff again."

"I hid it at the warehouse before the wedding."

Her throat works, but she doesn't speak.

Instead, she walks to the French doors and pulls them open. I follow her out to the deck where stepping stones lead to a grotto-style pool, a small waterfall spilling into it with a soothing rush. A fence offers a sense of privacy, but it's not necessary, considering the thick trees that press in on all three sides. Or the fact that we're miles and miles from the nearest neighbor.

Lexi gasps at the sight of the oasis. "This is…"

I grin. "There's a hot tub, too, around the corner. But this felt more like you."

She turns to me, eyes sparkling. "You did this for me?"

I step closer, brushing a lock of her hair behind her ear. "I did this for us."

"Why the pool?"

I lean in, my voice low. "Because I like seeing you in a bathing suit. Especially that blue bikini you wore at Dutch's."

Her lips part, mischief dancing in her eyes. "You like seeing me naked more."

"Obviously."

She laughs, and it's real and light, the tension melting from her shoulders. For the first time in a long time, I feel her relax in my arms. I hope that means this place will be a haven for us.

"Come swim with me," she says, tugging on my hand.

And fuck if I can say no to that.

The sun's almost down by the time we strip to our underwear and slip into the pool. The water is cool but not cold, a relief after the heat of the day. The waterfall splashes beside us, and the forest beyond the fence hums with cicadas and birdsong.

Lexi floats on her back, her hair fanning around her like a halo. I tread water nearby, arms resting on the rocks, watching her like I always do—like I can't believe she's real and mine.

She suddenly flips upright and swims toward me, water streaming down her face.

"What?" I ask, instantly wary of some threat.

She splashes water in my face.

I blink, stunned. "You did not just—"

Before I can finish, she's swimming away, laughing.

I chase her, grabbing her waist beneath the water and pulling her back to me. She squeals then gasps when I spin her to face me and pin her to the edge of the pool. I realize I like this version of her—of us. The playful, carefree version where we get to horse around in the pool. I haven't seen much of this side of her, but I'll do just about anything to make her safe enough that I get more days like this.

"You're in trouble," I murmur.

Her eyes sparkle at my threat. "I regret nothing."

I press her against the rock, my hips grinding into her and transforming this moment from playful to sexual because damn if I can stop myself. Her legs wrap around me without hesitation, her hands slick against my shoulders.

I dip my head and kiss the hollow of her throat, noting her pulse beating strong like a siren call for my wolf.

She's breathless now. "Grey…"

I raise my head. Her eyes are dark, dilated, lips parted. So fucking beautiful it makes my chest ache.

"What is it?" I ask softly.

"Are you okay?" she asks, concern in her expression. "With everything that's happening to you. With your wolf? Is this okay, I mean?"

My fingers tighten on her hips, and my erection strains against my boxers. "This is exactly what I need, princess. You anchoring me by giving me your body. Can you do that?"

"Yes." Her answer is breathless.

Concern melts into need. I know because I can scent it, and I nearly groan at how delicious her need is.

She looks like she might say more, but I shut her up with a kiss. Slow and deep. I pour everything into it. Every shattered piece of me that she held together these past few days. Every breath I've taken since meeting her that has only been because of her existence and presence in my life.

When I pull back, I press my forehead to hers. "My wolf needs this, Lex. You're the only thing that keeps him strong enough to fight this darkness."

Her breath hitches. "My wolf feels the same way."

"I don't want distance from you," I say, my hands roaming over her smooth, wet skin. "I want to be buried in you. I want to feel you everywhere until I don't know where I end and you begin."

Lexi rocks her hips against me. "I want that too," she whispers.

That's all the permission I need.

We stumble inside, dripping wet, a tangle of limbs and

mouths. My desire to take her right there in the pool is overwhelmed by the need to taste her on my tongue.

Just inside the bedroom, her bra peels away easily, and I drop to my knees to drag her soaked panties down her thighs, licking the drops of water from her skin as I go.

She grips my shoulders for balance, one foot braced on the wall, and when I dip my head between her legs and run my tongue along her center, she moans so loud it echoes through the empty house.

"Grey—"

Her hand tangles in my hair, pulling me tighter against her. Fine by me. I could die right here and be perfectly happy about meeting my end. So, as she moans my name, I don't stop. I devour. I worship. I work her clit with slow, circular pressure, then faster, then slower again until she's shaking against the wall, panting, pleading.

When I push a finger inside her, she comes on my tongue with a cry, her entire body trembling.

I rise and scoop her into my arms. She buries her face in my neck as I carry her to the bed. I drop her onto the comforter, scattering half a dozen pillows to the floor, and follow her down, my hands sliding over her curves, over her hips and breasts. I bite her shoulder, her collarbone, the inside of her thigh.

"I need you inside me," she whispers, voice hoarse, eyes unfocused.

She looks like a wet dream lying here spread out for me, her hair splayed against the bedsheets. A dream I never want to wake from again.

I sheath myself and slide into her slowly, both of us gasping at the stretch, the way her body clenches around me like she was made to take me.

We find our rhythm easily. Naturally. Like wolves running in sync. She meets me thrust for thrust, her nails digging into my back, her eyes locked on mine.

She's not afraid. Not of my wolf. Not of me. And that undoes me more than anything else ever could.

I shift slightly, angling deeper, hitting that spot that makes her eyes roll back. She clenches harder around my cock, breathless curses tumbling from her lips.

"You feel like fucking heaven," I growl, thrusting harder, chasing that edge.

She shudders beneath me. "Don't stop. Please don't stop."

"Never."

She tightens around me again, her cries turning desperate.

With a final thrust, I push her over the edge, and she pulls me with her, both of us spiraling together in heat and light and every promise we wish we could make for our future.

Then I collapse in a satisfied heap beside her.

Later, when the only sound is our breathing, I pull her against me, her head resting on my chest.

Her fingers trace lazy circles over my skin.

"Is this house really ours?" she asks sleepily.

"Yes."

She exhales, sinking deeper into my arms.

"I've never had a home before," she murmurs.

I kiss the top of her head. "You do now."

She lifts her head and kisses me softly, reverently. "So do you."

20

LEXI

The first thing I notice upon waking is the quiet.

No reporters. No staff or pack members in and out. No one banging on the door to tell me that I'm late to something or alerting us to some new threat. Just silence, thick and soft like a blanket over my ears.

Then warmth. The feel of Grey behind me, one arm heavy across my waist, his body curled around mine like I'm something precious. Protected.

His breathing is deep, steady. I can tell from the way his chest moves against my back that he's still asleep. I wonder if he's getting the same restful sleep I did. There's something about this house. About the way we are with each other here. It's like magic. The good kind.

Last night, after I'd had about three hundred orgasms, we shifted and ran together. It was what my first shift should have been. No blood or gore coating my fur. No violence in my wake. Just me and Grey, mated and running side by side.

It grounded my wolf in a way nothing else has. By the

time we returned and fell into bed, I started feeling like she and I might finally be on the same page.

Comforted by that thought, I keep my eyes closed a few more seconds, savoring the stillness. The illusion of safety. Because I know, the second I open them, it'll all come rushing back.

And it does.

Vincenzo's press conference. The video footage of me at the lab. The claims he made about me being something worse than Franco.

Then me, walking into that reporter's office with my chin up and my past on my sleeve.

Telling the truth.

About the foster homes. About Franco. About being alone.

About Indigo Hills.

About me and Grey.

I squeeze my eyes shut again, this time against the flood of memories. And the way my voice almost cracked when I said the city had become my home. When I looked into that camera and told them I wasn't just a science project. That I was a wolf like them.

That I would use the strength those experiments gave me to protect the people they tried to turn me against.

I hope I can keep that promise.

I hope I get to keep this life.

Grey stirs behind me, his fingers twitching against my stomach before settling again. I tilt my head back just enough to feel the weight of his breath in my hair.

The air in the room smells like us. Like sex and salt and sweat and something sweeter I can't name.

Whatever it is, it's real.

Just like him.

Just like this.

I roll onto my back carefully, trying not to fully wake him, but his arm tightens instinctively, his eyes cracking open as I settle again.

"Hey," he says, voice raspy with sleep and something deeper. "You okay?"

"Yeah." I nod, though the word feels too small.

His hand lifts to brush a strand of hair from my face. "You were amazing yesterday."

"Do you mean the live interview or the sex?"

He grins. "Both."

"Thanks," I tell him, sobering as emotions hit me with a force that feels unfair for so early in the morning.

"For which part?" he shoots back.

I swallow hard. "You were there. When I needed you. At the end."

He smiles faintly. "I always will be."

That breaks me a little. Because I believe him. And I've never believed that kind of promise before. Then again, no one's ever made a promise to me like that before.

I snuggle closer, pressing my forehead to his. "Thank you. For the house. For being there. For... not trying to fix me."

"I don't want to fix you, Lex. I just want to stand beside you while you fix the world."

I laugh softly, even as my eyes sting. "No pressure."

He kisses my temple, then my cheek, then the corner of my mouth. Then he's planting kisses so fast and sloppy, I can't help but laugh and wiggle away.

"Come on," he says, like he's satisfied with my happiness—like that was his goal all along, "Let's get coffee and breakfast, and then I'll have you for dessert." His wink has my body tingling in anticipation.

THE KITCHEN in the new house smells like cinnamon and dark roast. Grey stands at the counter in nothing but his boxers, hair a mess, tattoos on full display. He's flipping pancakes like some kind of domestic sex god while I sit on the stool by the island, watching him with my chin in my hand.

"You know," I murmur, "this whole hot alpha wolf thing really works when paired with maple syrup."

He shoots me a look over his shoulder. "Noted. Should I add bacon to the rotation?"

"Bacon's a sex toy now. Officially."

Grey barks a laugh, and something warm and fizzy bubbles in my chest. I can't get enough of this. The normalcy between us. The teasing and laughter. It's stupid to think we could have a life like this, but I can't help wishing…

There's a knock at the door.

My smile fades.

Grey puts the spatula down, instantly alert. "Stay here."

He walks to the front of the house, his stance shifting into predator mode so fast it makes my head spin. But the tension drains the second he looks through the peephole.

Relaxed, he opens the door.

"Morning," Dutch says casually, stepping inside with his hands raised. "No need to shift and maul, big guy. Just bringing news."

Grey grunts. "Next time, text."

"I did. Three times. You were too busy playing house to check it."

Dutch winks at me as he steps into the kitchen, dropping a folded newspaper on the counter beside me. "You made the front page."

I unfold it slowly, heart thudding. The headline reads: SHE-*WOLF TELLS ALL: LEXI GIOVANNI IS ONE OF US.*

Below it, a still from the interview. Me in that green dress, eyes steady, mouth mid-sentence. I stare at the picture, trying to recognize the version of me I see there. She looks… brave. Bold. I'm awed by it. By her.

I exhale shakily. "They didn't twist it."

"Nope," Dutch says. "Savannah's a real one. And public opinion's starting to tilt. Slow, but steady. You convinced people they can trust you."

"How does it change the numbers?" Grey asks.

"Defections are on the rise. Andy says a non-stop stream of people have been showing up at the gate since the interview aired." He doesn't look nearly as happy as his words make it sound.

"So what's the problem?" I ask.

"It's not enough. Not yet," Grey says knowingly. He hands me a mug of coffee before taking the stool beside mine. "What's my asshole father doing about it?"

Dutch grimaces. "We don't know yet. Rumor is he'll try to hijack Franco's funeral tonight."

The funeral I asked Andy to expedite, mostly so we could concentrate on the memorial services for our fallen security guards. They're the ones who deserve to be honored, but this city is steeped in sick traditions, and honoring a dead alpha is one that might as well be written into law.

I stop with the coffee halfway to my mouth. "Hijack how?"

Dutch shrugs. "Photos. A speech. Maybe even a call to arms. Paint himself as the true heir to Franco's legacy. Undermine you with nostalgia and fear."

I grit my teeth. "And everyone will be there."

Grey's hand settles over mine. "Which means we need to be too."

"I'm not letting him use Franco's death to rally support."

Dutch leans forward. "That's why we need to hit him back. Not with violence. Not yet," he adds when my expression tenses.

"Then how?"

"The interview you did was a hit, so Mia and I agree we stick with optics."

Grey nods at the newspaper. "We build on this."

Dutch flips open the folder he's still holding. "Andy sent over the guest list for the funeral, and it's a fucking goldmine. Half these people are connected to Vincenzo's various criminal schemes, including the money laundering."

"Wait, I thought that was Franco," I say. "It's why he framed Ramsey's dad. Shot him."

Dutch and Grey share a look.

"What?" I demand.

"Franco siphoned money from the city's coffers," Grey explains. "Taxes that should have gone to schools and child development programs. My father…"

He hesitates, and my entire body tightens. Whatever it is must be worse than Franco.

"Grey, just tell me."

"He makes his money from his own dealings," he says at last.

"What does that mean?"

"He sells magic-based weapons and enhancement serums."

"What? To who?"

"Mostly foreign shifter militias or black-market buyers. Really, anyone with enough money to fund a supernatural war."

My jaw drops. "How did he manage that without Franco knowing?"

"Franco knew," Dutch says grimly.

I look from him to Grey, trying to understand how this has been going on all along, and no one told me. "And the people of Indigo Hills—do they know?" I ask.

"Some do," Dutch says.

"And they don't care?"

"He pretends the funds go to security or infrastructure, but really, it's an arms trade," Grey says.

"And you forgot to mention it until now?" I can't help but feel like this is something they purposely left out.

Grey refuses to meet my eyes.

I look at Dutch, who looks guilty enough for both of them.

"Talk," I snap, not caring which one does it first.

"I was going to," Grey says. "But then he threatened to trigger your wolf, and you were so determined to let him. I thought if you knew he really did have access to shit like that, you'd go behind my back."

I blink, struck by that. And now I'm the one feeling guilty. Shit. That's exactly what I did.

"The point is, we didn't tell you because we were trying to protect you," Dutch says, trying to smooth it over.

I sigh, putting aside my initial anger. Not like I can blame them for keeping it from me now, when I did far worse by taking that serum. Speaking of which…

"Not to sound completely reckless here," I begin carefully, "but if Vincenzo has access to hex magic, maybe he has something to counteract whatever's going on with us—"

"No," Grey snarls at the same time Dutch practically yells the word in my face.

"Okay, okay." I hold up my hands in surrender.

"Anything my father touches is only meant to do us harm," Grey says in a voice packed with enough conviction that I nod in agreement, shoving aside any possible ideas I might have had.

"You're right," I say. "Forget it."

"So, about the plan," Dutch says pointedly.

"You want to expose his true business dealings at the funeral," I say, refocusing on the whole reason they brought this up.

"If we're smart about it, we can turn the whole night around on him. Expose him for what he truly is. After that, his whole pack will defect to us. To you," he amends, flicking a glance at his own alpha.

"To Lexi," Grey confirms. "No one knows yet what we are. And I want to keep it that way for a while longer."

"Agreed," Dutch says.

I look at Grey, hope rising. "Do you think this could work?"

"I do." He meets my gaze, calm and lethal. "We let the asshole have his moment onstage. He'll think he's won.

Then we expose his true business. The money. The corruption. We can use that reporter who interviewed you."

"Savannah," I say, already thinking ahead to how we'll orchestrate it.

Dutch grins. "Franco will be rolling over in his grave."

"Bonus," I snort.

Grey lifts his glass. "To turning grief into justice."

I lift mine too, and Dutch follows. We toast in silence, the air heavy with purpose.

Today, the city mourns Franco Giovanni. Tomorrow, it will pledge loyalty to the one who took his place.

21

GREY

St. Andrews smells like fresh flowers and expensive cologne. A cloying mixture that fills my head with memories. A lifetime of weddings and funerals and baptisms; of gatherings filled with fake smiles and self-righteous pride. All of it wrapped up in a pack where corruption is the uninvited guest filling every empty pew.

Franco's funeral flowers aren't the usual muted, tasteful arrangements. They're bright to the point of being overstated. Blood red roses so steeped in color and scent, clearly on the verge of rotting.

Fitting, really. Franco Giovanni deserves nothing less. Lexi says Andy planned the details, but I have to wonder who decided on the macabre color scheme that is crimson bouquets set among dark gray balloons.

It sends a message. Not just to the guests crowding the pews as we gather one last time for the monster who ran this city. But to the corpse of that man now lying inside the open casket at the front of the room.

Even so, it's not him I'm looking at.

It's her.

Lexi stands at the back of the church near the main entrance, a vision in black. Her shoulders are stiff, her expression solemn. It's not the broken kind of mourning that comes with losing a loved one. She wears her grief like armor—fitted, sharp, and tailored to draw every eye in the room. She looks like pure power.

She hasn't spotted me yet. Good. I don't want her to see the way my hands won't stop flexing. The way my wolf paces just beneath the surface, agitated and alert. The way I've already marked every possible exit and every armed man in this building. And it's not just my wolf I'm wrestling with.

The creature inside me is awake.

I can't stop thinking that this public arena is the perfect place to make some kind of move against us. I'm not sure my father will come at us so directly in front of witnesses, but if it were me, I would. So I can't let my guard down. And I can't let her out of my sight. Not even to fight off the darkness inside me.

The pews are nearly full. Family. Pack. Civilians. Reporters. Enemies dressed like mourners.

And my father.

Front row. Polished shoes. Custom suit. Snake-oil smile.

He sits like he owns the place, like this church exists for him alone. Like Franco's body is his final prop in a show designed to smear Lexi and manipulate the crowd.

But he's not the only one with theatrics up their sleeve.

I spot Dutch and Mia halfway down the left side. Razor and Crow flank the aisle, eyes sharp, shoulders stiff. Andy stands close beside Lexi, her gaze watchful for any kind of threat. A few of Lexi's lieutenants line the wall in the vestibule, Donahue and Camila among them. Dutch says they're the most loyal so far.

She's protected. I keep reminding myself of that since it's the only grip on control I have left. Lexi is mine to protect. Mine to keep safe. As long as I do that, I stand a chance of holding onto my sanity until this thing ends.

And then—

My mother walks in.

I've been calling her since the wedding with no answer. My worry for her is only second to my need to remain at Lexi's side. But I scan the sight of her, looking for evidence of harm.

She's in a knee-length black dress with a matching jacket. The cut is conservative with long sleeves and a high neckline that doesn't show much skin. Something in her posture is off. Slumped, worn, not like her usual queen-on-her-throne elegance. When she finally takes off her large sunglasses, I can see that she's pale with dark circles under her eyes. She bears no visible bruises, but I've seen what my father can do.

They either healed already, or she's hiding them well.

The anger flares white-hot.

My mother was once mine to protect too. My failure to do so drove me from this city once. Seeing her now brings it all back. I clench my fists and force myself to breathe through it.

But it's getting harder to hold the leash.

I can feel the alpha power in my blood like static under my skin. A yawning darkness that threatens to swallow me up. To take me over. To rule everyone, including me.

I shake my head to clear it.

This is not the time to lose control.

And if it slips the leash here, in front of all these people? There will be blood. I might not have control over whose.

Lexi's gaze sweeps the church. Our eyes lock.

And the chaos inside me stills.

Fuck, she's beautiful.

Not just in the way that makes people stare. But in the way she carries the future of this city on her shoulders like it belongs to her. Like, no matter how many knives are pointed at her back, they won't pierce her.

And I'm lucky enough to be married to her. Not just married. Mated. The realization steals my breath and evaporates my worries.

For one perfect second, I forget where we are. Or what dangers lurk.

Then something catches my eye from above. I look up.

And freeze.

A shadow on the balcony.

Tall. Golden. Familiar.

My heart stutters.

Ramsey.

The hallucination hits so hard I have to grip the edge of the pew in front of me.

It can't be.

He wouldn't be this stupid.

And yet, for that heartbeat, I see him clearly. That casual slouch. That smirk. A flex of his muscles as he presses his fist into his palm in a silent promise.

I blink.

The spot is empty.

The mirage of my former packmate gone as quickly as it came.

Maybe it was nothing.

Maybe it was everything.

My chest aches. Not from rage this time. From grief.

He was my brother. Maybe not by blood, but in all the ways that mattered. I miss him.

Even now.

But thanks to his betrayal, loyalty has never meant more than it does today.

The priest calls everyone to their seats.

Lexi makes her way down the aisle to where I wait at the front. I take her hand in mine, refusing to look at the balcony again. Instead, I walk across the aisle and drop a kiss on my mother's cheek. Squeeze her shoulder in a silent hello. She gives me a forced smile from where she sits beside my father.

"I love you," I whisper in her ear.

She doesn't respond, and my father doesn't so much as blink.

Lexi steps up behind me and takes her hand, offers a quick smile of her own, then steps back again. We take our seats across the aisle from them. My pack and hers fill in behind us.

When everyone is seated, the priest speaks. Something about legacy. About Franco. About the man who built an empire. I don't let myself hear it, not really. If I did, I'd likely lose it. Nothing about Franco's legacy is worth keeping—or honoring, for that matter. But apparently, we're going to pretend otherwise for one more day.

When the priest is finished, he nods at the first guest speaker, and my father stands.

I tense.

He walks slowly up the aisle, face somber. Controlled. Every step calculated to draw the eye.

He mounts the stage like a fucking politician.

The crowd quiets.

"Franco Giovanni was a titan. A leader. A father to us all," he says, voice deep and practiced. "He was an alpha whose presence commanded respect and whose vision shaped this city."

He pauses, no doubt for dramatic effect. "I had the honor of standing beside him through the years. He was a mentor to many, and to me, more than that. He was family."

Bullshit.

My wolf strains beneath my skin.

The darkness whispers in my ear.

"Today, we mourn him by honoring the work he did in the past. But we must also look to the future." He lifts his chin, scanning the room. "This city deserves leadership forged in loyalty. In strength. In understanding. Someone who puts the safety of our people before their own ambition."

His gaze slides pointedly toward Lexi. Subtle. Measured. Poison dipped in politeness. "Not those who court chaos. Who stumble into a position of power they barely understand, carrying a name and a title they didn't earn."

A low growl rips through my chest before I can stop it.

Lexi squeezes my hand, her thumb brushing over my skin.

It helps. A little.

My father doesn't acknowledge my outburst. He just keeps going.

"We need leaders who remember what it means to serve. Not reign. Leaders who will protect the balance between our kind and theirs. Who won't let blood and legacy be tainted by experiments and ambition."

My nails dig into my thigh.

I know exactly what he's doing.

And so does Lexi.

But she doesn't move. Doesn't flinch. Just watches him with that same regal stillness she possessed on our wedding day. Like the eye of a fucking hurricane.

My father bows his head. "Franco Giovanni was devoted to this city, and so am I. As a tribute to his memory, I can only hope to be as great a true alpha as he once was."

He steps down to a smattering of applause.

My wolf still claws under my skin, impatient. I can feel the shift threatening at the base of my spine.

But I breathe through it.

For her.

She came here in full view of her enemies to honor the man who tried to control her and the system that tried to break her. And she did it not to mourn Franco but to show she's not afraid.

She's ten times stronger and better than my father will ever be.

So, I sit. I wait. I keep my wolf on a tight leash. And I let the darkness wrap itself around my heart instead of someone else's throat.

At a nod from the priest, Lexi rises.

The moment she takes the podium, the church quiets.

"Franco Giovanni built this city on strength of will," she begins, her voice even, warm. "He made hard choices, some of them to the detriment of the people affected by them. And while I didn't agree with his actions, I respect the pack he built."

I watch her. Every syllable honest, every word genuine. She's not pretending. She's doing what so few of them ever could—telling the truth without making someone bleed for it.

"There are those who think leadership is about dominance. That it comes from inheritance or tradition. But leadership, real leadership, is about responsibility. About listening. About fighting for people who may never thank you for it. People who can't fight for themselves."

A murmur of approval ripples through the crowd.

Lexi looks out at them all, letting her hands rest flat on the podium. "This city deserves protection. Compassion. A future that doesn't bury its past but learns from it. Franco showed us his way. Now, let me show you mine. Because I will fight for the people of Indigo Hills every damned day you allow me to lead it."

When she's finished, there's no applause. Just stunned quiet.

And then someone near the back stands and places their hand over their heart. A silent pledge of loyalty.

Another follows.

Then another.

Until most of the room is standing and pledging.

Not a cheer. Not a roar. But respect.

22

LEXI

After standing up front to shake hands for what feels like hours, Grey and I are the last ones out of the church. The doors creak closed behind me, a final breath let out by the building like it's relieved the funeral is over. Me too. My hands still shake a little from the speech I gave—not because I regret it but because the adrenaline hasn't stopped buzzing through my veins.

People keep coming up to shake my hand, their expressions tight with grief but softened with something else. Approval? Acceptance? A few even give me half-smiles, like they believe what I said about change, about strength, about a future that looks different than what Franco would've allowed.

I clutch Grey's hand tighter as we linger on the steps of the church, away from the crowd gathering around Vincenzo below. Up until now, the questions have all been about how he's coping with the loss of his longtime friend and leader. Or what he thinks about my proposed changes for healing this city from corruption. I know because Andy has texted me updates and because those are all questions we fed the press through back channels.

I wasn't here to witness his answers, but I can guess they've all been politician-smooth and egotistical. For once, I don't even care what bullshit he's fed them. The real show's about to start. And for once, I'm not the one in the crosshairs.

Anxious, I scan the crowd and spot Andy near the news van parked at the curb. Our eyes meet, and I give the slightest nod. She says something to a guy standing on the outskirts of the crowd gathered. The cameraman from yesterday's interview.

He responds and then heads over to where Savannah stands with the other reporters surrounding Vincenzo.

Mia appears at my other side. "Is it happening?" she whispers.

"Wait for it," I murmur.

Off to the side, half a dozen of my pack enforcers, including Donahue and Camila, stand ready and waiting to take Vincenzo into custody. But not before he's blindsided with exposure.

Savannah shoulders her way to the front. Her cameraman is rounding the fringes, his camera pointed at her and Vincenzo.

"Mr. Diavolo, can you comment on the financial records I received this morning linking you to illegal arms deals, including arming a rogue pack in the northeast for magical warfare last spring?" Savannah asks.

Before the funeral, Andy delivered a thick file to her that contained all the records necessary to expose Vincenzo for who he really is. Bank records. Names of the packs he's sold to. Dates of the meetings. There's even a written statement from a hex witch with data on the lethal ingredients in some of his weapons.

At her question, the crowd erupts with shocked demands and urgent questions of their own.

Vincenzo's surprise is evident on his slack face.

My pulse jumps.

Here we go.

"I have no idea what you're talking about," Vincenzo says, but they ignore his denials in favor of more questions.

"Can you tell us where you go for the money to fund production of this magnitude?" Savannah presses. "The bank records we obtained show no trail between your accounts and the production costs themselves. So, who paid for these weapons?"

"Did Franco know about this?" another reporter shouts.

"You hear that?" Dutch says under his breath, the corner of his mouth twitching. "That's the sound of a man whose empire is falling."

"Shhh," I whisper, even as a grin tugs at my lips at the sight of Vincenzo's obvious floundering. I can't help it. It's petty. It's dangerous. It's everything I've been waiting for.

Grey leans in closer, brushing his mouth against my ear. "You're enjoying this."

"Of course I am," I whisper back. "Taking him down without shedding any more blood in the process is all I could hope for."

He chuckles low in his throat, and I can feel the vibration of it against my side, warm and grounding and all mine. The last time we were in this church, it was to exchange wedding vows. To promise each other a future together. I can only hope this moment leads us closer to that future.

The reporters' questions reach a fever pitch. Then—finally—one voice cuts through the noise.

"Those documents are forgeries," Vincenzo says, voice loud and sharp. It's not so much the denial in his words but the alpha power reverberating through his tone.

Despite the fact that half of them aren't even his pack, the crowd shuts up.

"This is a smear campaign," he goes on, cheeks flushing with the only sign of his rage, "An orchestrated attempt to discredit my leadership during a time of grief and transition."

Smooth. Confident. The voice of a man used to controlling the room.

"They're not forgeries," a reporter says. "We've verified the accounts with three separate sources."

I blink, surprised. We knew Savannah would distribute the files to the others, but fact-checking so quickly is impressive.

"Mr. Diavolo, how do you explain the transfers of funds earmarked for community support to shell companies under your wife's maiden name?" Savannah asks.

My heart lurches at that.

Grey's mom?

I look over and find Grey stony and tense. "She probably has no idea," he murmurs.

I search the crowd for Serena, but she's nowhere to be found. I exhale. Good. Hopefully, she's already slipped away from him.

"Is it true you used your access to city funds to launder over thirty million dollars in the last decade?" another reporter asks.

My shock deepens. Thirty million?

I didn't even realize…

The crowd keeps pressing in, more voices, more accusations. Cameras flash. Vincenzo's voice starts to splinter, his answers growing shorter, clipped with rage.

Grey squeezes my hand. "It's working."

I nod, breathless, ready to give the signal to Donahue and Camila to move in. Because, for a moment—just one stolen breath of clarity—I actually think this might be enough. That maybe we can win this without another bloodbath. That exposing Vincenzo publicly will fracture his support and give our people room to breathe. That we can rebuild something better.

Something real.

Maybe even something… safe.

But then—

"Since you're all so interested in transparency," Vincenzo snarls, voice louder than before, "Let me share something that's not yet public knowledge. I am officially declaring my general, Alvaro Martinez, a missing person. He hasn't been seen in seventy-two hours, and all the evidence my pack has uncovered points to foul play."

My stomach plummets.

Grey doesn't move.

"I've submitted his cell phone data to my best trackers," Vincenzo continues. "The last known location for Alvaro was a warehouse under the jurisdiction of the new alpha, Lexi Giovanni, and her mate, Grey Diavolo. Now, I know our packs live by a code that the strongest survive. But abducting a general and killing him in cold blood is not part of that code. If the evidence proves true, I will have no choice but to retaliate with the full force of my pack."

The silence that follows is deafening.

And then—

Flashbulbs.

Gasps.

Shouted questions.

Not aimed at him anymore but at us. Like a wave surging, the sea of reporters suddenly flocks up the steps toward us.

Grey's grip on my hand goes steel-tight.

"He did not just do that," Mia hisses.

"Shit," Dutch mutters.

I look out over the heads of the crowd and find Vincenzo already watching me. Our eyes lock, and his flush of triumph morphs into something darker. Smug. Vengeful.

He knew exactly what he was doing, letting those accusations against him build and build. All so he'd have their full attention when he accused me of murder—the only thing worse than the things we'd said about him.

The adrenaline from our near-win is still thrumming inside me, but now it turns to nausea. Acid claws at my throat.

Because, for a minute there, I'd started to believe victory without a war was possible. Now, I remember what I should have never forgotten: Fighting men like Vincenzo will never be without bloodshed.

Not in this city. Not in this life.

And I might be a fool to wish for it now.

"Start walking," Grey says, his voice low and insistent beside me.

I do.

He's right—we can't afford to linger. Not when Vincenzo's just painted a bloody target on our backs with perfect media optics. He doesn't have to prove we did anything. He only has to suggest it.

Let the public do the rest.

Reporters follow us all the way to the limo waiting. They press in around me, shouting questions, snapping pictures, demanding answers. I keep my head down and ignore them, clinging to Grey's hand like a lifeline.

With Mia and Andy offering cover from behind, we reach the limo and slide into the backseat. Dutch climbs in front with Crow, who drives. Across from me in the backseat, Mia and Andy are both already pulling out their phones as they talk about how to "start spinning the narrative."

Grey rests a hand on my thigh, grounding me as the car pulls away from the church and back into the city traffic. I glance over to find him staring out the window, jaw tight, his other hand clenched in a fist against his leg. His wolf is close. I can feel it in the air between us, simmering just below the surface. The darkness is there too. I can feel it through our mate bond like a toxic cloud.

But he hasn't let go of me.

Not once.

And even if everything else feels like it's slipping, his touch doesn't.

"I'm sorry," I whisper.

His eyes cut to mine. "For what?"

"For believing we could win so easily. For thinking, if I gave the right speech or exposed the right lie, we could come out of this without more blood on the floor."

His gaze softens, and he shifts to face me more fully. "You were right to hope."

I shake my head. "Hope's a liability in this game."

"No," he says, fierce now. Andy and Mia both look up from their phones. "Hope is what keeps us from becoming them. I need you not to lose yours."

The words land harder than I expect. My throat tightens, but I nod.

He curls our fingers together more tightly, like we're not already fused at the soul.

"You did good today," he tells me. "That speech? The way they looked at you after? They saw their alpha."

I shake my head. "I don't know about that."

"Grey's right," Mia says firmly. "I watched their faces, and they saw the future in you."

My skepticism must be obvious because Andy chimes in, "Vincenzo's stunt doesn't change that either."

"If they believe I'm capable of killing Alvaro and covering it up…"

"You're not like him, and they know it," Mia says. "You think a pack this tired of old blood wants to go back to someone like him?"

I don't answer.

Because I want to believe them. But I've seen what fear and hate can do. I've watched it crush people under its heel. Strong people. Survivors like me.

Grey must sense it—because the next thing he says is a whisper, meant only for me, even though Andy and Mia and everyone else can hear every word.

"I love you, Lexi Giovanni. I would tear this city apart for you. And anyone who's decent only has to be in the same room with you to feel the same."

My heart stumbles.

He leans in, pressing his forehead to mine. "But I'd rather build it with you instead."

Tears sting behind my eyes, but I don't let them fall. I just breathe him in again. His wolf, his fury, his faith in me.

"I love you too," I whisper. "And I'm not letting him take this from us."

His fingers flex around mine.

"That's my girl," he says.

And even with the war, even with Vincenzo's accusations rising like smoke behind us—I let myself believe him.

Just for one breath.

23

LEXI

We return to Franco's mansion—or as I'm determined to call it, the estate, mostly because it sounds only slightly less pretentious—for a quiet reception open only to pack members. No media. No rival families. Definitely no one from Vincenzo's side. Not when Alvaro's name is in a missing person's report and my name is listed alongside it.

Despite my doubts to the contrary, the Giovanni pack shows up. Not just the security teams and their families, or the lieutenants whose presence is required, but regular citizens too. They bring casseroles and hugs and wary glances. They offer condolences for Franco, yes—but mostly, they come for me.

They come to meet their alpha.

I shake so many hands I lose feeling in mine. Smile so many smiles my cheeks hurt. My wolf stays alert, pacing under my skin. Watching for signs of betrayal, or challenge, or both.

I'm beginning to realize those are the moments she'll

take me over. Part of me wants to appreciate the protection she offers, but the other part, the one whose will is taken over if that happens, would rather not.

"You looked good in that interview yesterday," someone says. "Strong."

I nod, murmuring an automatic thanks, but then the person smiles, and recognition strikes me.

"Bobby, right?" I ask warily.

He nods.

The bartender from Altobello's. One of Franco's most trusted…associates. If anyone's going to be pissed at how things have gone, it's him.

"What can I do for you?" I ask warily.

"Well, since you brought it up, what are your plans for the restaurant?"

I blink, absorbing his words for longer than necessary. Mostly because it's not the I-want-to-kill-you vibe I expect. "What do you mean?"

"Well, the place belongs to you. So, I guess it's your call, but it's a community staple, you know?"

"What's my call?"

His brows knit. "Whether to open it or keep it shut down. It wasn't you who gave the order to close?"

I shake my head. "No. Honestly, that place hasn't even been on my radar yet. Lots to figure out."

"Yeah, I get that." But he still looks confused. Or suspicious. I tense again, trying to decipher how much of that is a preamble to declaring himself my enemy.

"Well, I guess we'll just wait and see," he says finally before sauntering off toward the kitchen.

I watch him go and can't help but mutter, "I guess we will." In more ways than one.

After that, more pack members come to offer their well-wishes. Joan Balistrieri stops to tell me she's proud of me—as if she had some hand in all this—along with her husband, Fortuna, who apparently is now my financial advisor.

"Come by the office or call me when you're ready to meet," he says. "I'll make room for you whenever's convenient."

"I'll do that."

"Of course, Franco and I used to meet over whiskey and cards." Fortuna laughs hoarsely, and I wonder how many cigars are included in those "meetings" he's had with Franco over the years. "But you get to do things any way you want, boss."

Boss.

I don't come up with a response to that before they get distracted by Andy, and Joan rushes over to gush about her new promotion.

"Aunt Joan…" Andy meets my eyes, and I bite back a conspiratorial smile. Joan's only a loyal pack member to me. To Andy, she's an aunt who thinks she's a mother hen.

More guests come to tell me I did well to land my new position and have handled the opposition impressively so far. At first, I think they mean Vincenzo, but enough comments slip for me to realize they're talking about how I took out three generals in one meeting all by myself. That's when I realize the compliment is code for: You survived what should've killed you. It's impressive. Terrifying. A little unnatural.

And I don't blame them. I feel unnatural too.

Though he stands far enough away to avoid speaking to anyone, Grey hasn't let me leave his sight. He's stiff and silent, his gaze locked on every single person who gets too close to me. I can feel the way that dark creature inside him pulses under his skin like static, just barely contained.

It's getting harder for him to hide it. Harder for me to pretend it doesn't scare me. But we're still no closer to figuring out how to stop it. I'm hoping, after today, things will quiet down long enough for us to go searching for answers.

I'm grabbing another glass of wine from a server's tray when my phone buzzes in my hand. Andy gave it to me this morning when she had to learn I'd spent the night safely away with Grey from Dutch. She wasn't happy that I was unreachable, and I can't blame her for it. The phone she gave me—or forced on me—is already programmed with "all the important numbers," according to her. Grey watched the entire lecture she gave me—and approved.

Now, the caller ID flashes with **Security, Front Gate.**

I answer immediately. "Yes?"

"Alpha Giovanni," the man says, voice clipped and tense. "We've got Diavolo visitors."

My heart stutters, "Turn them away. No one from that pack is allowed through the gate. You already have your orders."

"Yes, ma'am. Thing is…" He clears his throat. "You might wanna come see for yourself."

I glance at Grey. He's already watching me, jaw tight, and I have a feeling he probably heard everything the guard just said.

"Fine," I say. "We're on our way."

I tell Andy where we're going and then slip away from the guests, heart pounding at the thought of what kind of attack we'll face. At the door, Grey pauses to nod at Mia and Dutch, who stand chatting with Claire. They take one look at their alpha and break away from Claire to follow us outside.

"Where's Razor and Crow?" Grey asks them.

"Patrol," Dutch says.

"I'm texting them now," Mia adds.

After that, we're all silent as we round the curve and get our first look at the visitors standing just beyond the checkpoint.

I stop dead.

Charlie Reyes stands front and center. His red hair gives him away even from this distance.

And behind him stand a dozen other Diavolo wolves. None of them wear colors or family insignia. They've shed their uniforms, their armor. But I know enough of the faces.

Elio. Cruz. Darius. One of them guarded my suite when Vincenzo held me hostage at his home. Another drove Grey and me to our engagement party.

What are they doing here?

"What the hell," Dutch mutters.

"Dad," Mia says, increasing her pace.

The surprise in her voice tells me she didn't know he was coming. Dutch says something to her, and she hangs back rather than closing the distance to where her father stands.

Charlie's eyes find mine. He steps forward, hands visible, no weapons, no challenge in his posture. "Alpha Giovanni," he says, "we've come to pledge our loyalty."

"What do you want to do?" Grey asks.

"Let's hear him out," I say.

Grey nods and motions at the guards to let Charlie

through. They open the gate far enough to allow him entry then shut it again, their weapons still aimed at the rest of the Diavolo pack members. Charlie approaches us warily, but he doesn't seem hostile. Just unsure.

Grey glances at Dutch, who takes Mia by the elbow and steers her out of range. She doesn't look happy about it, but she lets him. I turn to Charlie, arms crossed.

"Why are you here?" I ask him, keeping my voice low.

Charlie inclines his head toward the gate. "Because it's not safe for me out there anymore."

"Does my father know you helped us?" Grey asks.

"He's close to figuring it out. He's ordered interrogations for me and Rocco, which means he knows it was someone close to him."

"Word will reach him that you've come here, and then he'll know for sure," Grey warns.

But Charlie's expression doesn't waver. "Yes."

He's clearly already made his decision.

I study him. "Are you sure about this? I can't guarantee your safety here either," I tell him honestly. "Not with so many here who will only remember you as Vincenzo's general."

"I've got a little money saved up," he admits quietly. His gaze flicks to Mia. "I think it might be best if I leave the city. I'm just asking for a safe place to stay until I can get through the wards."

The wards. Another thing I haven't had time to think about since becoming High Alpha. Grey said only the alphas had access to them, but I have no idea how it works. And now Charlie wants to get through them. To leave.

"Have you talked to Mia about this?" I ask.

"Not yet."

I bite my lip, wishing there was an easier way.

Charlie's not a direct threat. He proved that when he got us the records we needed to expose Vincenzo's laundering. But him showing up here isn't part of the plan. Giovanni pack won't accept him without knowing what he's done for us, and I won't call him out as a rat without his permission. But the fact remains that he stood by while Vincenzo had me kidnapped and held prisoner. He did nothing while I was forced to be a puppet caught between two men vying for power over this city. And he allowed his daughter to grow up in a city where her life was threatened daily if she didn't comply with whatever orders she was given.

Charlie isn't a threat, but that doesn't mean I trust him. I hope Mia can understand that.

In the end, I nod. "You can stay here until you go." I glance past him to the dozen or so others. "What about them?"

"It's all I could gather on short notice," he says. "They want to swear loyalty to you."

I blink. "They'll renounce Vincenzo as their alpha?"

Charlie's eyes spark with something like hope, and he speaks loud enough for everyone to hear. "They want a new leader. A better future for their children."

For some reason, Grey snarls at that.

I glance at him, and my chest tightens.

His pupils are blown wide, his wolf too close to the surface. His hands shake at his sides, and his entire body vibrates with the kind of rage that only comes from too much buried power.

"Grey," I say quietly.

"They are … my enemy," he says in a strained voice.

Shit.

He's not going to last long with this many of his father's pack members breathing his air.

Behind him, the others nod at Charlie's words.

"We swear our loyalty to the high alpha," the woman says, voice shaking.

The others echo her words.

It's great news. Exactly what I wanted. For the city to turn. For the ones hiding in Vincenzo's shadow to see the light and choose differently. Choose *good*.

But Grey is unraveling beside me.

His fingers dig into my arm suddenly, breath ragged.

"Don't trust them," he grits out.

"They're not lying," I say. "I can feel it."

The alpha power inside me swells as they declare themselves my pack. Their intentions are pure, their words true.

But Grey's wolf is beyond reason.

"I need to leave," he grits out. "Lex—"

"I know," I whisper. I turn, cupping his face, forcing him to meet my eyes. "Go home. I'll meet you there when I can."

His gaze flickers at the word "home," and at least I know he understands my meaning.

"I can't leave you alone," he says.

"I'm not alone. I'll have my pack and yours."

Charlie makes a sound of surprise at that, but I focus solely on Grey.

He hesitates.

I can feel everyone's eyes on us, on him. Trying to understand what's happening. Dutch presses in close, and I know he's preparing to put himself between us like he did at the warehouse.

"You need space," I say. "I'll be okay. Besides, there's someone waiting for you there."

Or I hope there is.

His lips crash into mine—rough and desperate. A promise and a plea all at once.

Then he's gone. Shifted into his wolf and running so fast for the trees that he's nothing but a blur by the time he vanishes through the tree line.

"Do you want me to follow him?" Dutch asks.

"Just…make sure he gets there safely, but don't stay."

He nods, and then he starts jogging toward the woods.

Partway there, I see Crow intercept Dutch, and my shoulders sag in relief. Between the two of them, I know Grey will be in good hands.

I turn back to Charlie.

"You're not coming inside. Not until my guests are gone."

He nods like he expected that.

"But there's a guest house in the back." I hesitate, wincing at the irony of my next words. "I'll have to put guards on you. For your safety."

"I understand," Charlie says.

"I don't trust you," I tell him plainly. "Not entirely. I'm sorry."

"Don't be sorry about that."

I motion to Mia, who approaches us with enough relief that I know she was listening after all. "I'll get him settled," she says.

"And assign Donahue and Camila for watch."

She flashes me a look of gratitude. "Done."

~

LATER, after the defectors have officially sworn loyalty and Andy has found a safe place for them to go where Vincenzo can't find them, I finally let myself breathe.

Kind of.

Andy finds me on the back patio where I'm nursing a glass of wine and hiding from any remaining guests.

She sits in the chair beside mine and holds out a piece of cake.

"It's got rum in it," she offers.

I take it without hesitation. "You're a goddess."

"I know."

We sit in silence for a minute.

Then she says, "Dutch asked me out."

I choke.

She pats my back, smiling ruefully.

"What did you say?" I ask when I can breathe—or talk.

She shrugs. "I haven't given him an answer."

"Why not?"

"I was waiting to see if we survived the day."

Fair.

I glance sideways at her. "Are you going to say yes?"

She shrugs, expression softening. "I don't know. Maybe. He's hot. And weirdly sweet for a guy with permanent murder face."

I laugh. "He's not that scary."

"You're right. I mean, out of that entire pack, he's the least scary one. Mia, on the other hand…"

"Yeah."

As if summoned, Mia appears in the doorway, arms crossed.

"If you tell him I said this, I'll deny it with every breath in my body," she says dryly. "But Dutch is one of the good ones."

Andy smirks.

"And you're not wrong. I'm definitely the scariest."

With that, Mia disappears again like a cryptid.

Andy and I both share a look and then burst out laughing.

In the silence that follows, I get to just sit and eat my cake. It's nice. Not relaxing, exactly, considering how many ways the world is currently on fire. But everyone I know is safe. Even Grey. Dutch texted me to let me know he'd made it to the house after a long run as his wolf. No sign of the darkness in him at all. So, for now, we're all still ourselves.

Andy leans back in her chair, head tilted toward the darkening sky. "I don't know what we're building here, Lexi. But it's starting to feel like something good."

24

GREY

The second I walk away from the crowd at the gate, something snaps loose in my chest. Not like a clean break. More like threads tearing from the inside out, unraveling everything I've been holding together with gritted teeth and willpower. I don't bother with cars or keys. Instead, I head for the woods.

The moment I'm moving, my wolf claws at my skin, desperate to shift. To run. To *move* in some way that lets him out—and lets the pain out with him. Somehow, I know this is the only way to avoid the darkness taking me over, to let my wolf have full control over me, mind and body.

I shift quickly. The force of it is hard, brutal. The kind of shift that hurts more than it should. Muscles tear, bones snap, and the air splits around me as my wolf takes over and launches into the woods.

And I run.

The wind roars past my ears. Trees blur past, and earth churns beneath my paws. My wolf howls—high and wild and feral. Not because he's angry.

Because he's scared.

We're not right. Haven't been since Franco. The power I took from him is still inside me like rusted iron—corroding everything.

I don't know how to fix it.

I don't even know if it can be fixed.

So, I keep running. Long enough that the sun starts to dip behind the trees, dragging the sky with it.

Then I smell him.

Crow.

He doesn't sneak up on me. Doesn't have to. He just runs alongside, quiet and steady. Matching pace like we've done this a hundred times—probably because we have. None of the others know it, but Crow and I used to run together a lot before I left the city. He's the only one who actually knows how to sit in silence, and not just as a beast but as a man. So, even on the nights I told everyone else to stay away, Crow would show up, and we'd run just like this. Never saying a word. Never needing to.

We slow and shift almost in sync near the river. I drop down to the mossy bank and sit, uncaring that we're both naked. Sweat coats my skin. Adrenaline courses through my veins. My wolf is only mildly placated, but I need to see if I can maintain control on my own.

The current of the river is steady, crystal water washing over the smooth stones. I watch it for a moment, the words I want to say sticking in my throat.

Beside me, Crow doesn't say anything. Just stares at the current, arms dangling over his bent knees.

Eventually, I ask, "You mad at me?"

He looks up then. "For what?"

"Finishing him off like that."

He shakes his head. "No."

I wait.

Then he says, "I'm not sorry he's dead. But I don't feel better, either."

I nod, waiting, giving him space to get his words out.

We haven't talked about what happened in that warehouse. And even though I know Alvaro isn't the first man Crow has killed, we only kill our own father once.

Crow leans forward, flicking a stone into the water. "I used to think, if I could just make him see me, respect me, I'd finally matter."

"And now?"

"I don't care what he saw." He looks over at me with haunted eyes—it's a look I recognize. "But I don't know who I am without that fight."

His voice is raw. Like a scab just peeled back.

"I get it," I say.

He glances sideways. "Yeah?"

"For a long time, my whole identity was tied to surviving my old man. Outsmarting him. Beating him. Hating him."

Crow nods slowly. "It keeps you alive. But it doesn't teach you how to live."

We're quiet again.

Then he says, "When I was a kid, cooking felt a little bit like living."

"Makes sense. Eating your food feels like living to me."

He grins, and it's a bright light in the darkness of his expression. There and gone way too fast before the ghosts of his past return. "My mom taught me to cook, you know. Made everything from scratch and insisted I do the same. It was annoying as hell at the time." He snorts at some memory then immediately sobers again. "She always dreamt of opening a restaurant of her own."

I don't say anything.

I know we're both thinking how fucked up it is that she didn't get to live long enough for that dream to happen. That Alvaro did—but squandered his life by being a fucking monster.

Finally, he adds, "Sometimes, I still think about opening a place. Just mine. Small. No blood on the floor, you know what I mean."

I look at him. "You should."

A muscle in his jaw twitches. "I don't even know what that kind of life looks like."

"Maybe that's the point," I say. "You get to find out."

He doesn't say anything to that, and the silence lasts for a long while after that.

At the end of it, we don't hug. Don't do some dramatic goodbye. Crow just stands up, shifts again, and disappears into the trees like he never stopped running.

I wait a minute.

Then I pull out my phone and type a message.

Need your help. Just you and Mac. Location incoming. —G

Then I head for the safe house. Home.

The sun is nearly gone when I get there. Dusk casts long shadows across the front porch, the whole place soaked in stillness.

But it's not as still as it should be.

I'm not alone here either.

I slip into the backyard and let myself in through the door off the master bedroom. Silently, I snag a pair of shorts and pull them on. My wolf paces under my skin, not with rage this time but something heavier. Anticipation. Exhaustion. Dread.

I step through the bedroom door, expecting some assassin from my father's pack.

Instead, I freeze at the sight of my mother.

Serena Diavolo stands at the stove, stirring a pot like she's lived here for years, though her hand trembles as she sets the spoon on the counter. Her hair is down. She's wearing one of Lexi's old hoodies. She looks... softer. Less like the regal, put-together woman I know and more like some girlish version of herself I've never met.

She turns, though I've made no sound. Her eyes meet mine, and in them live all the memories of my failures.

I can't move. I'm not sure I'm breathing. What's she doing here? How did she find it? Not that I don't want her here, but her presence means this place is no longer safe. When she returns to my father, we risk—

"Hi, Grey," she says softly.

"What—how are you here?"

She steps toward me slowly, as if she thinks I might bolt. "Lexi slipped me a note at the funeral."

She holds out a scrap of paper. I take it and read Lexi's handwritten words: *If you want out, come.* Underneath it are coordinates to the house.

And then I realize: the quick greeting we gave her at Franco's funeral. Lexi's hand in my mother's, squeezing. Slipping her a note, apparently.

My mate did this.

In the middle of her grief, amid fighting a war with my father, under the weight of leading a pack that didn't ask for her—she still thought of my mother. Of me.

A knot forms in my chest. Not just for my mom, who made it out, but for Lexi, who made it happen.

"I didn't know," I whisper. "She didn't tell me."

"She said you wouldn't let yourself hope if you knew. Said you'd try to talk her out of such a risk."

"Wait. When did she say all that?"

"She told Razor to come find me after the funeral. He helped me unbind myself, and then he drove me here. I didn't even go home to pack a bag."

Her smile wavers. The dark circles beneath her eyes are suddenly more pronounced. She's afraid.

Her words hit me like a ton of bricks. "Wait, you left the pack?"

She nods. "It was the only way, right?"

I swallow hard, knowing how much pain her wolf must be in without an alpha to ground her. "Yeah."

As a kid, I'd begged her to do it. But she could never bring herself to take that final step. Like it was too painful. But I realized what she'd meant was it would be too permanent. And now…

My legs finally start working again, carrying me forward. I grab her shoulders, squeezing. "You're safe now. He can't reach you here."

"I know," she says. "I'd like to join your pack. If you'll have me." Her lip wobbles.

"I would be honored," I tell her.

I fully intend to be the one to hug her. But then she opens her arms, and I step into them like I'm ten years old and my father has just finished a tirade and stormed out. Like we're both just trying to pick up the pieces of ourselves after he's gone. Like, even though she's the one who bore the brunt of it, she's still the one comforting me. But this time—finally—we're the ones who left him.

25

LEXI

The funeral reception seems to last forever, the last guests lingering so late I wonder if I'm supposed to offer them a room or kick them out. Elena makes the choice for me, not-so-subtly shooing them out. Finally, sometime after nine p.m., the house is empty again.

In my room, I sit on the edge of the bed and kick my heels off, trying to work up the motivation to shower. A quick glance at my phone reveals Grey still hasn't sent any new updates since the last one two hours ago, when he texted: She's here. Settling in. Thank you.

I set the phone aside and try not to give in to the urge to ask when he'll be back. He deserves this time with his mom. She needs him more than I do right now.

My phone vibrates on the nightstand, and I grab it only to deflate when I see it's just another text from Andy. She and Mia have sent a barrage of updates over the last hour, including a schedule change for the patrol unit on duty tonight, a written report from the gate guard about all activity over the last three hours (none of it threatening), and a heads-up about Charlie's guard assignments.

I ignore them.

For one second, I want to pretend I'm not the high alpha.

That I'm just Lexi Ryall, a girl who isn't struggling to survive but also isn't in charge of anyone but herself.

The door clicks open, and I already know it's him. I feel it before the sound. The way the air thickens. The shift in gravity.

When I look up, Grey stands in the doorway like he's braced for war. But his eyes… fuck, his eyes are soft. Tired. Hollow.

"Hey," I say.

He closes the door behind him and crosses the room in three long strides.

I stand just in time for him to catch me. His arms come around my waist, and I bury my face in his shoulder.

"You're back," I whisper.

"I'll always come back, princess."

We stand like that for a long time. It's the first time I've felt steady all day.

He pulls back just enough to look at me. His thumb brushes my cheekbone.

"How's your mom?" I ask.

His throat works once before he answers. "Safe. She's staying at the house until we can find something more permanent. She left his pack. Said she's not going back to him."

"Good." I press my forehead to his. "I'm glad she got out."

His palm cups my cheek, his thumb stroking the corner of my mouth. "You did that. You gave her the way out."

I shrug, but my chest aches. "I thought maybe… if she had the chance, she'd take it."

"You were right. And I—" He swallows hard. "Thank you."

A beat passes. Then I ask, quieter, "Does that make up for letting someone else know about the house?"

A small, wry smile twitches at the corner of his mouth. "Yes."

"Even though Razor also now knows where our private sanctuary is and probably won't ever give us a moment's peace there?"

He snorts. "That asshole's never given me peace anywhere else." His gaze darkens, not with anger but something else. Something predatory.

I blink against the sudden sting behind my eyes.

"You okay?" I ask him.

His brows furrow. "Not completely."

"Grey…"

He shuts his eyes and opens them again. They're clearer now. "But I'm better when I'm with you."

The words hit me like a heartbeat I forgot I was missing. I lean in and kiss him—soft and lingering.

When I pull back, his hands find the zipper on my dress.

I don't stop him.

"I missed you," he murmurs as the fabric slips down my shoulders.

"I'm right here."

"You were amazing today." He kisses the curve of my neck. "A true leader."

"I couldn't afford to fall apart."

"You can now. If you need to."

I grip the hem of his shirt and tug it up.

He lets me, his skin warm under my fingers. He cups my face as I lean in, our lips brushing again and again until I can't remember what air tastes like without him.

We move toward the bed in a slow, reverent tangle. My wolf is quiet for once. Soothed by his scent, his touch.

We climb into bed, half-dressed and half-drunk on each other. His hands are on my hips, mine in his hair, and our breathing turns shallow.

We talk between kisses. Fragments of our feelings. Fears. Dreams. As much as I don't want to talk about Vincenzo while we're naked in bed together, it's where the conversation inevitably leads.

"He accused us of murdering Alvaro," I whisper. "On camera. In front of the press."

Grey's jaw tightens. "Let him. It's not like we didn't do it."

I snort. "That's not comforting."

"I talked to Crow."

"How is he?" I ask.

"He's trying to figure out where he goes from here. What's left for him besides his anger." He pauses, then adds, "Vengeance isn't very fulfilling."

"He needs hope," I say quietly. "We all do. But your father—"

"Will not win."

I start to say something else.

Then the door bangs open.

We break apart like guilty teenagers.

Andy stands there, out of breath, still in her funeral

dress. "Sorry," she says quickly. "But you need to come downstairs."

Grey is already up, pulling on his shirt. "What happened?"

"Dr. Severin escaped."

"What? How?"

"Some kind of distraction outside his home. The guard was knocked out from behind. And the doc is gone."

"We should have put him in a cell," I mutter, echoing Mia's sentiment since the beginning.

"What about the witch?" Grey asks.

"We're checking now."

Grey grabs his phone.

"There's more," Andy says grimly, and I brace myself.

"Report came in five minutes ago. A patrol reported movement at Capo."

I'm out of bed and rifling through the closet for something other than a dress. "What kind of movement?"

"Patrol says someone was there. Maybe more than one person. And the power's back on."

My blood goes cold. "I told them to shut it down."

Her expression is hard. "Sounds like they didn't listen."

An hour later, the SUV carrying me, Grey, Andy, Mia, and Dutch rolls to a stop outside the rusted chain-link gate. Same gate we shoved through last time. And just like before, the lights are all on. It's more noticeable at night too. Fluorescents buzz behind two grimy windows, casting a ghostly glow that shouldn't be there.

The place was supposed to be shut down. Condemned. Watched.

Instead, it looks ready to welcome us back like we're expected.

My stomach turns.

Dutch steps out first, weapon drawn. He pushes through the sagging gate. It swings open with a creak that drags across my spine. We follow him single file, boots crunching gravel.

Behind us, Crow and Razor climb out of their car and meld into our group like shadows.

The lab looms ahead like a concrete monolith—same cracked paint, same broken windows.

Andy tests the main door. Unlocked. She glances back, face pale.

"Be ready," Mia mutters.

We step inside.

And I stop breathing.

Everything is gone.

The rooms that previously contained hospital beds. The medical coolers. The equipment. Even the security doors and swipe pads. All of it—gone.

But the power's still running. The air hums with electricity. The scent of disinfectant clings to the walls like they just finished cleaning up. Like someone wiped the place down and left ten minutes ago.

Dutch peels off down the left hallway. Andy takes the right. Mia and I move straight ahead, into the central lab room.

And it's just... empty.

Not just cleared.

Scrubbed.

No monitors. No files. No restraints. Even the shelves have been ripped out of the walls. A steel bracket swings loosely from one bolt above the empty counter.

"What the hell," Mia whispers.

My wolf stirs. Uneasy.

"It's Vincenzo," I say. "It has to be. This is his way of getting what I promised him."

"Fuck," Mia says, frustration lining her features. "Where do you think he took it all?" she asks Grey.

He shakes his head. "No idea."

Andy returns, frowning. "They stripped the data storage room. Backup drives are gone. Server racks. All of it."

A pressure builds behind my ribs. Tight. Buzzing.

"They were supposed to shut this place down," I say. "We had a plan in place. Security patrols."

"Apparently not enough," Mia mutters.

I round on her. "Don't."

Her brows lift. "Don't what?"

"Make it sound like this is *our* failure."

"I didn't say—"

"You implied it."

"Lexi—"

"No." My voice is lower now. Edged with a growl.

Dutch returns, frowning. "Lower level's cleared. Not even a fucking bed pan. They took *everything*."

The pressure in my chest spikes. My claws scrape the inside of my skin.

"Lexi," Mia says carefully. "You need to breathe."

"I *am* breathing."

But I'm not.

The shift comes hard and fast.

Pain rips through my arms. My jaw snaps wide. My vision sharpens—and goes red.

My wolf surges to the surface with a snarl, fangs bared, claws out.

Dutch freezes, hands up. "Lex…"

My limbs coil, ready to lunge. I can smell his blood. His pulse. His fear.

I blink.

This is Dutch.

I wrench myself backward, biting down a scream as the shift retreats just as violently. My bones grind. My claws vanish. I'm left panting, sweating, shaking.

The silence is a living thing.

Andy stares, wide-eyed. Mia looks like she's stopped breathing.

Dutch exhales. "You good?"

I force the words out. "I'm fine."

Mia steps forward slowly. "You're not."

I glare at her. "I said I'm fine."

"You lost control."

"No, I—"

"That was your wolf, not you." Mia's voice is gentle. That's what makes it worse.

"I'm sorry," I whisper.

"Don't be." Mia's voice doesn't waver, but she's looking past me, her gaze sweeping the room. "Where's Grey?" she asks.

No one answers.

I look down at my hands.

Still human.

Barely.

But only because my wolf senses the true threat.

26

GREY

I smell them before I see them. Diavolo stench thick on the wind. I'm halfway out the front door when I see movement in the trees.

Then the howls start.

"Ambush," I roar, already shifting.

My bones tear and reform mid-sprint, pain shearing through me as my wolf bursts free. I don't stop to give orders. Don't check whether the others are behind me.

I know they are.

We've done this before. Most of us anyway.

Already shifted, Dutch appears on my left—fast and lethal, the blade of our formation. On four legs, Razor is behind him, solid and brutal, our shield. Sleek and fast, Mia takes the right, precise and sharp like a scalpel. And Lexi—

Lexi is at my side. Already full wolf.

Her white fur blurs in my periphery as we charge the clearing. There's no hesitation in her. No fear.

Only fury.

They hit us like a wave.

Fangs and claws and snarling bodies crash together in a chaos of teeth and blood. I tear through the first wolf that lunges for me—rip his throat and fling his body aside. Lexi takes the next, leaping high, jaws locking around the spine.

It snaps like dry wood.

Another wolf goes for her flank.

I'm there before he makes contact.

I slam into him, jaws crushing down on his skull. Blood sprays across my muzzle, hot and metallic.

Lexi doesn't thank me.

She doesn't need to.

This is what I was made for. Not speeches. Not strategy.

Death.

On my left, Mia flips a wolf onto his back and rips him open with surgical precision. Razor barrels through two more, flinging one into a tree. Dutch is a blur of claws and snapping jaws—his wolf moves like smoke, cutting down enemies before they know he's there.

And then—Crow arrives.

He joins the fight from the far side like a wrecking ball. No warning. Just a howl and a flash of dark brown fur. He slams into a Diavolo brute twice his size and shreds him to pieces.

The ground is wet now. Mud and blood and fur.

Lexi and I tear through another pair trying to circle back. Her fangs sink into one's shoulder while I take the other's throat. They fall together, twitching.

My pulse is wild. I'm not tired. Not even winded.

I'm *alive*.

Magic buzzes inside me like adrenaline. Franco's voice echoes in my mind to show no mercy. I have a vague sense that my form is different somehow. Not quite my wolf. Not quite human. But then there are more things to kill, and I forget all about what I look like.

I am pure darkness.

Death incarnate.

Another wolf stumbles, blood pouring from his side. He raises a paw, whines—surrenders.

I glance at Lexi.

She doesn't hesitate.

Neither do I.

We lunge.

He dies between our jaws.

There's no room for mercy.

Not anymore.

Not when my father keeps coming. Not when they keep hurting our people.

When the last enemy wolf falls, the clearing is a graveyard.

Panting, shaking, I approach her, lungs burning. Lexi's still a wolf, pacing beside me, blood soaking her white fur like paint.

She's beautiful. Terrifying.

Mine.

Somehow, that thought is enough to make the darkness recede. My wolf returns. Then my human form. Until I can feel my control returning over my own thoughts.

All that matters is her.

"Shift," I whisper. "Come back."

She stops.

For a long moment, I think she might refuse. Or that she's stuck, unable to find her humanity again. But then she shudders. The fur melts away, leaving her naked and blood-slicked, crouched in the dirt. She lifts her head, and her striking green eyes are all Lexi again.

I drop to my knees beside her, fingers brushing her dirt-streaked cheek. "You okay?"

She nods once. "You?"

Despite the carnage, I almost smile. "Better now."

Around us, the others are shifting back, some groaning, some limping. Crow helps Mia to her feet. Razor wipes blood from his arm, scanning the tree line for stragglers.

I do a quick count.

Razor. Mia. Dutch. Crow. Lexi.

"Where's Andy?" Dutch asks.

Silence.

Everyone freezes.

I look to Dutch.

He shakes his head slowly. "She was next to me when it started. Then I lost sight of her."

Crow steps forward. "I caught her scent when I first arrived. She was fighting. Then… nothing."

My stomach drops.

I sniff, but there's no sign of Andy anywhere nearby.

Lexi stands, her legs wobbly but her voice low and lethal. "They took her."

I can feel my claws again. The darkness whispering that I was too slow, too merciful.

They didn't come here to win.

They came to *distract* us.

And it worked.

27

LEXI

Andy's gone. The realization hits me hard, standing in the blood-soaked clearing, breathing in the aftermath of the attack. Bodies litter the ground, but all I see is the empty space where Andy should have been standing with us. My hands shake, adrenaline burning through my veins, twisting into guilt and panic.

She's my second. I was supposed to protect her.

"Lexi," Grey's voice is low, careful, like approaching a cornered animal. "This isn't on you."

I whip around, eyes wild. "Then who the hell is it on? She trusted me."

Mia steps up beside me, jaws clenched, eyes blazing with fury. "Fuck that. This is Vincenzo's doing. It has to be. Revenge for what we did to Alvaro."

My heart pounds. Mia is right, but it doesn't make the ache any easier. Andy was taken because she was mine—my responsibility. My pack. My friend.

"We need answers," Dutch says, voice sharp with tension. He looks at Mia. "Charlie might know something."

"Fine." My voice cracks, bitter and raw. "Let's go."

Mia, Grey, and I drive back to the mansion in silence. Razor remained behind to run the clean-up with the security team we dispatched. Dutch and Crow opted to shift and run back. Said their wolves needed to blow off steam. I already know nothing will make my wolf settle, not until we find Andy.

Back at the estate, the three of us pull on clothes and then head straight for the pool house. Donahue is standing at the door. He takes one look at our faces and snaps to attention.

"What happened?" he asks.

"Come with us," Grey says, and Donahue follows us inside.

In the small living room, Charlie sits in a plush chair, but the comfort is wasted on him. His face is pale, exhausted, the eyes of a man who's played every wrong hand.

"Hey, Dad," Mia says softly.

"What's wrong?" he asks, gaze darting between our faces.

"Andy's missing," I say flatly, not bothering with pleasantries.

Charlie sits straighter, his jaw tightening. "Vincenzo?"

"We think so," Grey says.

"You tell me," I snap.

"Lexi," Mia murmurs, but I don't let up.

"He accused us of killing Alvaro in front of the media. And all but declared he was going to retaliate. Now, Franco's lab has been cleaned out, and Dr. Severin is missing, which suggests he's likely found a new home for his fucked-up science projects. And I only know one person more fucked up than Severin. So, hold up your end of this and tell me where he is."

Charlie hesitates, and I step forward, snarling. "Don't. Don't protect him."

His eyes flash, not with defiance but resignation. "I'm not. I'm just… If he took Andy, it means…"

"It means what?" Grey snarls.

Charlie winces. "Vincenzo's working with Dr. Severin, has been for a while. They're developing a serum. Something to make him a super alpha beyond what Franco did to himself—to you."

"Are you fucking joking?" Grey's voice comes rough, incredulous from behind me.

Charlie shakes his head, slow and heavy. "I don't know the science or how close they are to perfecting it, but it would make him stronger than you, stronger than Lexi. Powerful enough to challenge you both—and win."

The air is sucked from my lungs. Of course Vincenzo decided to take matters into his own hands. I'd stupidly thought that withholding my blood samples would thwart his attempts to do something so horrible. I should have known he'd have a backup plan. Or maybe I was the backup plan. Maybe he's been capable of this all along.

"Doesn't he realize the side effects Grey and Lexi have been feeling? The instability of their wolves?" Mia asks.

"He thinks he's stronger," Charlie says tiredly.

I stare at Charlie, stomach roiling. The idea of Vincenzo becoming something like that makes my wolf pace restlessly beneath my skin.

"What does Andy have to do with any of this?" I ask.

"It could be a simple act of vengeance," Charlie says, but his tone makes it clear it's more than that.

"What aren't you saying?" I ask.

"He likely plans to use her as a test subject," he says quietly.

A snarl rips from my throat. The wildness I felt earlier slams through me again, and it's all I can do to remain human.

"Where is this place?" I demand.

"There's an office building across from Altobello's."

"In the middle of the fucking city?" Mia asks incredulously.

Charlie looks away. "Vincenzo believes hiding in plain sight is the best strategy. Always has." His voice is hoarse as he adds, "He's been moving equipment there in pieces, quiet, secretive."

Grey curses, low and vicious.

"Dad," Mia says, her voice breaking. "How do you know?" But disappointment is already written into her expression.

Charlie takes one look at her, and his shoulders sag. "I helped him secure the lease and set it up, before…" he trails off, face crumbling into shame. "Before I knew how far he'd go."

I leave Charlie in silence, my stomach turning as I walk out the door and into the starlit night. The others follow, all except for Mia. Whatever she's saying to him in there, I can't hear it—and that's fine by me. I don't envy her pain, but I also can't watch her look at him like that anymore. Like she wants to forgive him. I'm not sure I feel the same way.

"What do you want to do?" Donahue asks, and it takes me a moment longer than it should to realize he's talking to me and not Grey.

Dutch and Grey hover beside him, everyone looking at me. Grey nods as if to signal he's letting me decide what comes next.

"Call Camila and fill her in," I tell Donahue. "And anyone else you trust. We need them to be ready at first light."

He doesn't question me, simply nods and returns to his post outside the pool house, already dialing on his phone.

Dutch and Grey follow me into the house where I prowl through the darkness toward the study. It's the one place in the house Andy's presence still lingers. Maybe because she and I have already spent so much time together in here. But it makes me feel closer to her. Less like I've lost her already.

Grey follows me into the room but doesn't say a word, simply lets me pace like a caged animal. A moment later, Dutch appears with three glasses and a bottle. I can smell the whiskey from here and take it gladly when he passes the glasses around.

The liquid burns my throat, but I welcome it. The way it slices through my senses. I hold my empty glass out for a refill. Dutch pours it, but not without murmuring a warning, "If you want a buzz, you're going to be disappointed. Wolf metabolism's going to burn it off too fast."

I empty the glass, exhaling against the burn in my throat. For the first time since becoming a wolf, I wish I were still human. If only so I could lose myself to the numbness of the alcohol. But hiding has never been my style before, and I'm not going to start now.

So, I set the empty glass aside and force myself to focus on a plan.

"Hey," Razor says as he and Crow arrive. "Did Charlie give us anything?"

Dutch holds out a glass. "Yeah, but you're going to want one of these."

Razor takes one, but Crow shakes his head and takes up a spot against the shelf by the window.

I listen as Grey tells them what Charlie said about Vincenzo and his new lab.

"How could he be stronger, though?" Razor's eyes narrow skeptically. "You can't just become more alpha. I mean, I'm not a scientist, but even I know that's not how it works.

Dutch folds his arms, tense and restless. "Maybe Vincenzo knows something we don't. Dr. Severin clearly held back information when we spoke to him before. He was hiding something even then."

"He never intended to fight with politics," Grey says quietly, voice edged with grim realization. "He always planned to use brute force. He just wanted to be strong enough first."

I stare at Grey, dread pooling in my gut. He's right. All the posturing, the accusations, the media—a political battle was never Vincenzo's endgame. It was always violence. Always bloodshed.

"What's the play?" Razor asks, restless already, and I know he wants to fight. Right now, tonight.

"We need to verify Charlie's information," I say, and Grey nods. "But once we do, we're going to get Andy back, whatever it takes."

"Fucking right we are," Dutch echoes.

Crow steps forward. "Razor and I will go now to scout."

Razor nods in agreement, face grim. "That asshole's just fucked with us for the last time."

I meet each of their eyes, heart swelling with gratitude and fear. "Be careful. We don't know how many guards he has, but I think we should assume he'll be watching for us."

"We should double the patrols around this place for tonight," Dutch adds.

"I'll go talk to Donahue," I say wearily.

"I got it." Razor starts for the door.

"Thanks," I tell him gratefully. When they're gone, I turn to Grey. "Someone should check on your mom," I say.

"I'll do it." Dutch drains his glass again too, before setting it aside. "My wolf could use a run right now."

"Thanks, call if there's anything," Grey tells him.

"Back at you, brother."

When we're alone, Grey's expression is tight.

"I want to go tonight," I say.

"I know."

"What if something happens to her before we get there?"

"It won't."

"You don't know that."

"You're right," he admits. "But I know my father. And if we go in there before we have a solid plan, we'll lose. And that won't help her either."

I swallow the frustrated scream that builds in my throat. He's right, but it still sucks. Around us, the house feels suddenly much quieter and emptier. The shadows longer.

"We should try to get some sleep," I say reluctantly.

"You go ahead. I'll be up soon."

I hesitate, trying to read his mood through the bond. But it's clouded, like he's got some kind of wall up between us. We haven't talked about the way he became some darker, deadlier version of his wolf earlier tonight. Or the way his bloodthirst filtered through our bond, seeping into me. I don't bring it up, even though I should. Without answers, it just feels exhausting to discuss.

And it's not like we can afford for him to sit out of the fight.

But I study him now, worry spiking that, one of these times, he'll shift into that *thing* and won't be able to shift back. "Do you need anything? If your wolf needs to run, we can—"

"No, it's not that." He drops his head. "I just… I think I need some time alone. Before tomorrow. When I face my dad, I think it's going to be for the last time, and I… I just need some time with that."

I nod, and for the second time tonight, I'm honestly glad to avoid the pain. Not having a father is bad enough. Having one betray you, or worse, try to kill you, is far beyond what I've felt over losing my own father so young. Even Franco never actually tried to end my life. He sent others to do it for him. But this is different.

Tomorrow, Grey will kill his father.

That's not a thing I can begin to understand.

"Take all the time you need," I say, rising on my toes to press a kiss to his cheek. "I'll be here waiting."

28

GREY

The moon hangs low tonight. Its glow filters through a thick canopy of trees, casting the small clearing in silver shadows. The air is muggy with the scent of pine and damp earth. But beneath it, I scent the tang in the air that is the ward line. Meeting out in the open is a risk, but it can't be helped. The wards still haven't been changed since Franco died, and I'm not naïve enough to think Levi and Mac will slip in and out unnoticed. But we're far enough out from any roads or even running trails that there's no chance of other wolves spotting us. It's quiet here. Peaceful.

My mind is neither of those things.

I wasn't lying when I told Lexi I needed some time before tomorrow's inevitable battle. Somehow, it's always felt as if my father and I were headed toward this finality. A moment one of us won't walk away from. And while I've known it would eventually come to this, and that he won't be stopped any other way, it's still a heavy thing to face.

I've done a lot of hard shit. Took down a lot of bad

people. But taking out my own father is next level. And the worst part is that I already know I won't even hesitate.

What if that makes me the same kind of monster as him?

I can't bear to ask that question aloud. Or to even think about what that kind of kill might do to my wolf or my own sanity. Not to mention the dark creature whose grip on me grows with every hour. Destroying my father would satisfy that *thing* in a way I'm not sure I can come back from. But the worst part is, even knowing I might lose myself won't stop me. Nothing can change my mind about doing whatever it takes to protect my people and my pack.

The soft crunch of footsteps snaps me from my thoughts, and two figures emerge from the shadows. I tense out of pure instinct, muscles coiling, but even before my hands form into fists or my wolf can stir inside me, I know it's them.

Levi and Mac, walking side by side, moving like extensions of each other. Mates. Partners. Co-alphas.

The Black Moon Pack once thrived on rejecting their own mates as a show of strength, but Mac and Levi fought to change that. Now, they're the strongest mated pair I know. After five years fighting alongside Levi for his right to choose his mate, I know he'll understand what's at stake for me.

"Hey, stranger," Levi says, his expression friendly despite the cool calculation in his gaze. Levi's the only other person I've known who is constantly assessing the threats in a space and adjusting accordingly.

"Good to see you, Grey," Mac adds, stepping forward to embrace me, but I hold up a hand, and Levi tugs her back.

"It's best if you stay on that side of the ward line," I

explain. "Crossing it would bring others, and I don't want to explain what we're doing out here."

Mac looks defiant, like she wants to argue and do it anyway, but Levi nods at me. "We're on your turf. We'll do it your way."

I exhale. "Thanks for coming," I say gratefully.

"You didn't give us much notice," Levi says, the corner of his mouth pulling into a half-grin. "Something big must be going down if you're asking for help."

"You're enjoying this," I say wryly.

"The first and only time Grey asks me for a favor?" Levi snorts. "Damn right I'm enjoying it."

I roll my eyes. The fucker is never going to let me live this down. "I'd say I'm owed more than one," I remind him.

"I owe you my life, brother," Levi says, instantly serious.

The memories of battles we fought together are a barrage inside my head, but I just nod at that.

"You look good," Mac says softly, studying me. "Tired, but good."

"It's been a rough few weeks," I say, my voice tighter than I intend.

"Is that why you asked us to consult a hex witch on that research you sent us?" she asks.

"I need to know if alpha power mixed with hex magic can poison someone."

"Poison how?" Mac asks.

"Make them go mad," I say quietly, and her eyes widen.

"Grey, what the fuck is going on?" Levi asks.

"It's better if you don't know the details—"

"No way." He shakes his head. "You kept quiet about your past all these years, and I respected your privacy, but this isn't something we can help with blindly. What's happening? Is it your family? Is someone in trouble?"

I exhale heavily, looking away before forcing myself to meet his gaze. "It's not my family. It's me."

I tell them everything as quickly as I can—about how I helped Franco try to kill my old man five years ago but failed miserably, about my father's orders to kidnap the heir in a coup attempt, about falling for Lexi while I held her prisoner. Then I tell them about the experiments and the poisoned power I inherited when I killed Franco.

It feels both wrong and right to finally tell them everything. Levi and I spent years fighting a rebellion together, and even then, I never uttered a word about who I really am. How I grew up. The shock of it registers on their faces as I talk, but neither of them interrupts. They keep their shit together, which is just evidence of everything we've been through.

When I finish, Levi shakes his head. "I knew you had some darkness behind you, Grey, but *the* mafia pack? Damn."

Mac nods, her expression gentle. "It explains a lot. Why you were always so careful, always watching our backs. You've been in survival mode your entire life."

"Yeah," I say quietly, throat tight. Their understanding is bordering on pity, and I can't take that, so I steer the conversation back to what I need most. "But this alpha power—I feel it, twisting inside me. Franco was evil, but it's more than that. I think it has to do with the serum that turned on his LAG gene. It was laced with hex magic, and I think it's what was killing him before I… Whatever was wrong with him is infecting me. Can alpha power do that? Corrupt you? I mean, we all saw Crigger."

"No," Mac says firmly, her voice calm but unyielding. "Alpha power amplifies who you already are. If you're an asshole, you're just a bigger asshole. *That* was Crigger's problem."

Levi opens his mouth like he wants to make a comment about their former alpha, but Mac shoots him a glare that has him closing his mouth again. "But you, Grey," she continues, "You're one of the good ones. Alpha power can't turn you into something you're not."

Levi nods, the humor gone. "She's right. You're strong because of your own integrity and your commitment to protect the people you love. Don't confuse that with corruption, even if it means you have to get your hands dirty."

I blow out a breath.

Their certainty helps, but it doesn't erase my fear entirely. I run a hand over my face. "So, whatever's causing this, if it's not me, then it's something from Franco's alpha essence. Something in that serum that made him so strong—and so fucking dark."

Levi exchanges a glance with Mac, something unspoken passing between them. "We showed the research to Chloe from the Forest Hills coven. She's a hex witch and an herbologist who studies medicines for shifters—"

"Did she find anything?"

They exchange a look, and something passes between them. Some silent conversation only fated mates can have. It sends my fear skyrocketing.

Levi cocks his head, studying me. "You said you're already mated to Lexi?"

"Yeah."

Another look exchanged. I fist my hands to keep from smashing one of them into Levi to get him to talk.

"We can't really smell her on you," Mac says.

"What the hell are you talking about?" I growl. Their words feel like some kind of threat against my mate. Or, at least, that's how my wolf takes it. Because it doesn't make any sense.

"Your scent is…" Mac shakes her head. "I smell a she-wolf on you, but not like a mated pair."

"That's impossible," I snap. "We claimed each other days ago."

"But she's the alpha of the Giovanni pack," Levi says carefully.

"Yeah."

"And you're the alpha of your own pack now," he adds.

"What the fuck does—"

"Mates—true fated mates," Mac says softly, "are meant to share a bond that goes deeper than any pack bond ever will."

"I know that," I say, my words clipped. Had they come here to insult and lecture me?

"However," Mac says carefully, and Levi angles himself closer to her, "a pack bond is still a necessary part of the equation."

"No shit."

Mac lifts a brow. "You just said your pack doesn't include Lexi."

I blink then shake off her insinuation, even if it does raise my wolf's hackles that someone is questioning our devotion to our mate. "Lexi is my mate, which makes her my pack by default. You don't understand our hierarchy—"

But Mac shakes her head. "Maybe for another wolf, that could be true, but this alpha power you both have with the hex magic woven into it… We think it's changed the way you bonded. Chloe said the gene mutation elevated your wolf so there would be no equal, so the wolf in power could rule alone—"

"Lexi has it, too, though," I say quickly.

"Right. Which is why I think you have to claim each other as pack to fully seal it—to truly share it."

"Share it?" I echo, "You want me to let this darkness inside her too? No way. Absolutely fucking not."

"Your bond with Lexi," Levi interrupts. "Do you feel it right now?"

"Of course I do."

"Where is she?"

"She's at the estate."

"Do you know that in your head, or do you feel it through your bond?"

"I..." I blink, realization dawning. My sense of Lexi's location points vaguely east and suggests a distance of several miles... but that's it.

My gaze snaps to theirs. "What the fuck," I breathe.

Mac's eyes glimmer with sympathy. "These injections your former alpha gave himself, between the gene mutation and the hex magic...Chloe said it's too much power for one wolf. Trying to contain it in a singular shifter—even an alpha—is basically only ever going to end badly."

"Shit." My chest hurts as the hope I'd begun to feel is stamped out.

"But you can stop containing it in just one wolf," Mac adds.

My head snaps up. "What are you talking about?"

"Alpha power is meant to be shared." Mac looks at Levi, love shining in her eyes as bright as the fucking moon. "Two alphas—fated mates—stabilizing each other."

I stare at her. No, I stare past her. My head spins. My hope reignites.

"You've closed yourself off from the bond with your mate," Mac says, "But the key to stopping the madness is to let her in."

"Franco never would have done that," I say.

"Maybe it's the missing piece in the research. The reason why he could never make it work properly," Levi says quietly.

"Because he didn't understand how loving someone can make you stronger," I say, laughing, but there's no humor in it.

Mac grins, a wicked glint in her eye. "When are these idiot alphas ever going to realize fated mates are the key to everything?"

"How do I let her in?" I ask, impatience and frustration sending me pacing back and forth along the boundary line. "We claimed each other. I don't know what else I'm supposed to do."

Another exchanged look, and I have to bite back curses at the way they seem so in sync with one another. They're right, though. Lexi and I aren't this connected. Not yet.

"According to Chloe, magic helped create the problem, so magic should be able to fix it."

"And if I don't have a witch lying around?"

He frowns. "The only other thing I can think of is a hex blade, but they're impossible to—"

"I have one."

They both blink at me.

Mac just shakes her head.

Levi snorts. "Of course you do." He looks at Mac.

"He's still the most mysteriously resourceful person I know. And that's saying something, considering Tripp."

"There's nothing mysterious about Tripp," Mac retorts, but the shared joke is lost on me.

I can't think about anything except the hex blade. About using it to remove whatever magic is allowing my wolf to be held hostage by this creature it's borne inside me. To be free of that, to deepen my bond with Lexi, and feel the kind of connection with her that Levi and Mac have—I'd risk my own life for that. But not hers.

I swallow hard, stomach clenching as reality crashes in around me. "Lexi's wolf is already unstable. Isn't it a risk—giving her more power?"

"I don't think so," Mac says. "You and Lexi—you're mates. Your true bond, without hex magic clouding it, could stabilize both of you. Nature intended alpha pairs to share the load, offer strength to the other when necessary. It's why our very lives are tied together. She can handle this, Grey."

Can she? My heart races. Lexi's fierce, strong, but her wolf… it's barely under her control as it is.

"Look, Grey," Levi says, "we can't make this choice for you. And even though I haven't met your mate yet, I'm willing to bet that, if your wolf chose her, she's not just any wolf. She's special. And strong as hell. Trust that. Trust her. Hell, trust yourself."

"I do," I whisper, emotion thickening my throat. "I trust Lexi with my life, but I'm terrified of hurting her."

"You're not going to hurt her. You'll protect her. Just like you protected us." Mac sounds so sure.

A lump rises in my throat, memories flooding back—the battle we fought together, the rebellion they endured.

How I'd guarded their backs, watching them find each other, becoming stronger together. And now, they're doing the same for me.

"Thanks." For one fleeting moment, I allow vulnerability to show. "Both of you. I missed you."

"Missed you too, brother," Levi says quietly. "You deserve to be happy, Grey. You've spent your life fighting, protecting everyone else. It's time someone had your back. Your wolf picked Lexi for a reason. Don't be afraid of that."

Their words sink deep, calming the storm inside me. I stand, grateful we've had this time together. It grounds me, reminding me of who I am—who I could be without my father's constant threats and violence.

When we part, Levi gives me a knowing look. "You need any backup, just say the fucking word."

"I appreciate that. But I think I have to face this on my own."

Mac smiles, eyes fierce. "If he's anything like Crigger was, he underestimates you. Let that be his downfall."

Their confidence bolsters my own, and as they turn to leave, the ache in my chest eases slightly. I glance toward the sky, breathing deeply as I note the blue hues of dawn lightening the horizon. My heart speeds as I think about everything that awaits us today.

The hex blade's location pulses in my mind, calling to me like a siren.

This has to work. If it doesn't… I don't let myself think about what will happen to our mate bond if that creature takes me over for good.

~

THE SUN's just beginning to rise when I return to the estate. Lexi's in the kitchen, pacing between the sink and the stove, a mug clutched in both hands. Her eyes snap to mine the second I enter, and relief softens her features.

"You're back," she says, like she's been holding that sentence in for hours. Dark circles line her eyes, and I feel a stab of guilt for being responsible.

"I am."

I wrap my arms around her and breathe her in. Steady and warm and mine.

"Where were you? You never came to bed," she says.

I let her go, knowing we're running out of time. "I met a friend of mine out near the wards."

"Who?"

"Levi and Mac. They're the co-alphas of the Black Moon Pack. The ones I told you about."

"I remember," she says, wary now. "But if you're going to try to make me stay with them while you—"

"Nothing like that, I promise," I say quickly.

"Then what?"

Before I can answer, footsteps sound—heavy boots moving fast.

A second later, Razor and Crow appear.

They're both flushed and out of breath, dust and blood on their clothes.

"Vincenzo's already dosing himself," Razor says without preamble. "We got a guard to talk."

Crow jumps in. "He's using something Dr. Severin made. Something that enhances alpha power. Like, way beyond normal."

"Where is he now?" Lexi asks.

"At his lab," Crow says. "Charlie was right about the location, by the way."

"We have to go," Lexi says, pulling away from me, but I hold her tight.

"What's my father doing?" I ask.

"He's passed out from the first injection," Crow says.

"But who knows how long that'll last?" Razor puts in.

Crow doesn't disagree. "The guard thinks he'll wake up stronger than ever. That Vincenzo claims he'll be invincible."

Lexi looks horrified.

Dutch and Mia enter next as if the scent of bad news pulled everyone in. Crow repeats the information for them.

"What about Andy?" Lexi asks, worry etched into her expression.

"The guard didn't know details," Razor says. "Only that she's being held." He casts Dutch an apologetic look.

"We have to move soon," Mia says.

"It's going to be a hell of a fight," Razor warns. "Guard says they have two dozen posted up with full pack back up waiting the moment the alarm goes off. He knows we'll come."

Lexi looks at Dutch, jaw tight. "Do we have the numbers?"

He shrugs. "Enough. If everyone who pledged to us actually shows."

"We'll need them all," Mia says. "Giovanni loyalists, Vincenzo's defectors, new pack, old pack—every able wolf."

It's not the worst news. But Lexi's wolf is pacing under her skin. I can feel it even from here. The tension rolling off her. She's losing control again.

She grips the edge of the counter until her knuckles go

white. "I can't do this if I keep fracturing every time I shift."

That's when I know. This is the moment. Levi and Mac were right. It's time to trust my mate and our wolves.

I step forward. "I might have found a way to fix that—for both of us."

Everyone goes still.

"That's why Levi was here?" Lexi asks, searching my gaze as if she'll be able to read the answers there. It reminds me of Levi and Mac—their connection. And now I see how much of our bond never really took.

"Uh, not to interrupt a good thing, but who the fuck is Levi?" Razor asks.

"Levi and Mac are co-alphas of the Black Moon Pack in Virginia," I say quietly. "They're friends of mine."

Crow's gaze on mine is intense and knowing. "That's where you were," he says. "All the years you were gone." I nod. "You fought with them in their rebellion, didn't you?" Crow asks, but his tone suggests he already knows the answer.

"Seriously? That story is already legendary," Razor says, eyes wide as he looks me over like he's seeing me for the first time.

"Levi and I trained together for a year. And then fought together for several more," I say. "Outside of you all, he's the only wolf I trust to help us."

"What did he say?" Lexi asks.

"They sent the research to a hex wolf in Forest Hills. She doesn't think this is about genetic modifications or poisoned power. She thinks the problem is that we're not bonded deeply enough."

Lexi only stares at me, and I remember the last time she

looked at me like that. When she found out I'd become an alpha of a pack that technically didn't include her. She'd felt like an outsider in my world all over again.

I'd hurt her that night.

And I'm hurting her now.

It's the last piece I need to know this is the right thing. Even if it's dangerous to use a hex blade without a witch to do the spell. Lexi's only ever wanted to belong. Hell, she's fighting for her place here as much as I'm fighting for my home.

This is what I can do for her. To show her she belongs to me. Body and soul—and wolf.

"You think we're not really bonded?" she asks, and the pain in her voice stabs me right through the heart.

"We are," I assure her. "But true mates…that bond is deeper. It's more powerful than what we're sharing now. If we can open it, we'll share more than just our emotions or even our thoughts. We'll share my alpha power. And yours."

"Share our alpha power?" Lexi echoes, brows knitting.

"Mac says it's what packs were always meant to do. Two alphas. Balanced. Bonded. Leading together."

"Now that you mention it, the Lone Wolf Pack did the same thing," Dutch says.

I nod because I heard the same story. Kai and Ash, leading together. It's one of the reasons I think Mac is right about this being the answer.

"My mother used to talk about this," Mia says softly. Her eyes fill with unshed tears, which is a rare sight and shuts us all up. "She says our shifter ancestors believed in this kind of balance, too, but it was lost when the human world's patriarchy bled into our own hierarchy." She smirks, blinking back her tears. “The Black Moon Pack is the perfect example of what happens when an egotistical, power-hungry alpha tries to rewrite how we were meant to live and lead.”

“Didn’t he try to outlaw fated mates at one point?” Razor asks.

“He tried,” I say quietly. “And it got him killed.”

“Well, I for one want to meet this Levi and his mate, Mac, someday,” Mia says. “She sounds like a badass.”

“When we get through this, I’ll make it happen,” I tell her.

She gawks at me. “Seriously? You’ll let all your compartments overlap? Who are you?”

Dutch snorts.

I shake my head and turn back to Lexi.

She blinks at me. “But I’m still unstable. What if my power isn’t safe to share?”

I soften at the hope and fear that shines in her eyes. “Maybe that’s because you’ve been carrying it alone.”

Mia crosses her arms. “What about the hex witch from the lab? Davina. Why didn’t she say anything about this?”

“That’s a good question,” I say. “One I’d like to ask her myself.”

“We sent Broderick and a few others to retrieve her,” Crow says. “But the house was empty when they got there.”

“What about the guards?” I ask.

He shrugs. “Also missing. No sign of any of them.”

“She must be with Vincenzo,” Razor says.

Lexi exhales slowly. “So, we can’t wait.”

“No,” I say. “We do the ritual. Now.”

“Wait. Ritual?” Mia echoes. “Like with magic?”

"The magic used in the gene serum is likely what's clouding our bond," I say.

"Don't we need a witch to break a hex spell?" she asks pointedly.

"Not if we have a hex blade," I tell her.

"Fuck," Razor mutters, and I can't blame him. The hex blade packs a punch none of us have likely forgotten.

"You're seriously going to do this," Mia says, and I don't miss the way Lexi takes in Mia's reluctance.

"If I don't," I say slowly, "Whatever darkness this is inside me—killing my father will only feed it. And if that happens, I'm not sure I can find my way back to myself again."

No one says anything for a moment.

Lexi looks at me, really looks. "You're sure this will work?"

"I'm not sure of anything," I admit. "Except that you have been the only steadying force since the moment that creature took hold of me. If we can strengthen our bond, I think I can shut him out for good. If we don't..." I can't bring myself to finish.

Lexi pulls my face to hers and rests her forehead against mine. "Okay," she breathes. "Then we do it."

I kiss her hard and fast. From here on, we give each other everything.

29

LEXI

The warehouse is chilly, thanks to its concrete walls. Or maybe it's an internal shudder at the memory of all the nightmares I've witnessed here. Last time I stood in here, Alvaro's blood was still wet on the floor. Before that, it was Trucker's and, from what I'm told, Ramsey's. This isn't exactly the place I would have chosen for a magical ritual that will hopefully stabilize our wolves, but it's the perfect place for bloodshed. And apparently, that's the main ingredient necessary, so I guess it fits after all.

Thankfully, we don't use the tiny room in the back where we've kept prisoners. Instead, we remain in the larger space where there aren't already blood stains on the concrete floor and where light filters in through the high, albeit dirt-coated, windows.

It's the least magical feeling ambience I can imagine. But it's remote and undisturbed enough that, if this doesn't work and one of our wolves loses it, hopefully they can contain us.

Grey's been notably silent since we left the house. There's worry lining his brow. I know he thinks he's risking me by doing this, but maybe that's what I appreciate about it. He's letting me protect him just as much as he's protecting me.

Finally, after everything, he's making me feel like his equal partner. Like he considers me capable of fighting alongside him instead of hiding in the background while he fights for me.

It's all I've ever wanted.

I hope to hell this works.

Mia, Dutch, Razor, and Crow stand in a wide circle around us. The hex blade rests on a worn metal table between Grey and me. Apparently, it was stashed in a gym bag in the janitor's closet this entire time. The same bag Grey once showed me and told me to run away with if anything ever happened to him. I guess a hex blade would have gotten me through the wards—and anything else that stood in my way. I just hope it's strong enough to get through to my wolf. And to kill that dark creature inside him that keeps taking him over.

Outside, the wind whines through broken siding, but in here, it's calm.

Calm. And terrifying.

I take a steadying breath and look up at Grey. He stares down at the blade between us as if it's a snake ready to strike.

"We don't have a witch to guide us," I say, voice shakier than I mean for it to be. "How do we know what to do?"

He meets my gaze, eyes dark but clear. "We didn't have one last time either. We just need each other and the blade."

My chest tightens as Mia adds, "And blood."

He nods. "That too."

I glance around the circle—Mia watching with open worry, Razor nodding once when I meet his gaze, Dutch and Crow still and unreadable. These people have followed Grey through thick and thin. And now they do the same for me.

Grey picks up the blade. Even in the dim light, it gleams. Some of my worry must show on my face because he sets it down again.

"We don't have to do this," he says. "If you're not sure—"

"I'm sure," I interrupt, stepping forward.

Because I am. Terrified, yes. But sure.

We're out of time. And this—this is the only thing that's ever made sense. Him. Me. Together. If we're going to stop Vincenzo, it's not going to be through sheer force. It has to be through balance. Through unity. Through power shared. Through love and trust freely given.

Grey draws the blade across his palm first, no hesitation. Blood wells and spills over his hand.

Then he hands me the hex blade.

It's heavier than I expect. The jewels encrusted in the hilt sparkle, even in the dimness. There's a buzz beneath my skin as I hold it.

Magic.

The blade is sharp despite its age and disuse.

My hand doesn't shake when I draw it across my own skin.

Grey holds his hand out for mine. We press our bleeding palms together.

I feel it immediately.

A tug. A pull.

Not pain. Not even magic.

Just *connection*, pure and deep. It's so much bigger than what I felt that night we claimed one another in the woods. Colors and scents and emotions whirl inside me, burrowing into the deepest places. Hidden parts of me that I only ever felt awaken the day I found my wolf. And now, those places belong to Grey just as much as they belong to me.

My wolf rises, opening, letting that connection pour into her. She surges with it—an energy all its own. And I know she's found strength from it already.

Grey gasps, and I watch the way his veins suddenly glow bright blue as magic flares to life inside him.

The air shifts.

Grey groans, and a second later, darkness pours from his mouth, rising above us like an angry cloud. It blots out the light from the windows, darkening the room until we're standing inside a roiling storm. Suddenly, the sound of the wind against the building isn't coming from outside but from within the cyclone above our heads.

I have no idea whether to be relieved it's out of him or worried that it's become something sentient and separate—something capable of hurting us.

"Uh, not to interrupt, but what the fuck," Dutch calls.

"Stay where you are," Mia tells him. "It's not finished yet."

"This is some serious Wizard of Oz shit," Razor says.

My wolf surges to the surface—but not violently. Not wild. She rises like a tide. Strong. Steady. Awake.

Part of me.

Grey's eyes flare silver. His power floods toward me—but it doesn't hurt. It doesn't burn. It *settles*.

This is what it was always meant to be.

"Do you feel it?" he says, nearly shouting to be heard above the wind.

I nod, the magic already nudging me to speak aloud what's woken inside me. We never needed a witch after all.

"We should say it out loud," I whisper, breath catching.

Grey nods, his voice low and reverent. "I pledge my wolf's strength to you, Lexi Giovanni. Not just as your mate but as your equal. Your co-alpha. A bonded pair; a balance. Shared strength, wolf to mated wolf. As it was always meant to be for our kind."

The words hit deep, anchoring something inside me I didn't know was still floating.

"I pledge my wolf's strength to you, Grey Diavolo. As your equal. Your mate. Your co-alpha. A bonded pair; a balance. My strength freely shared, wolf to mated wolf." The darkness seethes at that, but I finish the words that are building inside me. "What we've joined, nothing can ever break apart."

And then, just like that, the full weight of our bond clicks into place—not just emotional but *physical.* I feel Grey's wolf in a way I've never felt before. His strength. His steadiness. His unwavering love. And beneath it, his fear. His pain. His desire to protect me. His commitment to never hurt me.

And I let it all in.

Just as clearly as I can feel Grey and his wolf, I see my own wolf standing on the other side of a door, shut and locked between us. She watches me in my mind's eye. Waiting. She doesn't ask me to open the door, but I know instinctively that is the choice I have to make.

To fully let her in.

To allow her to become part of me.

To embrace both halves of my soul and no longer define myself as either human or wolf. From this moment forward, I'm both, always.

Shoving aside the fear, I reach over and yank the door wide open.

Because she's mine. And I'm not just Grey's; I'm hers. And our wolves belong to one another just as fiercely as they belong to each of us.

My wolf crosses the threshold, and something inside me bursts wide open. Power, love, unity, flashes of white, of magic, of futures—all of it fills my mind, and I gasp, blinking against the sheer enormity of it all.

Around us, the air audibly hums with a power too big to contain inside us any longer. Suddenly, the darkness is met with a white cloud so pure and blinding, I have to shield my eyes from its brightness. The dark cloud screams and writhes before sizzling out of existence.

A heartbeat later, the air clears, and any trace of magic or sentience winks out.

Mia lets out a sharp exhale. Razor mutters a string of curses that are aimed at "The Wicked Witch of the Hex Blade" and other nonsensical accusations.

When I look down at my palm, the wound has already sealed shut. Only a small scar remains to prove I didn't just hallucinate the entire thing. I exhale, feeling both drained and energized. Grey looks back at me, the same stunned expression on his face. We stand there for a long moment, just holding each other's gaze.

Then Grey steps forward, sliding an arm around my waist, pressing his forehead to mine. "You okay?" he whispers.

I nod. "I don't feel broken anymore," I manage, my voice thick with emotion. "I feel… grounded. And strong."

Grey lets out a shaky laugh. "Good. Because we're about to face hell."

"Is that thing… is it gone?" I ask, but I already know the answer because I can feel it—the pure, absolute presence of Grey and his wolf through the bond between us.

The power that radiates from them both leaves me breathless, and for the first time in my life, I realize what a true predator Grey really is. No wonder my human ass ran from him that first night he shifted and hunted me.

His eyes gleam with mischief, and I realize he's probably already sensed my train of thought. The bond is that powerful now.

It's going to take some serious getting used to.

"I'd never hurt you, princess," he says, teeth flashing in a tease of sorts. "But I'd hunt you down anytime you want to be chased."

Despite everything, my cheeks heat, and my core aches. I am instantly turned on. Is this what a full mate bond feels like? Because I could really go for a quickie right now, maybe a little hide and seek first—

Mia clears her throat. "Not to ruin the moment, but we should get moving. Everyone's already waiting at the restaurant."

Her words are the splash of cold water I need to remind me where my focus should be. Grey merely winks and sends something down the bond that feels a lot like *we'll get to that later.* He releases my waist only to thread his fingers through mine. His touch grounds me, and I follow the contact all the way through to the invisible tether between us. It's a wealth of information too. His quiet determination to win today, to protect his pack, whom he loves beyond words. And his completely depthless love for me. The emotion he feels…it's overwhelming in the best way.

While Crow returns the hex blade to the closet, Dutch claps a hand on Grey's shoulder. "You look different."

Grey smirks. "Feel different."

I meet Mia's gaze. She doesn't say anything. Just nods.

We leave the warehouse together.

United.

30

GREY

Altobello's is bustling by the time we arrive. Lexi was right; it makes the perfect staging area for what we have planned, considering my father's lab location is the old attorney's office across the street. It's a fucked-up message my father sent by choosing this location. The high-rise building, and the entire block it sits on, has been considered neutral territory for my entire life. It's like he wants us to know nothing is off limits anymore.

It's the same reason we made the call to the city police chief on the way over, filling him in on our plans. And why we asked him to set up a five-block perimeter, evacuating everyone inside it so there won't be collateral damage in the form of innocent lives. Luckily, Fletcher is in favor of a regime change, so he agreed to help us. I try to remember the last time Indigo Hills Police worked together with any one of the city's alphas, but I can't. They've always remained outside of our jurisdiction and let us operate outside of theirs.

It's a new day for sure.

By the time we arrive, uniformed officers are already taping off the block and evacuating the businesses nearby. Police cruisers block off both ends of the street. News vans are parked along the curb just outside the boundary line. Reporters are already giving on-camera updates with the information we fed them.

By now, the whole city knows something's coming.

And that's the point.

No more secrets. No more shadow plays. If my father's going to fight us for this city, he can do it in full view of every single one of us.

"There's no going back now," Lexi says as we step out of the car onto the busy sidewalk.

"There never was," I tell her and then take her hand and bring it to my lips for a quick kiss before leading her inside.

Being back inside Altobello's brings a strange sense of nostalgia. When Franco was alive, I was ready to burn this place to the ground. Almost did once. Now, it's our war room. I'm not sure if that's ironic or if it makes total fucking sense.

The restaurant is already full of people getting things set up for us.

Donahue and Camila stand to one side, quietly directing the newer members of the Giovanni pack, organizing teams. They're not just showing up—they're leading. And they're looking at Lexi with a respect that doesn't need words.

I brace myself for the violent jealousy to hit. But my wolf merely smiles at the knowledge that the strong alpha female beside me is his. And Franco's ghostly voice doesn't utter a peep. The ritual changed something inside me. I just hope it means I'm back in control—for good.

I go back to sweeping the room just as Lexi tenses beside me. I sense her awareness of him through our bond before I even see him. Charlie. He stands by the back wall as if he's just come through the kitchen door. His wrists are bound, and two guards flank him.

"I want in," he says as we approach him.

"Who gave the order to bring you here?" Lexi asks.

"I did." Mia steps up beside her dad and shoots me a pleading look. I shift my gaze pointedly to Lexi. Through the bond, I can feel her skepticism. She doesn't think having him here is a good idea. I don't disagree.

"He wants to help," Mia says to Lexi. "I think we should let him."

"Helping us stop Vincenzo is one thing," Lexi says. "But if you go in there, you'd likely have to harm the men you once considered brothers. Are you sure you're up for that?"

Charlie nods, eyes hard. "I helped him build this nightmare, and that's something I'll have to live with. But now, I need to help tear it down." He glances at Mia. "Brothers or not, it's time I fight for my daughter."

Lexi hesitates, and I watch the decision play out in her expression even as I feel it through our completed bond. Holy hell, it's so much stronger than it was before. She looks up at me as if she's thinking the same thing.

"What do you think?" she asks softly.

We both know everyone can hear us. But it won't matter once the decision has been made.

"He's here. Choosing us," I say. "That has to mean something. Besides, we're all fighting our family today."

Lexi nods and looks back at Charlie.

"Can you get to Rocco?" she asks. "Make him stand down?"

"You would show him mercy?" Charlie asks, clearly surprised.

"Of course," she says. "If we can avoid just one person raising a hand in violence against their own blood, it will be worth it."

Dutch steps forward. "Lexi, you don't have to do this. I made my choice."

"I know," she tells him. "But we'll let your dad make his."

They share a look, and finally, Dutch nods. "I'll take Charlie with me. If my father refuses his offer to surrender…I'll handle it." He looks at Charlie, daring him to argue.

Charlie nods. "I'd expect nothing less."

Dutch turns back to Lexi, expression hardening into a stony resolve. "And I'm not leaving that building without Andy."

"That works for me," Lexi says.

"I'm coming with you," Mia says.

Lexi nods. "Okay."

"Take a team," I say. "If anyone surrenders, someone from your team escorts them directly here to swear loyalty to their new alpha, or the police take them into custody until they're banished."

"Got it." Dutch and Mia call out for a couple of the others, and they all disappear into the back room together.

Savannah walks up, camera crew in tow. "You sure about this?" the reporter asks. She looks equal parts nervous and thrilled at being so close to the action.

Lexi glances out the window, where the office building across the street is deceivingly quiet considering our obvious mobilizing. "The city deserves to know what's really happening."

"Yes, but in real time?" She glances at me. "You know this will bring a crowd."

"That's what we want," I tell her. "Let them pick a side."

Savannah nods, then tells her crew to set up just outside the barricade. "We'll go live in ten, just over there."

The moment she's gone, I feel the shift behind me in the air. I whirl just in time to see two women enter, the scent of my father's pack coming off them strong enough to set me on edge.

Alvaro's wife, Gloria. And Rocco's wife, Sonesta.

I tap Razor's shoulder to get his attention, and he stiffens. Crow swears under his breath. Not angry, just worried.

"Mom?" Razor says uncertainly.

Gloria just looks him up and down. "You look like hell."

"What are you doing here?"

Sonesta lifts her chin. "You're my son. Where else would I be?"

Razor blinks, clearly caught off guard. "Dad's…not here."

"I think I know exactly where your father is."

Razor tenses.

Crow is frozen beside him, a deer in headlights. It might be funny if it weren't so fucked up—seeing Crow thrown off by someone so harmless.

Gloria flicks him a glance. "I'm guessing you had your hand in that."

"Yes, ma'am." Crow's answer is instant and unapologetic.

Gloria is silent for a long moment, her mouth set in a hard line. She turns back to Razor. Then she steps forward and pulls him into a hug.

"Good," she whispers. She pulls back and pats his cheek. "I expect you for dinner when this is over."

"O-okay," Razor manages.

She turns to Crow and softens. "Both of you."

Crow blinks. Then nods. "Yes, ma'am."

The moment is weirdly domestic and comforting—exactly what I didn't know we needed.

"And my husband?" Sonesta asks quietly. "Has anyone heard from Rocco?"

Razor and Crow look to me with matching "it's your turn now" expressions.

"Our intel says he's inside the lab," I tell her.

She just juts her chin. "He's the enemy now."

It's not a question, but I understand what she's asking me.

"Dutch and Charlie plan to find him and try to convince him not to fight us," I tell her. "But I can't make any promises."

She inhales shakily but nods. It's not exactly the first time these women have seen their husbands go off to battle. It *is* the first time their sons have been on the opposite side of that battle, though.

"All right, then," she says. "The rest is on him."

"Would you both like to wait in the back office?" Lexi asks. "There's a couch and a screen where you can watch Savannah's broadcast. And we can have someone bring you some tea or coffee."

"You got any vodka?" Gloria asks, eyeing the bar that's clearly fully stocked.

"I'll send a bottle," Lexi says, already directing them to the back room where I know for a fact Franco used to host poker nights and strippers. So weird doing this here.

"You're an angel," Sonesta tells her, squeezing her hand before they walk away.

When they're gone, Razor lifts a brow. "You're an angel? Crow's invited to dinner? Is this the apocalypse?"

"Guess we shoulda' kicked our old man's ass years ago," Crow tells him. He offers Razor the ghost of a smile.

Razor grins. "I better go find that bottle of vodka, or we'll ruin everything."

He stalks off toward the bar, and I turn to Lexi.

"You ready?" I ask.

"I'm ready to put this part behind us," she says.

"You and me both, princess. Come on."

I take her hand, and we make our way to the center of things. The room quiets instinctively. But I wait for Lexi to speak first. She stands taller than I've ever seen her, power radiating off her in waves. My wolf has never been prouder. The bond never more potent.

"You all know why we're here," Lexi says. "Vincenzo has declared war on anyone who does not pledge their loyalty to him. And now he's kidnapped an innocent woman.

"He's injecting himself with an illegal serum that he will use to cause more violence and bloodshed. And he will not rest until he's made every single person in this city bow to him. He doesn't want to be an alpha. He wants to be a king. A dictator. Today, we fight for our freedom."

The soldiers in the room roar a cheer.

"When Grey and I give the order, we go in together," Lexi says. "Our goal is to rescue the captives, apprehend Dr. Severin, and take down Vincenzo before the serum turns him into something worse than he already is."

A murmur of agreement rolls through the room.

"Anyone who asks for mercy gets it," I add. "No senseless killing. We're not here to prove we're stronger. Strength comes from unity. From a pack that doesn't fracture ever again. We're here to prove we're better than the monsters who came before us."

Elio—a recent pack addition who used to be one of my drivers when he followed my father—steps forward from the back. "Why show him mercy?" he asks. "He wouldn't do the same for you."

"I know," I say. "That's exactly why we have to."

Lexi nods, and there's fire in her eyes. "This is our city. And we're not fighting for only ourselves but for the ones who come after us. Let's show Vincenzo and his pack what it means to truly protect each other. To truly be a unified pack."

"What do you mean by unified pack?" Elio asks. "You're both alphas of your own packs, aren't you?"

I can't help but think of Mac and Levi. Or Kai and Ash—even though I've never met them. I can't help feeling a bit like this moment is wrapped in destiny.

"Lexi and I are both alphas, but we're also bonded mates," I tell him.

"A bond made stronger when we rule as equals," Lexi adds.

The group gasps.

Halfway out the door, Savannah whispers something to her cameraman, and he steps back into the room, camera aimed at us. I have a feeling everyone watching from home is hanging on our words—just like everyone in this room now is.

"Two alphas ruling together?" Donahue asks. "You'd give up your title so easily?"

"Our pack is stronger this way," Lexi tells them. "And I'm not giving up anything. We're gaining more strength, more equality—"

"A pack that's rooted in family," says another voice.

My mother. She comes forward and stands on the other side of Lexi. She smiles at my mate, warmth and acceptance radiating.

Emotion clogs my throat.

From the back, a new voice cuts in. "I'll fight for a unified pack."

The crowd parts, and someone approaches.

Claire.

The girl we rescued from Trucker.

She's flanked by two other girls, both of whom I recognize as rescues Mia helped after either my father or Franco tried to hurt and use them.

Claire smiles gratefully at me. "You and your friends saved me. I owe you everything for what you did for me that night. And I'm not going to hide while you do all the saving again."

"Claire, you don't have to fight," I say gently.

"I do," she insists. "Because I want to be part of the world you're building. The one where girls like us aren't prey."

I glance at Lexi. Her eyes are glassy.

"Then you're with us," Lexi says, her voice soft but sure.

I turn and look around the room. All of them. Not just my pack but my family. No more drawn lines. No more feuding amongst ourselves. Just all of us in this together.

Whatever happens next, it was all worth it.

Uncaring that the entire room—and city—is watching, I pull Lexi into my arms.

She smiles up at me, fierce and glowing.

And I kiss her.

It's not slow. It's not tender.

It's a promise.

Then I turn back to the room and raise my voice.

"Let's go take our city back."

A roar rises like thunder.

The doors open.

Wolves shift all around us.

And I go hunt for my father one last time.

31

LEXI

The second Grey and I give the signal, our wolves surge forward in synchronized motion, a blur of claws and muscle through the city streets. The scent of fear already hangs in the air—ours isn't the only force aware this battle has begun. But this time, it doesn't matter. We're not hiding. We're not sneaking in.

We're walking through the front door.

As we cross the street, I register awareness through the mate bond. Grey's attention draws my gaze up, too, and I see movement on the rooftop—guards. Three, maybe more. Likely with weapons.

I shift mid-run, body twisting, snapping into form, and the relief of my wolf surging forward is instant. She's not fighting me anymore. We are connected now. One mind. One purpose.

Grey is beside me, black fur brushing mine as we tear through the final barricade. Behind us, the pack follows—our pack. United. Wolves we saved, wolves who defected, wolves who chose this fight.

And I feel them.

Not just their presence but their anger. Their fear. Their courage.

Then the door looms, and I drop the connection as we push inside and up the stairs to the second floor where our intel says Vincenzo's lab begins. Levels two through seven, according to the recon Crow and Razor did last night. It's a lot of ground to cover.

The stairwell is dark and crowded as dozens of wolves race upward. At the second-floor landing, one of our guards, still in human form, holds the door open. We race through to find all the lights out and the entire floor wreathed in shadows.

Unlike at Capo, there are no sterile white lights. No hum of machinery. Instead, red emergency lights pulse overhead like a heartbeat. Someone's pulled the alarm. They know we're inside.

Donahue and Camila and my other lieutenants give a snarl. Our eyes meet, and then we split up. Everyone knows their role.

Dutch and Mia take the upper level with Charlie and the rest of their team. Razor and Crow sweep floors in between. Camila and Donahue lead a search team with orders to find Andy and Davina and get them out.

Determined to find Vincenzo and end this, I race forward with Grey at my side, carving a path down the main corridor. We encounter several armed guards. Most of them take one look at our numbers and try to run, but a couple raise their weapons or try to shift. One drops his weapon and holds up his hands.

We let him live.

Another lunges for Grey's throat.

I kill him before he can touch my mate.

By the time I'm ready to run again, there's an ear-splitting *boom*, and the entire building shakes beneath our feet. Parts of the ceiling come loose and rain down on our heads. Grey's teeth snag my shoulder as he drags me into an empty cubicle and shoves me underneath the desk.

Overhead, a siren wails. Glass explodes, and I realize the windows along the far wall have just blown out.

Smoke fills the air, and my wolf whines with the desperate urge to run.

Suddenly, Grey is human again. Naked and crouched beside me. Pure adrenaline coats the bond.

"Are you okay?"

It takes me only a few seconds more to find my human form too. "What was that?" I ask.

"He rigged the entire fucking place," he says. "It was a trap."

I blink, dazed to realize he's right. And we walked right into it. Our entire fucking pack. All our soldiers. Our friends, the city block full of innocent civilians—

"You have to go," Grey insists. "Get back outside before this place collapses. Tell them to evacuate the area. My mom—"

Around us, steel groans. Concrete cracks. More of the ceiling falls on the desk above our heads. I wince.

"What about you?" I ask, tears brimming, both from the smoke burning my eyes and the fear gripping me at leaving him.

"I have to find him," Grey says, a snarl in those words. "He won't be far."

"You think he's still here?"

"He's here," Grey says in a voice that brooks no more doubt from me.

"Then, I'm coming with you—"

"No!" He grabs my face, kisses me hard, fast. "Get everyone to safety. Find my mom. Tell her—tell her I love her."

And then he's gone.

My heart stutters. But I make myself move.

I shift back to my wolf, navigating by scent and instinct. The air is thick now, choked with smoke and ash and something acrid. Chemical.

The guard at the stairwell door motions for me to hurry, but I hesitate as a familiar scent hits me. It's nearly lost to the other smells coating this place, but it's there.

Andy.

Slipping past the guard, I follow it up to the third floor. There are no cubicles up here. Instead, there's a narrow hallway that opens into a space lined with reinforced glass cells. All of them are empty except for one.

"Andy!" I shout, shifting back into my human form so I can reach the keypad mounted beside the door.

She's slumped against the wall, blinking slowly at the sight of me. "Took you long enough."

Relief punches through me so fast I almost drop to my knees. "Are you hurt?"

"Drugged," she slurs. "Woozy."

The keypad doesn't respond to my thumbprint, and trying to crack the passcode would take time we don't have. I look around for another wolf or a guard with a weapon that can break this lock, but there's no one else here. Desperate, I call on my wolf. Half-shifted, I rip the panel off the wall and shove my claws into the wiring. Sparks fly. The lock disengages.

Andy stumbles out, and I catch her before she can hit the floor.

Already, the smoke is becoming too thick to see through. It clogs my nose, leaving us both coughing.

"Can you shift?" I wheeze.

"Not yet. But point me in the direction of that asshole Severin, and I'm sure my wolf will find her claws again."

We start back toward the stairs.

And then he steps into view. Not Severin.

Vincenzo.

Except that he's… wrong.

Taller. Broader. His skin looks too tight, like it's trying to contain something boiling underneath. His eyes glow gold —not a natural color. More chemical.

"Going somewhere?" he growls.

I shove Andy behind me.

"Move," I snarl.

He smiles. "Now-now, *principessa*. Is that any way to speak to your future king?"

Through the bond, I send a warning to Grey. A call for help. Because I know there's only one way this can end. And something inside Vincenzo's eyes tells me that serum has done its job. He's powerful. More lethal than I'm equipped to take on.

Even my wolf knows she's met her match. She can't do this alone.

"Franco called himself a king too, and look how that turned out."

He steps closer, and the scent of chemicals grows stronger.

"I heard about your little ritual," he says. "Two alphas. One soul. How romantic. But unnecessary. All you needed was one last dose of my new serum—binding your genes to his. Kind of like I did with her. And then you would have been unstoppable."

Andy growls behind me.

Shock ripples through me at what he's saying, but I hold my ground.

"You're still a mortal," I say.

"Am I?" His eyes glitter with the promise of death. "Only one way to find out."

He lunges.

And I let go.

My wolf rips free, faster than ever before. Cleaner. Sharper.

We meet him mid-air.

And I don't think about what happens next.

I just fight.

32

GREY

My father's scent isn't on the second floor, so I go back to the stairwell and race all the way up to the seventh, intent on working my way down until I find him. Flames consume the far side of the building, which is apparently where the explosives had been rigged, just waiting for us all to get inside before they detonated. Up here, the walls are already scorched, the floor buckling. This place isn't going to hold for long.

Racing through the space, I stop short when I see Mia and Dutch in what used to be a conference room—now full of overturned tables and scattered debris. Charlie stands with them, but the rest of their team is missing.

Facing off with them is Rocco.

He stands at the far end, arms folded, flanked by two guards who look like they're unsure if they should be fighting or running. The general's face, so similar to Dutch's in the shape of his nose and set of his mouth, is stone, cold, and unreadable. But his hands tremble either with fear or rage. Or both.

At the sight of me, Rocco snarls, but Dutch steps forward, clearly trying to continue whatever conversation they've already begun. "Mom's across the street. She came to support our side. She's with us now."

Rocco sneers. "Sentimental bullshit. That bitch should've stayed home like I told her to."

Dutch flinches. But he holds his ground.

"I'm not here to fight you, Dad."

"No, you're just here to betray me. To tear down everything I built."

Charlie steps forward then, jaw tight. "Everything you built—you did it with bloodshed and pain. You made something that is killing our children to keep it. Don't you want to fight for your son instead of against him?"

Rocco's laugh is sharp. Cruel. "Of course you'd say that. You were always too soft for our pack. All this talk of letting women lead. Of feelings. You were never a real Diavolo."

Rocco turns to Mia, and the fury in his voice spikes. "And you. You're a disgrace. Your mother should've drowned you at birth."

Mia doesn't move. Doesn't blink.

Charlie does.

He lunges—but Rocco is faster. He slams into Mia, claws out.

Dutch moves fast as a whip.

He intercepts the blow, shifting mid-air and crashing into his father, and they go down hard.

I start forward, but Mia blocks me. "Let him."

Dutch's wolf uses its teeth and rolls Rocco over just as Rocco shifts, snarling. Blood coats their jaws as their teeth tear into each other. It's feral. Ugly. Not a fight—a reckoning.

But then Rocco gets his teeth around Dutch's throat.

And Dutch's wolf responds in kind. Fast, too fast, Dutch rakes his claws across Rocco's eyes. The older wolf snarls and rolls away, exposing his throat. Dutch sinks his teeth into his father's neck, through muscle and sinew all the way to bone.

The snap echoes through the burning hall.

Rocco slumps.

Dead.

Dutch shifts back, panting, blood soaking his arms, his chest, his face.

He doesn't look down at the body.

He looks at Mia.

"You okay?" he asks, voice raw.

She nods once. "Yeah."

"And you?" he asks Charlie.

Charlie nods, pulling Mia into a hug.

Dutch meets my eyes. My wolf howls its approval and sorrow. But the sound is cut short when I feel it.

Lexi's fear slams into me like a sixth sense. I don't need words to tell me it's my father she's afraid of. That he's found her and he's not going to let her go. Already running, I scream her name through the bond.

No answer.

Just a flicker of panic. Determination. Fear.

Hoping it's enough, I send as much of my own strength down the bond as I can, and then I run like hell, hoping it'll be enough to strengthen her until I get there.

At the stairwell, I race downward as the bond calls me toward her like a beacon. Pulsing with her presence. But

I'm running out of fucking time, I can feel it. Behind me, Dutch and the others have shifted and are running now too.

We race onto the third floor, and I duck low beneath beams that dangle from crumbling ceilings. Smoke fills my lungs, my paws pounding over scorched tile. I don't stop to think. Just move. Just *find her*.

I hear them before I see them.

Snarls. Growls. The crash of breaking glass.

I round a corner—and see her.

Andy slumped in a pile of broken glass; shards embedded in her skin.

Lexi. Bleeding. Fighting.

And my father, his wolf coated in power and violence.

He's changed. Warped by the serum. There's a darkness in him now too. It radiates off him.

I don't hesitate.

I leap.

With teeth and claws out, I hit him hard enough to crack bone. We roll, a tangle of fur, and land hard against the far wall. Plaster crumbles around us at the impact, but he doesn't slow. His teeth gnash at my throat, missing by inches. His paws threaten to pin me. He's strong—stronger than before. But he's not *better*. He's not stronger than the bond I have with my mate.

He slams me into the wall, his claws raking down my shoulder and splitting my flesh open.

Lexi screams.

I launch forward. My father feints right, but I see it coming and match it, my teeth ripping a chunk from his shoulder. Muscle and blood rip free, and he makes a sound of pain, his leg buckling when he tries to land on it.

I take the opening and lunge again, this time ripping a chunk from his flank. His legs give out, and he falls.

I loom over him, ready to end this—at last.

Lexi's hand lands on my shoulder.

"Don't," she rasps. "If you kill him, you'll absorb all that power. All that darkness. It could kill you—or worse."

Fuck. She's probably right. I stop and look down at my father cowering on the ground. He's wheezing. Bleeding. Not quite dying, thanks to that stupid serum, but rendered immobile.

"Let's go," Lexi says quietly. "This place is falling apart."

And I realize what she means to do.

I turn away from my father as Dutch kneels beside Andy. She's bleeding, barely conscious, and covered in glass. It's not until he lifts her into his arms that I see the body behind her.

Severin. Still in his lab coat, which is now coated in blood. A large piece of glass protrudes from his throat.

"You did good, baby," Dutch tells her. "You did so fucking good."

"Can we get the fuck out of here?" Mia asks.

"Yes, please," Lexi says.

I look back at my father.

And I let him go.

Lexi's right. Killing him would mean inheriting his alpha essence. And there's no part of him I want surviving in me when this is all over. So, instead of taking my vengeance on the one man who deserves it the most, I shift back to my human form so I can take the hand of the woman I love.

"You'll die alone," I tell him. "It's no less than you deserve."

Then I turn my back on him forever.

A moment later, his voice stops me. "I knew you couldn't kill me," he rasps. I look back to see he's shifted to his human form. A form that will make healing impossible. All so he can taunt me one last time. "You're too weak. I was always stronger than you."

A steel beam breaks loose and crashes through the floor.

Dutch curses, darting out of the way as more chunks rain down. He cradles Andy more tightly against his chest, his eyes wide with urgency now.

All around us, the walls crack.

The floor tilts.

"Out!" I shout. "Everyone out!"

We run.

The hall collapses behind us.

The ceiling buckles.

We don't stop.

We don't look back.

We don't breathe until the sunlight hits our faces.

33

LEXI

Two weeks later

The sign above the door still reads Altobello's, but only until a new one is ordered. Crow says he hasn't decided on the new name yet, but I catch him scribbling things in a little notebook he keeps in the kitchen—recipes, ideas, possible contenders. Andy swears she saw "Crow's Nest" written at the top of the page the other day. He denies it. Razor says he'll boycott if it sticks. Mia suggested "La Famiglia," but Dutch said that sounded like a pasta sauce. Crow called him an uncultured idiot and threw a breadstick at him.

For now, it's enough that the place smells like fresh bread and garlic, not strippers and cigars.

Tonight, the restaurant glows in the warm light of dusk. The dining room is empty except for us—our found family

—seated around two pushed-together tables near the windows. The glass is new, after the explosion across the street blew them all out. The street outside is quiet.

Safe.

Bobby is at the bar, polishing glasses. Claire is bustling between the kitchen and our table, topping off drinks, stealing bites from Razor's plate, and teasing Crow mercilessly about his inability to run this place without her.

"You missed the garlic on table three," she says, even though there is no table three tonight.

"Keep talking back, and I'll demote you to dishwasher," Crow warns.

"You'd have to pay me first," Claire shoots back.

"I *do* pay you."

She winks. "Is that what that envelope full of ones was?"

Snickers and hoots follow that. Then more jokes. Laughter breaks across the table, the sound of it like sunlight in my ears.

I watch it all, soaking it in. It's the first time I've ever seen Crow genuinely relaxed. There's no edge to his voice, no shadow under his eyes. It's almost like peace. He wears it well.

Across from me, Dutch sits next to Andy, their shoulders brushing every few minutes, and each time it happens, Andy pretends not to notice while blushing so hard I'm worried she'll combust. Dutch keeps passing her bites off his plate like a love-struck idiot.

"I swear, if you two don't stop making heart eyes while I eat these cannoli, I'm leaving," Mia says, pointing her fork at them.

"I'm not making heart eyes," Andy protests.

Dutch just smirks and holds out his last bite for Andy.

Razor leans back and mutters, "Whipped."

But Dutch just gives him a shit-eating grin and says, "It's called romance, Razor. Look it up."

"I think I'll pass and retain my dignity," Razor fires back.

Grey chuckles beside me, his hand resting on my knee under the table. Every time he looks at me, I feel like I can breathe a little easier. Like maybe, just maybe, the storm is finally passing.

"We should do this every week," Mia says, refilling her wine. "Dinner. Laughter. Light trauma bonding."

"I'm in," I say.

"Okay, but only after I've hired some help for the kitchen," Crow adds, wiping flour off his apron as he finally takes a seat to dig into his own plate. "You guys are pigs."

"My wolf resents that remark," Razor says.

"Your wolf resembles that remark," Mia corrects.

Razor throws his napkin at her.

The jokes keep coming, the food keeps disappearing, and for a while, it really does feel like we made it. Like the city is finally ours.

It's been two weeks since Vincenzo's lab fell. Like, literally the building came down a few minutes after we all made it out. Vincenzo's body was never recovered in the rubble, and I can see the way it fucked with Grey the way it all ended with his father. Or, more accurately, I can feel it. But I'm hoping it'll heal with time.

Since then, most of Vincenzo's loyalists have either gone into hiding or surrendered. The next step for the ones in custody will be exile. As soon as we find a hex witch who can help us gain control of the wards. Davina wasn't in the lab, and no one has been able to find any trace of her since.

The other hex witches left in the city have all disappeared too, though no one knows why. I tell myself it's a good thing. Davina was a prisoner, and now she's free. She deserves to be left alone. They all do.

Besides, we have our hands full with other things.

Elections are scheduled for next month—a mayoral race and a council of delegates that will provide oversight on budgeting and city policy. Grey and I plan to keep out of the governance of the city, especially in the ways that Vincenzo and Franco weaponized for so many years. In the interim, money has already been reallocated. Schools are being repaired. New after-school programs are launching, the kind that keep kids off the streets and give them something to believe in.

Crow's restaurant is even donating meals to local shelters once a week. Shelters I hope to volunteer at just like I used to do before coming to Indigo Hills. Serena, Grey's mom, is heading up the non-profit efforts. She's invited me to come help, and I plan to take her up on it.

I promoted Donahue and Camila to team leaders—we're not using the term generals anymore—so they share an equal position with Andy, Mia, Dutch, Razor, and Crow. We hold meetings now. Actual meetings. With agendas. And donuts. Razor keeps showing up late and eating all the glazed.

We've been rebuilding from the inside out. It's starting to feel more and more like family, a feeling that's less and less foreign with each passing day.

A knock on the restaurant door pulls me from my thoughts.

Razor calls out, "We're closed!"

But the knock comes again.

Grey and Dutch exchange a look.

"I'll get it," Razor grumbles.

He pushes to his feet and stalks to the door, turning the lock and yanking the door wide. Whoever's on the other side has him reaching out. He grabs them with a grunt and spins to face us.

"Uh, guys, anyone know who this is?" he asks.

No one speaks up.

When I see who it is, I jump up, recognition and fear hitting me in equal parts. "Violet?"

She's bruised. One eye swollen, her lip split. It's clear she can't stand up without Razor's help. The scent of blood radiates from her human body, and my wolf whines at the way she's been beaten.

She manages to lift her head and meet my eyes. "Hi, Lexi."

"What happened to you?" I ask, my voice cracking as my heart breaks for my friend and what she's clearly been through. Whoever did this to her will pay.

"I'm supposed to deliver a message," she whispers, the effort of talking clearly causing her more pain.

I go cold. "What message?"

"There's one more alpha you forgot to include… when you took the city for yourselves… and he's pissed."

"Who?" Grey asks, appearing beside me, voice low and dangerous.

Blood trickles down Violet's chin as she says, "Ramsey.

And he's coming for you. Starting with the people you love." Her eyes water as she says, "Starting with me."

Then she passes out in Razor's arms.

Find out what happens when Ramsey returns in Savage Wolf Vow, Mafia Pack #4, coming in 2026!

ABOUT THE AUTHOR

Heather Hildenbrand lives in coastal Virginia where she writes paranormal and fantasy romance with strong-willed heroines and dark, grumpy heroes who'll burn the world down for their mate. Her most frequent hobbies are cuddling with her giant goldendoodles, riding country roads on the back of her husband's motorcycle, and avoiding killer slugs.

You can find out more about Heather and her books at www.heatherhildenbrand.com.

Or find her here:

Online Store (get signed copies)
heatherhildenbrandbooks.com

ALSO BY HEATHER HILDENBRAND

Dark Wolf Soul

Deadly Wolf Bite

Broken Wolf Heart

Savage Wolf Vow (coming 2026)

Kingdom of Briars and Roses (Cursed Fae Courts)

A Glamour of Smoke and Shadow (Cursed Fae Courts)

Protect Me (Immortal Vices & Virtues)

Hunt Me (Immortal Vices & Virtues)

Consume Me (Immortal Vices & Virtues) - coming 2025

To Hunt A Wolf

To Kiss A Wolf

To Keep A Wolf

Midnight Cursed

Midnight Hunted

Midnight Bound

Wolf Cursed

Wolf Captive

Wolf Chosen

Wolf Revealed

A Witch's Call

A Witch's Destiny

A Witch's Fate

A Witch's Soul

A Witch's Prophecy

A Witch's Hope

Twisted Tides

The Girl Who Cried Werewolf

The Girl Who Cried Captive

The Girl Who Cried War

The Girl Who Never Cried

The Winter Witch

The Spring Witch

The Witch's Heart

Midnight Mate

One Dark Spark

Two Blazing Hearts

Three Scorched Kingdoms

Goddess Ascending

Goddess Claiming

Goddess Forging

Kiss of Death

Knock Em Dead

Death's Door

Dead to Rights

Dead End

The Girl Who Called The Stars

The Girl Who Ruled The Stars

Alpha Games

Alpha Trials

Alpha Chosen

Dirty Blood

Cold Blood

Blood Bond

Blood Rule

Broken Blood

Imitation

Deviation

Generation

Heather also writes small town contemporary romance as Violet Stafford.

Stay For Summer

The Breakup Bet

www.ingramcontent.com/pod-product-compliance
Lightning Source LLC
Chambersburg PA
CBHW020340310726
48979CB00015B/2438/J

* 9 7 8 1 9 6 1 4 5 5 3 5 1 *